Abigail's Redemption

Adda Leah Davis

WestBow
PRESS
A DIVISION OF THOMAS NELSON

ISBN: 978-1-4497-2285-2 (e)
ISBN: 978-1-4497-2286-9 (sc)
Library of Congress Control Number: 2011913229

WestBow Press books may be ordered through booksellers or by contacting:

WestBow Press
A Division of Thomas Nelson
1663 Liberty Drive
Bloomington, IN 47403
www.westbowpress.com
1-(866) 928-1240

Printed in the United States of America
WestBow Press rev. date: 11/04/2011

Acknowledgements

It is my desire to be found, as in the fifth chapter of Ephesians in the 20th verse of the King James Version of the Bible which says: "Giving thanks always for all things unto God and the Father in the name of our Lord Jesus Christ." So it is with the gift of writing. I did nothing to attain the gift and I know if I fail to use it my gift will be taken and given to another. I thank my God for the talent he has given me and the health to use that gift, to his Glory.

I wish to thank my dear friend and heartfelt sister, Jo Osborne, for giving up her valuable time to read the marked-through draft. Her opinion is very important to me.

Many thanks are also due to my friend and editor Rachel Riggsby. She has gone over this book numerous times and if there are errors it is due to my, once again, changing something at the last minute.

Finally I wish to thank my dear husband and my grandson, Jonathan for the many times they have wanted my attention, but left me to work. I hope they know that they were always in the back of my mind.

This book is dedicated to all those abused and traumatized individuals who have never found relief. It is my fervent hope and prayer that they may find some comfort in these pages.

ABIGAIL'S REDEMPTION

My Redemption
Once my soul was filled with darkness
And my tortured thoughts held fear
This daily parody of living
Became more than I could bear.
Then my God sent sweet deliverance
From loving hands as yet unseen
Images viewed from a distance
For the past was still too keen.
Months and years of shadowed living
While begging for HIS grace and peace
Then there beside the river waiting
My redemption came to me.

Chapter 1

Abigail's breath came in gasps and pain ripped through her chest, but she kept running. *He's drunk or crazy like that . . .* She shivered and wouldn't let her mind go there. Her current situation was scary enough.

She strained to listen for the roar of the truck motor or the taunting voice of its driver. The battered blue truck had come barreling around the curve as she approached the crest of the hill above the cemetery.

When Abigail jumped to the side of the road the truck screeched to a halt and a dark bearded face protruded through the window. "Scared you to death, didn't I? It's all right, little girl. Just come get in with me and I'll take you home."

Abigail's frightened green eyes had grown large in her ashen face. She stammered, "No, thank you."

The beard parted and white teeth showed through in a wide grin as the driver revved the engine. "It's a long way to the hardtop. I've an errand on down the road a ways, but I'll be right back to get you," he yelled as he went speeding down the rutted dusty road.

To get you . . . was like a pointed gun. There were no houses and Abigail knew she couldn't outrun a truck, but she had to try. *Jesus, please help me,* she prayed as she ran. She heard the truck go lurching down the rutted road, much too fast, as it descended the hill she had just mounted.

He's coming back to get me, she thought frantically as her mind leapt back to that awful day three years before. She couldn't hear the truck now, which was a relief. When he started back up Jack Murphy Hill she would know it.

It's about a mile to Walter Mullins's place. If I can make it there I'll be safe. Oh Jesus! Please help me, she prayed. Now, she had gotten her second wind and increased her speed. However, she knew it wouldn't take long for the driver to overtake her in the truck. The Mullins's place still wasn't in sight when she heard the roar of the truck laboring back up the hill.

He can't drive that truck down through these trees, she thought and immediately left the road. Fighting her way through briars and brambles, she lost her footing, and tumbled down the small slope to the level ridge below.

Scrambling hurriedly to a denser stand of bigger trees, large enough to hide behind, she crept out of sight. Abigail stood, trying to slow her labored breathing as tears seeped from her eyes. *Maybe he'll go on. Maybe he's just trying to scare me,* she hoped. As she stood listening, the truck went slowly on out the road that she had been on. She heard it slow and finally come to a stop.

Quaking in fear, she silently prayed. *Oh God, please let somebody come to help me. Please.* She stood like a statue, afraid to move or breathe.

"What in the world happened to that girl? I've had a drink or two, but I know I'm not that drunk. She's the prettiest little red-headed girl I've ever seen and she was walking right down this road. I even spoke to her. I told her I'd be right back," a voice said as Abigail tried to make herself smaller.

Three years ago she'd been told she had a ride home, but it was a lie. *I'm not taking a chance like that again*, she thought, shivering in revulsion. The voice seemed to be moving along the road, but Abigail was afraid to peek out of her hiding spot. She didn't know what direction he was moving in.

She had finished her week's work as a hired girl for Matty and Harve Collins and was going home for the weekend. The long rutted and dusty road out of Collins Ridge ran eight miles before it connected to Route 83. It was isolated, since there were only three houses that could be seen from the road. Most

2

houses were situated on some off-road that angled down to the creek, making it easier for farmers to water their stock.

Route 83 was the only paved road in the area and it ran the entire length of the long plateau, called the top of Bradshaw Mountain by the local inhabitants. Southern West Virginia was a picturesque display of hollows and high ridges with large stands of timber covering many of the mountain sides. This area was also touted as one of the richest coalfields in the eastern United States, and the numerous coal camps dotting the landscape supplied the labor for the mining operations.

These mining towns were located in the valleys, or ravines as the outsiders called them, but the farmers carved out a living on the rugged peaks of the sheltering mountains.

All through the week in summer, Abigail washed clothes, scrubbed floors, ironed, cooked, canned fruit and vegetables, and hoed the garden for the Collins family. They paid her ten dollars a week, but she had her own room and plenty to eat.

She had now worked for this couple for a year and nine months. Matty Collins was crippled from arthritis and had gotten worse, making her unable to do much of anything except churn or something she could do while sitting.

Harve had asked Abigail to continue working when school was out after the first year, and since she hadn't yet been able to save the money she needed for college, she agreed. She was often so tired at the end of the day that she thought she'd just quit, but her reason for working kept her there. Although Abigail had grown to like Harve and Matty she knew that as soon as she could find something better she would leave.

"Hey, little girl! If you are hiding somewhere around here, I wish you'd come out. I'd like to take another look at you. I don't believe a girl can be as pretty as I thought you were. I just want to get another look. Besides, if you don't come out, I'm going to go give Harvey Phillips the best thrashing he's ever had in his life. He's either sold me some bad whiskey or I'm losing my mind," the voice stated, getting farther and farther away. The last Abigail heard was, "Maybe I just thought I saw her. Maybe she wasn't there at all, but why did I stop to look for her on the way back?"

Abigail noticed that the sun was lower in the sky and thought that it must be nearing five o'clock. *If I don't get home by six o'clock, Daddy will swear that I've been fooling around with some man.* Knowing that soon the sun would sink over the horizon, Abigail fearfully started the slow and painful climb back to the road. With every step she prayed, *Lord, please let him be gone.*

She was on the road again before she even noticed the scratches on her legs or the muck on her shoes. Looking down, she saw long threads hanging from her coat, with briars still clinging. Her socks were snagged and were now sagging over her shoes.

She looked along the road, and not seeing anybody, she hiked up her dress and pulled up the rubber bands that held the socks above her knees. *I've only got one more pair of socks. I wish I could wear pants like boys, but Harve would think I was just like some of the other girls around here.*

Abigail knew that the year she graduated, some of her classmates had earned really bad names and some had even gotten pregnant and had to quit school. *If I'd been like that I'd never have gotten this job, for Matty wouldn't have let a bad girl around Harve, even if he is old,* thought Abigail.

She'd been so careful with her coat, since it was the first one she had ever owned. Now, she shook her head sadly and plucked the briars and twigs from her person. Not hearing any sounds, she started walking out the road.

About a quarter of a mile farther on, Abigail heard voices up ahead but she couldn't see anyone. *What if it's him and he has some buddies?* She didn't hear the sound of a car; only voices. She stopped and stood listening. Walter Mullins's house was just a little farther on up the road.

Are the voices coming from someplace this side of Walter's house? She wondered. Then she heard the roar of an engine. When she realized it was coming toward her, she plunged into the woods again.

4

Since the trees here were not close, she crouched down as low as possible and breathed a sigh of relief when the vehicle sped on down the road. She slowly climbed back to the top and soon was in sight of the Walter Mullins place.

Abigail went through the squeaky gate and up the plank walkway that led to the porch just as she heard a vehicle coming back down the road. She hurried onto the porch and knocked on the door. Thankfully, Mary Mullins let her in just as the battered Ford truck passed the house.

"Why, Abigail Dawson, you're tore all to pieces. What's happened?" Mary asked as she ushered Abigail into the living room. Abigail was so thankful she felt like falling into Mary's arms, but instead she shivered and sat down on a wooden chair near the fireplace.

"Mrs. Mullins, do you know who owns that truck that just passed?" she asked.

"No, honey, I don't believe I do. To tell the truth I was lookin' at you and didn't pay that truck no mind." Mary stood looking at Abigail, who was pale, disheveled, and now trembling. "What's the matter? Did somebody bother you?"

Abigail dropped her face into her hands as tears gushed from her eyes. Mary handed Abigail a towel. "Here, honey, don't cry. If somebody bothered you, I'll get Walter to go out to the road and get Francis Kennedy to call the sheriff."

Abigail raised her head and wiped her eyes. "No, Mrs. Mullins, nobody bothered me, but that man in the truck was drunk or something. He stopped and asked me to ride and I said no. He was going the wrong way anyway. He went on down the hill, but said he was coming back to get me. When I heard him coming back, I ran down in the woods and hid."

"You poor child! So, that's why you look like you've been pulled out of a hollow log back'ards. I'm going to pour you a cup of hot coffee. You jest set there and rest a spell. Then me and Walter will take you out to the road. "

Abigail sat drinking the coffee and soon the shivering stopped. "I think Daddy may come looking for me pretty soon, Mrs. Mullins. I don't want to bother you."

"That's all right. We don't mind a bit. We know how hard you work at Harve Collins's place," said Mary Mullins with compassion. She took the empty cup that Abigail offered and started toward the kitchen. "I'll bet that feller was going down to Dave Largen's place to get him some moonshine."

"I heard him say something about getting some whiskey from Harvey Phillips. Do you know anybody with that name?" asked Abigail.

Mary stood still with the coffee cup in her hand. "Harvey Phillips . . . hmm. There ain't no sech person on this ridge. I know that for a fact. That feller must not be from around here. What did he look like anyway?"

"I don't really know except he had a thick black beard and black hair I think. He just rolled down his window and asked me to ride. I said no and then he said he was coming back to get me," explained Abigail.

"Well, pon my honor! Ain't no wonder you was scared," said Mary, shaking her head. "Well, you ain't walking another step by yourself. I'll go all the way home with you 'fore I'll see that happen."

"I can't let you do that, Mrs. Mullins. Daddy doesn't like me to accept favors from people. You know how he is."

"I've heard how he is, honey. It ain't no wonder your sisters got away from there as fast as they could," said Mary with a grimace. Abigail had dropped her head and was still crying. "You ain't like the others are you? I mean, you don't flirt with boys, do you?" asked Mary.

"No. No, no. I don't like men or boys. They scare me," said Abigail in a trembling voice.

Mary Mullins looked at her and realized that she was almost in a panic and changed the subject. "We can take you. I ain't got nothing else to do, so we'll take you out to the road. Now, just calm down and don't think no more about it." Mary patted her on the shoulder. "All men ain't bad, Abigail. I've been with Walter Mullins for nigh onto fifty years and I swear he wouldn't never bother nobody; especially a young girl."

Abigail turned redder still and looked up at Mary with tears

6

in her eyes. "I didn't mean that Mr. Mullins was bad. Honestly, I didn't. I'm just so mixed up right now."

Mary smiled. "That's all right. I can see you ain't in very good shape."

Chapter 2

Sally Dawson took one look at Abigail and gasped. "Lordy mercy, girl. What has happened to you? Your coat is ruined and you're scratched all to pieces. Some boy has been after you, I guess."

Abigail put her hands over her face and dropped her head. "Mommy, I ran down through the woods and hid," she said between sobs. It was hard but she continued on until she had the whole story out. Her youngest brother, Damon, had met her at the mouth of Collins Ridge. She had asked him if he had seen anyone who fit the description of the man who had been driving the blue truck.

Damon had replied. "Nope, Sis, I've not seen him or his truck either."

Sally pulled Abigail's hands from her face and said. "Ain't no use you cryin' like that and you'd better not let your daddy catch you cryin' either. You know how he'll set in, so hide that coat. I'll look at it when he's gone and see if I can fix it."

Sally turned from Abigail, saying, "Wash your hands and face and help me get supper on the table. Your dad will probably know who that feller was. Why were you walking out of that ridge anyway?"

"I thought you always rode out of Collins Ridge with Noah and Lola Adair," said Damon.

"Yeah, I did too. Has he finally got a job? Since the mines have been on strike everybody around here has been out of work," said Sally.

By this time, Abigail had gone to the sink in the kitchen and pumped water into her hands to wash her face. She came back into the room drying her face and hands. "No, I don't think Noah has been called back to work. Matty Collins said something about Noah's wife, Lola, needing to go to the doctor today. I waited at the end of the lane, but they didn't come and I started walking."

They were discussing the area and who it could possibly have been when they heard Garson Dawson's logging truck come around the bend above the garden.

Sally pushed Abigail toward the kitchen. "Come on let's get supper on the table. Don't say nothing about this 'til after supper, else your dad won't eat a bite and his stomach will be hurting again. You know he usually takes it out on one of us when his stomach hurts."

Garson soon took his place at the head of the table and waited until they all sat down before he started filling his plate. Sally looked on stoically, but asked a blessing inside her head before she filled her own plate. After the meal was over, Sally got up to bring Garson's usual cup of coffee to the table, along with the strawberry cobbler she'd made for dessert.

Garson looked over at Abigail. "Well, little hired girl, tell us how the work went this week. Did Harve Collins have you pullin' the plow?"

Abigail looked at her mother and then replied, "The work went fine, Daddy. I usually get some free time to rest in the evenings."

When she didn't say anything else, Garson gave her a shrewd look. "What else? There's something else going on. I could feel it as soon as I stepped through the door."

Abigail felt herself choking on tears and was glad when Sally blurted, "A man scared her to death as she was walking out of Collins Ridge."

Garson Dawson lurched to his feet, his eyes blazing. "What man? Just tell me who he is. He'll be sorry he ever bothered my daughter."

"She don't know who he is, Garson, so just calm down. Besides he didn't get to her. He just scared her," said Sally calmly.

"What did he do, Abby?" asked her dad.

Abigail repeated her story once again and also told about Walter Mullins and his wife bringing her the rest of the way out of Collins Ridge.

"I'll have to do something for Walter to repay his kindness. We Dawsons don't take kindly to charity. Did Walter know who the man was?" asked Garson.

"No, Daddy. Walter Mullins didn't know him and neither did his wife. Mrs. Mullins didn't think he was from around here, especially when I told her about him saying Harvey Phillips sold whiskey," said Abigail.

"She's right. There's nobody by that name living around here. Believe me if somebody is selling whiskey the men working for me would know them and that's a name I've never heard," stated Garson.

"Why can't we fix it some way 'til she won't have to walk out of that holler no more?" asked Sally.

"Oh well, I'll just buy her a car," sneered Garson and looked at Sally as if he thought she was stupid. Sally didn't make any comment. She stood gripping the back of a chair and gritting her teeth, trying to control her growing bitterness.

Garson still sat at the table frowning. "I didn't want her to take that job in the first place, but since she has, I'll get Rob Baker to swing by here and pick me up on Friday mornings. That way Damon can take the truck and go out Collins Ridge to get Abby. He gets off work at the post office at 4:30 and Abby can wait with Harve and Matty until he gets there."

Garson sat back as if pleased with his way of settling things. Suddenly he gave Abigail a penetrating look. "I'll have to have a little extra for doing this, you know. Gas ain't cheap and that will be four extra trips each month. I guess two dollars a trip will take care of it."

Abigail thought wearily, *That takes eight more dollars from my savings, but I'll have to do it.* She nodded her understanding and rose from the table. She knew that was just another way her dad had to keep her from going to college.

That seemed to settle it to Garson's satisfaction and soon

they were all ready to retire for the night. They would have to leave early the next morning. Garson always went to Bradshaw on Saturday mornings and stayed all day; usually coming home half drunk.

Sally, Abigail, and Damon went to church either at Bee Branch on Route 83 or to Slate Creek Church in Bradshaw. A brother and sister in the church had asked Sally to go with them on the second weekend to visit a church over on Stone Coal Hollow in Virginia, a twenty-mile distance. Sally Dawson never missed a weekend in going to meeting somewhere, if she could help it. Sally was a member of the Bee Branch Primitive Baptist Church, which was only about three miles away. That congregation, like all Primitive Baptists, only met one weekend of each month, with services on Saturday and Sunday, and this was the weekend for Bee Branch to meet.

Abigail hoped it would rain so she wouldn't have to ride on the back of her dad's logging truck. Before she finished grade school she liked riding on the back of that big, high truck, but now she was so embarrassed. If it rained, Damon wouldn't ask to drive and he could sit on the back of the truck. It wouldn't hurt him anyway since his hair didn't blow all over the place and he didn't have to hold down a skirt all the way.

Tonight Abigail went to bed in a dread. She feared that she would have nightmares and again relive that terrible episode of three years ago. She had been so sick, and for months afterward, she was awakened nightly, screaming in terror. Sally always came in and gave her a dose of the nerve medicine Dr. Carr had given her. Garson Dawson had laughed at the idea of sending her to St. Albans Psychiatric Hospital, in Salem, Virginia as the doctors had insisted.

"She didn't get raped and she ain't crazy and I ain't got the money for no such foolishness," was his prompt reply when Sally had told him what the doctor had said. Garson had gotten really angry and Sally stood mutely by and allowed the tirade to wash over her like a beaten pup. Even though Abigail was traumatized she had felt sorry for her mother and wondered why she didn't at least defend herself. It was almost as if her dad had wanted her mother to cry or something. Sally didn't however. Instead she had gone to the source of all her help . . . She had called upon the Lord.

Now, Abigail realized that she had been too trusting. That man was old. He had white hair, like her grandpa. Abigail had trusted older men, but not anymore. Her grandfather had been the kindest, gentlest man she had ever known and also the most important person in her life, and he had been old.

Three years ago she had come home after spending Thanksgiving week with her brother Kyle, who lived at Union, West Virginia. She had been so pleased that Kyle and Marie, his wife, had wanted her to spend a week with them. It would be the first time she had been farther than Welch, the county seat of McDowell County, in her entire fifteen years. She was petrified at first when she learned that Kyle couldn't bring her home. Assuring her that she would be fine, Kyle had taken her into town to catch the bus to Bluefield which was the first lap of her journey.

"I've bought you a ticket straight through to Bradshaw. You only have to make sure you don't miss your bus. You have to change buses in Bluefield, Welch, and War so hang on to your ticket. The drivers will punch it as you get on the bus," explained Kyle worriedly. He knew that this was a first for Abigail and she was afraid.

She arrived at the Bus Depot in Bradshaw without mishap and heaved a sigh of relief, but that soon left her. She had been hoping that her dad would meet her in Bradshaw, but he didn't. Since there were no telephones in the area, she knew she had no way to contact any of her family and she became scared again. She waited for a little while and then decided to walk. It would only be seven miles to the cut off to Stateline Ridge, and since it was only four o'clock, she'd make it home by seven o'clock easily.

With her suitcase in one hand and her purse in the other, she stepped out with resolution and walked at a good pace for about two miles and then she began to tire. Several cars had stopped to see if she wanted a ride, but her sisters Virginia and Alice had repeatedly told her what men would do to her, if she let them, and Abigail refused every offer. All those offering rides so far had been young men, who she feared most of all. Sally had warned her constantly about accepting rides or being too friendly with young men, especially if they were not from the area. The area around Bradshaw and Bradshaw Mountain was safe. Women could go anywhere in the area and there hadn't ever been a case of anyone being harmed.

Abigail was trudging up a small incline when a shiny new Packard sedan pulled to a stop beside her. "Hello, young lady. You look like you're awfully tired. Would you like a ride?"

Abigail turned to look and a kind-faced, white-haired man was smiling at her. Abigail smiled in return. He reminded her of her grandpa.

"I'm just going to the top of the mountain. It isn't far," she answered.

"Well, I'm going that way and it would save you carrying that suitcase up that hill," he said, pointing ahead. Abigail stood undecided, but he looked so nice and kind, just like her grandpa.

Seeing her hesitation, the man said, "I wouldn't want a child of mine to be walking this road by herself."

Abigail smiled, thinking he really was just like her grandpa. She thanked him and got in the car, placing her suitcase on the floorboard at her feet.

"Do you want to put your case in the backseat?" he asked as he shifted into gear.

"No, this is fine. I have plenty of room."

"What's your name, young lady? You must live around here"

"Yes sir, I do. I'm Garson Dawson's daughter. I live on Stateline Ridge. I'm going home. I've been visiting my brother. What's your name, sir? I'll want to tell Daddy so he can thank you," said Abigail.

"I'm Jim Smith," replied the man as he accelerated. They had reached the top of the mountain and as the road leveled off the car began to move faster and faster. Abigail looked at the speedometer and saw that it registered sixty and was climbing. They had already passed the Collins Ridge turn off. There was four miles of straight road before it turned down the other side of the mountain. They went flying past Alvie Horn's beer joint and Abigail became wild with fright.

"Stop! Stop! We've passed my road." Abigail yelled, but to no avail. They were going so fast that she knew she would be killed if she jumped out. *Oh God! Help me! What must I do?* Abigail prayed as they came to the top of Bertha Horn Hill, where a wooded lane ran back into the woods. The car shot off the road and up the lane. Abigail knew there wasn't a house in hearing distance and not many cars came by at this time of the evening. The man stopped the car and turned toward her with a smile.

"I'm sorry I scared you, but I wanted to get to know you. I won't hurt you," he said, reaching out his hand. Abigail jerked back and hit the door lever. The door fell open and she turned to jump out but the suitcase caught her foot. She fell forward into the dirt with her foot still caught. Before she could get her foot free, the man was upon her. He grabbed her upper arms and started dragging her on out of the car. When her feet hit the ground, she screamed and kicked out, but he side-stepped and kept a tight hold on her arms. Now, she became frantic and clawed with her hands. She heard fabric ripping and felt a sharp slice of pain rip across her breast. She didn't know if it was her clothes or his, and her breast was hurting, but she didn't try to see if she had been cut. She was too busy fighting for her life.

"Merciful Lord, please help me," she cried aloud just as he threw her backwards on the ground. As he came down on her, she felt hands on her in places that nobody had touched since she was a small child. She grabbed a handful of dirt and threw it. She heard a loud curse as a fist hit her eye and she was slapped across the face. She screamed again but kept fighting. Blackness began to swirl around her, but with one last effort, she jabbed her fingers toward his face and made contact.

The man screamed and rolled off her. She frantically

turned over and scrambled on her hands and knees away from him. She jumped to her feet, and never looking back, went staggering and reeling toward the road.

Abigail didn't know she was almost naked as she made it to the blacktop. Tears were streaming down her face, but she kept repeating, *Thank you, sweet Jesus. Thank you, thank you.* She could barely see where she was going since her right eye was swollen shut. In fact, her entire face felt swollen. She stumbled along as fast as she could, fearful that the man would come after her. A car came around the curve in front of her and came to a screeching halt.

"Oh my Lord! Abby, what has happened to you?" said an astonished male voice. Recognizing the voice of her brother Charles, Abigail lost all her strength and sank to the ground in relief.

Chapter 3

Charles jumped from his car and plucked a sobbing Abigail from the ground. He didn't speak as he carried her to the car. He placed her gently on the front seat. "Who did this to you, Abigail?" he asked, and then turned red as he asked, "Did he r. . . uh, you know?"

"No, the Lord helped me get away from him. I-I think I must have jabbed him in the eye," replied Abigail between sobs, while looking at her fingers. They were bloody and two fingernails were broken and jagged.

"Well, he did more than that to you. You have a black eye, you're bruised and scratched all over and your clothes are gone," stated Charles.

Abigail gasped as she looked down at herself. The only clothes she saw were her panties, and the ragged shreds of her other garments hung about her. Convulsively, she tried to cover her nakedness with her arms. Charles took off his jacket and handed it to her as he turned to look down the road.

"He . . . he's still in those woods," she said, pointing ahead with a hand that trembled so badly that she could barely hold it up. "He's in a car. He was going so fast I couldn't jump out. He's old, but he's not like Grandpa. He's evil," said Abigail, who had cried so much she was now hiccupping.

Before she had finished, Charles sprang around the car and, in a loping run, headed for the woods. Abigail sat shivering in revulsion, and then she suddenly shoved the door open and vomited. She hadn't finished when Charles came back.

He didn't see Abigail because she was bent so low toward the ground. "Abby, where are you. You don't have to hide. He's gone," said Charles, hurrying around the car. When he saw Abigail bent over heaving, he rushed to her side.

"Give me something to drink," she moaned, trying to straighten up. Charles pulled her upright and rested her head against the back of the seat.

"I don't have any water but I have a case of Nehi pop in the trunk. I'll get you a bottle and you can rinse your mouth. That should help some." When he came back he had the pop and also a quart fruit jar with water, or so Abigail thought.

"Give me the water. I don't like pop."

Charles opened the lid and held it to her lips. "Don't drink much. It ain't water, but it may stop the shivers."

She took a sip and gasped for breath before she started coughing. When she had finally gained enough air to breathe, she gasped, "What is that?"

"It's corn whiskey. You didn't drink enough to hurt you. You've stopped shivering, so it's helped you. Now, I'm going to take you home. I found your suitcase and handbag as well as pieces of your clothes. Mom will know how to handle this better than I do," said Charles, placing her purse and suitcase in the back seat. He got into the car and started the engine.

Abigail was so tired, shocked, and bruised that she sat silent, but shivered violently every few minutes all the way along Stateline Ridge. By the time they arrived at home and saw Sally, delayed reaction had set in and Abigail was screaming and fighting so much that Charles had to hold her while Sally dressed her from the skin out. Sally was also shaking so badly that she felt she'd never get the clothes on Abigail. She looked at Charles with wildly blaring eyes and trembling lips. She tried to say something, but was trembling so badly that she couldn't speak. Charles knew she needed help, but didn't think he should help dress his sister.

"Mom, get hold of yourself! You're almost as bad as Abby. We need to get her to the doctor," scolded Charles and Sally drew herself up to a rigid posture and finished getting Abigail dressed.

"Thank you, Jesus, for helping her before he finished his

evil deed," whispered Sally in a choked voice as she walked Abigail to the car, but only with Charles's help. Sally sat in the back seat beside Abigail, whose arms had to be bound to her sides to keep her from fighting. Sally held Abigail tightly as Charles drove them to War, West Virginia to old Dr. Carr's office.

Abigail started screaming again as soon as she saw Dr. Carr's white hair. They couldn't calm her and he finally had to give her a 'knock-out' shot. "She needs to go to St. Albans hospital where they have doctors who treat this kind of trauma."

Sally shook her head. "My husband won't agree to that and we don't have the money, either."

"Well, you may have to bring her back tomorrow. I'll send her to the hospital if she's not any better. How did this happen?"

Sally, who was now in rigid control, told him all she knew in a stony voice. Dr. Carr gave her a strange look and sent his nurse to ask Charles to come in. Charles told of finding Abigail and her saying she hadn't been raped because she jabbed her finger in his eye. "Well, thank God, for that. He would have killed her if she hadn't. I hope she blinded the devil," said Dr. Carr vehemently.

When Charles went back into the outer office, Dr. Carr examined Abigail for broken bones, cleaned the cuts and scratches and swabbed them with gentian violet. He gave Sally a bottle of green nerve medicine. "I think you'll have to bring her back, but if not, gradually reduce the dosage from a teaspoon three times a day to twice a day, to one teaspoon a day, then a half teaspoon. Then you can drop it down to every other day and after two weeks stop altogether," ordered the doctor. "You don't want her to become dependent on it. She's in no state to hear this now, but she is a very lucky, young woman. She got away and many young women haven't." He looked at Sally, "I still say she may need long term counseling before she gets better."

Sally, had never heard of a counselor, but later that night, when she told Garson, he said, "Counseling! I can talk to her as good as any other man can. Besides you're the one that's always spouting about the Lord. We'll take her to one of them preachers you think so much of."

The next morning, Sally gave Abigail a dose of her nerve medicine and they took her to old Elder Oscar Lee Pruitt, who was visiting in the area, and he put his hands on her head and prayed. On the way home, Abigail fell into a restful sleep.

The sleep did her good and stopped the shakes, but even now, looking back she couldn't recall the next few weeks. She could remember, however, the weeks of terrifying nightmares that had her waking in cold sweat with a pounding heart. She didn't return to school the rest of that year, but her grades were so good that she was allowed to go on to the twelfth grade the following year.

When Sally told Abigail what Dr. Carr had said about her being lucky, she agreed with the doctor. Silently she thought, *I've also learned to never accept rides or trust any men even if they are old.* The family soon realized that Abigail avoided close contact with her father or any of the male members of her family and they were all concerned, especially Sally. Sally stoically watched every move Abigail made, but seldom made any comment.

Abigail gradually seemed better, but she realized that her experience had given her an unnatural fear of men, especially if they wanted to touch her. She knew her attitude was puzzling to her dad and her brothers, but since her family was never demonstrative with their affections it went mostly unnoticed.

Regardless of her feelings, she worked hard to overcome her fear and prayed constantly for help. Gradually the fear began to lessen, but she had withdrawn more than ever. Abigail couldn't remember when she had been laughing and carefree. She felt that surely she must have been happy at some time in her life, but a time when she wasn't afraid was only a nebulous memory.

She completed the last year of high school at seventeen, but never had a boyfriend; not even for the senior prom. She graduated with a four- point O average, but felt that had come about from all the studying she had done and not because she was overly intelligent. The principal, John Henry Adair, had called her into his office to tell her that she was eligible for a full four-year scholarship to Concord College.

Abigail knew she would need some clothes and other money for personal items as well as transportation to and from if she ever got to come home. She had no way of getting that money unless she worked it out. When she asked her dad about getting a job, his reaction was terrible.

"So, you're wantin' to work in a beer joint like your sisters. You never have been flirty around boys like the other girls. I thought you had more sense than that, but I was wrong again. Didn't that old man's pawing you learn you nothing? If you could get you a decent job and not shame me like your sisters have, I'd be glad to see you go," roared Garson, his eyes blaring wildly in a red face, while he glared at his wife as if accusing her.

Abigail was seventeen and knew she couldn't find work near her home that her dad would think decent. She was wrong though. She was in the post office two days later when she heard two women talking about Harve and Matty Collins needing a hired girl because Matty was so sick. Abigail hurried home and told Sally what she had heard.

"Mommy, don't those people live around Collins Ridge? Do you reckon Daddy would take me to see them?"

"Abby, do you know what hired girls have to do? You know how to do anything that needs doing around a place, but I'm always here to do the main part. There, you'd be expected to do it all by yourself," said Sally worriedly.

"I know, Mommy, but Daddy said if I could get decent work and that's decent work, isn't it?"

"Yes, girl, it is, but it is also back-breaking hard. You're not very big and I don't know if you could stand it or not. Do you really want to go to that college that much?" asked Sally.

"Yes, Mommy, I do want to go that much. Can you talk to Daddy for me?"

"Girl, you must be crazy. If I even mentioned it to your

daddy you'd never get to go. No, you don't want me to mention it. You'd do better talking to him yourself," answered Sally.

Abigail was afraid to ask her dad, but going to college was like opening a locked door and Abigail wanted to open that door. She caught Garson after he had come home from one of his Saturday trips into Bradshaw. With a few drinks in him, Garson Dawson sometimes became easier to agree to things the family wanted. She had picked the right time.

So Abigail went to work for Harve and Matty Collins in August after her high school graduation. Her mother was right. The work was from sun to sun and it was back-breaking. Sometimes Abigail was so tired she felt like just lying down and never getting up again. Then she thought of the letter she had written to John Henry Adair and the reply she had gotten from him: "If you can come up with three hundred dollars you won't need any more." Then Abigail would put one foot in front of the other and keep going.

Abigail had now worked one full year and nine months, but she only had one hundred and ninety-six dollars. She had to give Garson five dollars each month to take her back to Harve and Matty's each week and she had to buy a coat, boots, socks, and under clothes. Garson also insisted that she give Sally three dollars each month to wash her clothes. Sally didn't want it, but Abigail knew that was the only way her mother would be able to buy one thing for herself. Now, since that man had scared her so badly she would have to pay an extra eight dollars out of her meager pay.

Abigail worked all week and came home on the weekends. She went to church with Sally; sometimes they walked all the way. Many of the neighbor boys had offered to take her and Sally to church but Abigail always refused. Abigail hadn't wanted to date anyone before she was attacked, and now she was terrified for a man or boy to get near her. She sometimes sat on the school bus with Harold Jeffrey, also from State Line Ridge, before this had happened to her, but she refused to sit anywhere near him after that.

Abigail kept her fears hidden by telling would-be suitors

that she was so busy trying to work out money to go to college that she didn't have time to go out. That was true, but she had chosen to take on this job. Soon, the boys in the area stopped trying, even though they all talked about her long wavy red hair, emerald green eyes, and creamy skin. They talked about what a shame that none of them had a chance with her.

The teacher at Roosevelt School on Collins Ridge had advertised for a janitor and Abigail applied for the job. She had checked with Harve Collins to make sure he wouldn't object to her going in the evenings to clean the school house and then going early the next morning to build the fire in the winter.

"I don't care as long as you do your work here," said Harve, but Matty cautioned her that she was working herself to death. Abigail told her that twenty dollars more on a month was very important to her.

"I've never seen a young, pretty girl so eager to make money. Why don't you find you a good man and marry?" asked Matty.

Abigail shivered. "I'd rather work myself to death than marry."

"Well, I never heard the beat of that in my life. What's turned you sour on marriage? Does your daddy beat on your mammy?" questioned Matty.

Abigail said, "No, Daddy don't beat on Mommy, but I still don't want to marry."

"Well, what are you aiming to do? If you work the way you do here for many years there won't be nothing left of you," said Matty, who really hated to see her work so hard.

"When I get enough money I'm going to college and become a teacher," said Abigail.

"Well, bless my soul. You'd make a good teacher that's for certain. You're always showing my grand young'uns how to do things. You've got a way with young'uns," said Matty with a beaming smile.

Abigail thought the same thing. She knew she loved children and loved to watch their little eyes light up when she showed them something they hadn't known before. Grandpa had said that teaching was her calling in life. "A good teacher teaches more with her feet than they do with their mouths," said Grandpa when he talked of being a good example. Daily she prayed for guidance in setting a good example in all her walks, acts, and speech.

Everything had just seemed to fall into place the entire first year, and now she was into the second year. Even though she worked constantly, she had been healthy and had not had to miss any work. Now it was March, but still cold and she'd had to wear her new coat, her first and only coat.

Now, her coat was ruined and if Sally couldn't repair it, she would have to have another one. She had finally gotten past the nightly nightmares of that first episode and now this had happened to her today.

That night she dreaded going to sleep. She didn't want to relive that first experience, but that's what she had done. However, it didn't have the effect it had always had on her. She didn't wake up screaming and shaking to pieces. *I must be getting over it,* she thought, even though she was still afraid to accept rides and was still afraid of men. *The terror seems less, though,* she told herself the next morning.

God delivered me the first time and he heard me today, she thought. *Grandpa always told me that if God was for me who could be against me.* She sometimes wondered if she should unite with the church, but she wanted to be sure of her calling. She went to sleep, thanking God for watching over her.

Garson was as good as his word. Each Friday morning he rode with Rob Baker to work. Damon took the truck to work and went out Collins Ridge to get Abigail in the evening.

In April, all of Abigail's brothers and sisters came home with their families for a two-day Easter holiday. Kyle, the oldest brother, had written to tell Garson that he was bringing someone who was a forester and a timber appraiser with him.

"Dad, I told him that you knew more about timber and trees than any man I ever met. He offered to pay me if I'd introduce him to you," wrote Kyle. "He says he's been in McDowell County before, but only for one day. I hope you don't mind me bringing him with us," he'd continued.

Garson was anxious for Kyle's arrival since he loved talking about forestry. He had a love for nature, especially the trees. He was totally against clear-cutting and was a good timber contractor. With this kind of mindset, he had raised his family to love and respect nature. Sally often said, "I wish he'd feel the same about people, especially women."

Virginia, Abigail's oldest sister, with her two daughters, had arrived a day early, but late in the evening. Early the next morning, Abigail and her nieces, Cindy and Beatrice, went for a walk. They left through the orchard, stopping to watch a mother bird bringing twigs for her nest. Then they took the path through the woods leading to the creek that ran through Wall Plate Hollow. They dawdled along, picking mountain tea and pinecones.

"Help me gather these pinecones, girls. I'll take them back to Matty's and use them in some of the art projects I have in mind. Matty's grandchildren pester me to death to help them make things." said Abigail, filling the burlap sack she had brought with her.

They made it back home just as the first car pulled into the parking space below the house. Charles, Sylvia, and their two boys, Rick and Charlie, piled out, the boys racing to see who got to Grandpa first. Soon after that, Alice and Wilson with their three children, Janie, Jill, and Johnny, were parking beside Charles's car, but their car was new. Looking out the window, Garson said, "Would you look at that. Wilson must have got another raise. What kind is it this time, Charles?"

"It's a Cadillac, Dad. You've got a rich son-in-law," Charles said on a laugh.

There was an audible groan around the room. "Oh Lord, we'll all have to go out and look at it and listen for an hour to how he got such a good deal," said Charles's wife, Sylvia.

Jill, the youngest of the children, came skipping through the door. "Papaw, my Daddy has a Cadi . . .; uh what is it, Mommy?"

"A Cadillac, dear. I'm sure Papaw saw us pull up," answered Alice warily, since she felt Garson didn't care for girl children.

"Yep, that's right. A Cadi- lac. Daddy says it's the best car on the road, didn't you, Daddy?" Jill gloated, looking up at her Dad for approval.

"Well, come on, Jill, take your old Papaw out to see it," said Garson, walking out of the room. They all trooped out the door to stand gazing as Wilson opened the doors, offered opportunities to test the seats for comfort, to admire the chrome on the grill, to inspect the interior color scheme, and see how bright the lights were.

Charles slapped Wilson on the back. "You've missed your calling. You would make a first rate car salesman. You've almost talked me into trading my old station wagon for a Cadillac."

Before Wilson could gain a second wind, another car pulled into the spot behind the Cadillac. Kyle Dawson stepped out on the driver's side and stood looking at the gathered assembly. "Well, gosh I didn't expect all of you to come outside to welcome me. You could have waited inside." He laughed merrily, since he also knew of Wilson's pride in acquiring possessions; especially when nobody else in the family had them.

Garson laughed as he walked over and clasped his son's hand. "Good to see you, Kyle. Was the traffic bad?"

"No, not too bad except that road between Welch and Bradshaw. I guess that will never be any different though." Just then the passenger door opened and Marie, Kyle's wife, stepped out as did the passengers from the back seat. David and Randall, Kyle's teenage sons, everyone knew, but the tall black-haired man who unfolded himself from the back seat was a total stranger.

"Dad, here's that forester I wrote to you about. Lucas Sutherland, come and meet the tree wizard, Garson Dawson. Dad, this is Lucas Sutherland, a forester for Georgia Pacific Lumber Company." Garson looked up at this tall young man and smiled as he put out his hand.

Abigail was standing at the back of the crowd with her arm around Beatrice's shoulders. She caught her breath. She was looking at the handsomest man she had ever seen in her life. His coal black hair lay in waves and curls and his brown eyes twinkled. Her pulse raced as she watched him smile at her dad, showing beautiful white teeth, but when he spoke, a shiver ran down her spine. He sounded like that man in the blue truck. He couldn't be though. That man had been all hair and beard. He had also looked dirty and scruffy, or as much as she could see of him did. This man had short hair, was clean-shaven and looked prosperous. Kyle had just said he was the forester for Georgia Pacific. According to Garson, foresters made a good salary. *No, this couldn't be that man,* thought Abigail.

She turned with Beatrice and went into the house, leaving the others still being introduced to Mr. Sutherland. That voice was too much like his and Abigail didn't want him to be that man. "Let's go back to my room, Beatrice. I need some ideas of what to make with my pine cones."

They stayed there until her mother called, "Abigail and Beatrice! You two get in here. Supper is on the table."

Abigail pushed Beatrice. "You go on in front. You're taller than I am and nobody will notice me."

Beatrice laughed. "That won't work. Everybody always notices you, Aunt Abigail. Besides they've all already noticed you, except for . . . oh! That man. You don't want him to notice you, but I thought he was handsome, didn't you?"

Chapter 4

Beatrice was right. As soon as she walked into the well-lit room the man, who was seated at the backside of the table in front of the windows, almost choked. He hastily took a drink of water, but never took his eyes off her.

"Lucas, you look like you've seen a ghost. Ain't you never seen a girl as pretty as our Abigail?" joked Kyle.

"Were you walking out of Collins Ridge one evening about a month ago?" Lucas asked, looking at Abigail.

Sally looked at Abigail who was deathly white. "Yes, she was. She works around Collins Ridge. Why? Did you see her?"

Lucas felt the tension around the table. "Yes, I did see her. I was going down to a Mr. Murphy's house for my boss and she was walking along the road. I stopped and asked her to ride, but I guess she thought I was crazy. I was going in the wrong direction. I told her I would be right back, but I never could find her. I made five trips in and out of that ridge, but she'd just vanished. I finally decided I must have imagined seeing her. What happened to you, anyway?" he asked a stunned Abigail.

Abigail stood like a statue and everyone turned to look at her. "You scared me. You were drunk. I told you I didn't want to ride, but you said you were coming back to get me."

Sally spoke up. "She said that man was covered with beard. She was still all tore up when she finally got home." Sally turned to Abigail. "Come on and sit down."

Abigail slowly walked to her place beside her mother, but

didn't raise her head to look at Lucas. Everybody seemed to relax as Lucas explained.

"I wasn't drunk, but to be honest I'd had a drink or two. I'd been in the woods for nearly three weeks appraising a boundary of timber. That's why I looked like a wild man. I wouldn't have hurt you. It never entered my head that you would be afraid. I give people rides all the time. They expect to be given rides where I come from. I'm truly sorry. I hope you can forgive me."

Abigail didn't look up, but Garson said, "Of course, she forgives you. She don't usually walk out of the ridge, but the man and his wife that she always rides with went to the doctor that day. I guess it's just one of those things that happen for some reason, so just forget it."

Oh yes, thought Abigail. *The great Garson Dawson has decreed it and every knee must bow.*

Soon the talk around the table became lively and Abigail's quietness went unnoticed by everyone except Sally and Lucas Sutherland. Sally knew the reason Abigail was so quiet, but Lucas did not and he wondered why she was acting this way. *She must be at least sixteen, so surely she isn't that timid. There must be something else,* he thought.

When supper was over, the men all went back outside. Garson wanted to show Lucas some lumber he'd obtained from his stand of black walnut. Kyle, Charles, Wilson, and Damon went out to once again go all over the fine points of Wilson's Cadillac. Soon the women had the kitchen cleared and Abigail, and her nieces, had a jigsaw puzzle spread out on the end of the big kitchen table.

They were all totally engrossed in putting the puzzle together when the men came back in. Garson came to the door. "Abby, bring us four cups of coffee and some slices of that cake to go with it. We're going to watch wrestling on television and all that struggling will make us hungry."

Abigail got up and poured coffee, cut the cake, and put it all on a tray with cream and sugar and walked toward the living room. When Lucas saw her he jumped to his feet and came to meet her. "Here, that's too heavy for you. I'll carry it in."

He took the tray and Abigail thanked him. She turned back into the kitchen without once looking at him.

"I sure got off on the wrong foot with your daughter, Mr. Dawson. I'm so sorry I scared her. I wouldn't harm a fly much less a young lady," Lucas said as he watched Abigail's back going through the door.

"Give it time, son. Abby is awfully shy around men, but things have a way of working out. If you two were meant to be friends, you'll be friends some way," replied Garson in a firm assured voice.

Lucas looked doubtful but resumed his seat. He soon found that watching wrestling wasn't something he enjoyed. He stood and stretched. "I think I'll walk around outside. Sitting too long makes me want to stretch my legs. You want to show me around the farm, Kyle?"

Kyle nodded and eased out of his chair, knowing that Garson was so engrossed in the wrestling match that he wouldn't notice they had gone until it was over. They went strolling down through the orchard. "Abby loves this orchard. In fact she loves this entire farm. I'll bet that she has taken some of the girls on a walk to the creek already," said Kyle.

"She'll not offer to take me on a walk, that's for sure. She made it abundantly clear that she wants nothing to do with me," said Lucas.

"According to Dad, you scared her so badly that she ran down in the woods until you had gone on and then ran to Walter Mullins's place. She was scratched, her coat was torn, and she was shaking like a leaf, was the report Dad received. I think he even asked around to try to find out who had scared her and now he rides with someone else on Fridays so that Damon can have the truck to drive out Collins Ridge and bring Abby home."

Lucas walked along deep in thought. "Kyle, I swear I wasn't drunk, but I was tired. I didn't want to go down to the Murphy place. I was mad, but when I went around that curve and saw a beautiful girl walking, I . . . I don't know how I acted. I really just meant that I had to go on down the road, but when I came back I would give her a ride home."

Kyle slapped him on the shoulder. "I believe you, man. I'll get Marie to talk to Mom. If Mom is convinced, I think she might talk Abby around."

"Is she dating somebody?" asked Lucas.

"No. As far as I know she has never dated anybody. Of course, there aren't many eligible young men in this area, but I just don't think she is interested."

"You mean you think some boy broke her heart and she doesn't want to take another chance? She's awfully young for that to happen. Surely she'll want to marry someday. She seems to like children." Lucas was puzzled.

"She does. She loves children and I understand that she is planning to become a teacher. I just mean that she never mentions dating or being interested in any man. I don't know if some boy broke her heart or not," replied Kyle thoughtfully.

They turned and meandered among the trees talking about the different varieties Garson had growing. As they neared the house Lucas asked, "Will you try to find out something tonight? I'd like to ask her for a date, but unless something is done I feel like I would be wasting my time?"

Kyle grinned. "You're really interested, aren't you? Don't worry. I'll try to find out something for you." They stepped up on the porch just as Garson and Charles came out the door.

"Did your man win, Dad?" asked Kyle.

"No, that other man had something hid in his trunks and nearly put his eyes out. I wish I'd been there. I'd have helped him. I can't stand people not being treated fair." Garson's face was red and his eyes looked wild.

I wouldn't like to have him angry at me, thought Lucas, watching him.

Charles laughed. "Dad, they're just putting on a show. I'll bet they rode to the arena together."

"I can't see how anybody could act like that and not be mad. I certainly got mad, but that's the reason I wouldn't get involved in something like that," replied Garson soberly. "I'd probably end up in jail for killin' somebody."

Turning toward Lucas, he said, "Did you like my orchard? I reckon it's Abby's favorite spot on this farm. Quick as she learned to walk she wanted to go to the 'chard as she called it. Sally's daddy used to keep her out there pert nigh all day. He showed her how to graft limbs from one tree into another."

"She still does it, too, but I have better luck with a graft than she does," bragged Damon, who had come to join them.

"She must be a good teacher then, cause she's the one that showed you how to do it, wouldn't she?" asked Charles.

Damon grinned. "She taught me after Grandpa died. She said it made her feel close to Grandpa. I believe that's why that man scared her so bad that time. She trusted him 'cause he looked like Grandpa and . . ." Damon stopped when Charles punched his shoulder. He turned red and hung his head.

Charles tried to laugh. "Sometimes Damon gets carried away, don't you? We look over him since he is the youngest boy. Do you have any brothers, Lucas?"

Lucas had picked up on Damon's partial revelation, but he acted as if he hadn't heard anything. "I have three brothers and two sisters, all younger than I am," replied Lucas. They were all seated on the porch and now Lucas sat wondering what Damon had started to tell.

He realized that he wasn't going to learn it now, since the talk was centered on the coal industry. "The union has called a strike again down at Number Six. Gilbert Holt said he was going to Toledo, Ohio and work in the steel mills until the strike is settled," said Garson.

Kyle grinned. "Gilbert always did act like missing a shift's work was a mortal sin. I've known him to work in coal not two feet high if his mine was on strike. I'll bet he saves over half of every pay day he gets."

"'There's more in saving than there is in making it,' is what Grandpa always said," quipped Charles.

Alice's husband, Wilson, spoke up, "That's the truth. How

do you think I can afford a Cadillac? I put by so much out of every pay check for a rainy day."

Garson laughed. "Then you buy a Cadillac to keep out the rain, I guess."

Kyle, fearing that would hurt Wilson, said, "Well, he must be right. You don't see any of us with a Cadillac do you?"

Just then Sally stuck her head out the door. "If you men plan to go hunting tomorrow you'd better be getting to bed. Me and the girls are going to the meeting house. Services start at ten in the morning so we'll have to leave here by nine thirty."

Chapter 5

Nine-thirty the next morning found three cars pulling out of the driveway at Garson Dawson's farm. Wilson, of course, wanted Charles and Garson to ride with him; who better to impress than one's father-in-law. He was first in line. Next was Virginia in her Jeep Cherokee wagon. It was filled with her own daughters, Alice and her children, and Sally. Sylvia's boys had gone with Wilson and their dad, since they wanted to hunt. Abigail was left to ride with Kyle or drive her Dad's truck.

I'll just stay home, she thought as she realized how crowded it would be, and also that Lucas Sutherland would be her seat mate. Since Kyle's wife, Marie, had decided that her family was going to church, she had already ordered her boys into their car when Damon came rushing out the door. He stopped as he saw the other cars driving away.

"We can't all ride in your car, Kyle," he said in a disgruntled voice. He looked at Abigail, Lucas, and Kyle. "They must not have wanted me to go."

"You can drive Dad's truck, Damon. Lucas and Abigail could ride with you," said Kyle, thinking Damon would be proud to drive to church.

"I don't want to drive Dad's big old truck to church. Matthew Cantrell will laugh his head off. I'll ride with you and let Lucas drive Dad's truck. Abigail can ride with him," he said, pulling the keys from his pocket.

"Lucas can drive a truck, that's for sure," said Kyle, chuckling. "Abigail knows all about his driving, don't you, Abigail?"

Abigail turned red. She looked especially pretty in her pale green dress, which set off her green eyes and red hair to perfection. Her hair was hanging down her back in a shining cascade of waves and curls and drew attention to her creamy skin, arched eyebrows, and dark eyelashes. The dress had a framing collar and a belted waist with the skirt reaching to just below her knees.

"I don't think I'll go today, Kyle. I have some ironing to do. I can stay here and have dinner ready when all of you get back."

"Now, Abigail, you didn't get all dressed up in your pretty green, Sunday-go-to-meeting dress, just to stay here and cook dinner," chided Kyle. "Besides, Dad wanted some of that wood brought back from where they trimmed those trees at the back of the church and we'll need the truck for that."

Seeing no way that she could refuse without making a scene, Abigail shrugged and walked toward the truck. Lucas grinned and winked at Kyle as he strode jauntily in the same direction.

Abigail opened the door and climbed hurriedly into the truck. Lucas had started to that side to assist her, but seeing that she was already seated, he continued on to the other side. They didn't speak until Lucas had backed, turned, and pulled out in front of Kyle, who was settling the seating argument between his sons.

"I'll let Kyle eat the dust this big old truck will make," Lucas said with a laugh. "He'll learn to assign seats before he starts from now on, won't he?"

Abigail didn't say anything in reply and Lucas drove along as if deep in thought. As he shifted into gear to go up Cecil Kennedy Hill, he turned his head and looked at her. "Honestly, I meant you no harm that day. I live in the country too, and everybody knows me. I guess I just acted the way I would at home if I saw someone walking. I'd stop and give them a ride."

Abigail looked at him and knew he was sincere. "I believe you, but I had never seen you before. Besides, you were going the wrong way."

Lucas grinned. "Well, that is hard to explain. You see, my

boss wanted to make sure Mr. Murphy didn't sell his boundary of timber to anyone else and he sent me to get his option to buy signed. I knew I'd only be about ten minutes and I thought I was letting you know that you wouldn't have to walk any farther."

Abigail grinned. "I didn't walk. I ran."

Lucas saw her grin and was pleased. "I'm sorry. Could we just wipe the slate clean and start all over?"

"What do you mean? What do we start all over?" asked Abigail.

By this time the convoy was merging with the blacktopped Route 83 highway and everyone came to a full stop before pulling onto it. While the truck was stopped Lucas reached out his hand. "Hello. My name is Lucas Sutherland. I live in Ronceverte, West Virginia. What is your name?"

Abigail didn't put out her hand, but she did smile and Lucas dropped his hand onto the steering wheel. "My name is Abigail Dawson. I live in Paynesville, on Stateline Ridge Road." Abigail giggled. "I feel silly."

"I don't feel silly, Abigail. It's all right to call you Abigail isn't it?"

"I guess so, since you've already scared me half to death."

Lucas laughed. "We can always tell our grandchildren about that meeting."

"Our grandchildren! You mean yours and mine?" gasped Abigail.

"Well, you're apt to have grandchildren and I hope I have some so I meant it is a story we can tell our grandchildren."

"Oh, sure, I guess they would like to hear how some man scared their grandmother out of her wits," said Abigail, laughing.

Now, all the cars were traveling along the highway. Wilson and his hunting party would go on down Bradshaw Mountain and the rest would soon arrive at the meeting house.

"What happens when we get to this church?" Lucas asked. "I've never been to a Primitive Baptist service before. How come your mother calls it meeting instead of church?"

"Because that's what it is. The church or the kingdom is set up in the hearts and minds of believers when these believers meet, then the church has arrived. Lots of people get the physical building mixed up with the church. We go to the building to meet with our brothers and sisters who are members of the Lord's church," explained Abigail.

"Hm-m. I've never heard it put like that before, but it makes sense, I guess. You sound like you are a member. I guess you were baptized when you were christened, weren't you?"

"No. I'm not a member. We don't christen children and not many children join our faith. We think people are called into the church and we have to wait upon the calling of the Lord." Abigail felt so easy and relaxed talking about her belief that Lucas looked at her and smiled.

"You just seemed so sure, that I thought you were a member. How does one receive this 'calling' as you term it?" asked Lucas.

Abigail looked surprised. "I don't know. The Lord does the calling and I'm not his counselor. He calls whom he will and when he will. A person cannot draw the Lord nigh unto themselves."

Lucas drove on deep in thought. "I don't understand. What if the Lord doesn't call someone? Do they never attend church?" By this time they were pulling into the churchyard behind Virginia's station wagon. Lucas shut off the engine and sat waiting.

Abigail had been thinking while he parked. "Lots of people are regular attendees at church, but never become members. I don't know the answer to your question, though. I remember Grandpa saying that he believed that from the time that Adam was driven from the Garden of Eden and lost his fellowship with God that there had been an emptiness in man that he tried to fill all the days of his life. That, Grandpa said, contributes to drug abuse, alcoholism, and many other destructive things. Man, according to Grandpa, is trying to get back what he lost in Adam, but doesn't know it. The church members that I know seem so sure and content, even though they have problems

36

just like non-members. I guess that is why people attend churches. I think they are looking for peace and I think many find it because they have a 'family' of like-minded believers to be with, and this gives them a stability they wouldn't have outside the church."

Lucas smiled. "You are a deep thinker aren't you, Abigail Dawson?" Then he opened his door to get out.

Abigail opened the door and before Lucas could get to her side of the truck, she jumped to the ground. Lucas grinned. "Are you always in such a hurry or is it that you don't like me to help you?"

"I can't get out of this truck without jumping out. I didn't even think about waiting. I guess that's the reason Mom doesn't go many places with Dad; she doesn't like to jump from the truck. Dad wouldn't even think about coming to help her. I guess I just didn't expect any help," said Abigail and smiled.

Lucas started to grasp her elbow but she side-stepped. Lucas was puzzled at her action, but said, "Please don't make me enter by myself. Nobody knows me here."

Seeing Kyle approaching, Abigail said, "Here's Kyle. Let him introduce you."

Kyle walked to Lucas's side. "Are you two arguing?"

Abigail turned to walk toward her mother. "No, but I'll let you do the introductions. You know him better than I do."

Lucas started to protest, but realized she had her back to him and was already walking away. "I didn't even ask her out. Drat! "

Kyle slapped his back good-naturedly. "Don't despair, young fellow. You'll be driving her back home after service."

Lucas relaxed and followed Kyle toward the church doors. They were stopped along the way as Kyle made him known to many of the men who lingered on the outside until singing began.

Kyle stopped as someone tapped him on the shoulder. "Rob Baker, you old son-of-a-gun, I've not seen you in ages."

"Tain't my fault, Scooter. You just out-grew your raisin' I guess, and ain't got time for your old friends," replied Rob, spitting ambeer onto the grass beside the walkway. His eyes twinkled merrily above his neatly trimmed silver beard and moustache.

Kyle laughed and said. "Well, I want you to meet one of the best foresters that any lumber company ever hired. This is Lucas Sutherland. He is forester for Georgia-Pacific Corporation. Lucas this is Rob Baker, one of the orneriest woodsmen you could ever meet. He's got more tricks up his sleeve than a dog has fleas."

Rob guffawed. "Scooter ort to know since that's how he got his name."

Kyle laughed as several men gathered around. "This old scoundrel was the first man I ever worked for. He had a timber contract and took me on as a trainee, I guess. Anyway, I had to learn to do it all. Me and another boy had sawed down a tree and just left it. We were going on to saw on another tree, but Rob yelled at me, 'Get that tree lined up to be skidded' then I yelled back. "How do I do that? This tree landed sideways."

"'Scoot'-er around,' he yelled back. I went over to the end of that log and pushed and pulled with all my might and that log wouldn't budge. I'll bet I worked there for twenty minutes and couldn't move it an inch. Then here come Rob with a cane hook in his hand."

"'Can't you scoot it?' he asked.

"'No, and you can't either,' I blurted out completely disgusted.

"Then Rob walks up with that cane hook and grapples the lower end around. The first thing I knew that log was in place and went sliding down the hill at a push from his foot. He looked around at me and said, 'You ain't much good as a scooter are you?'"

"I guess Scooter became your name after that," said Lucas laughing.

"It sure did. If I had stayed in the timber industry in this area people would have never known that I had any other name." Kyle grinned and put his arm around Rob Baker's shoulders. "He's a pretty good old cuss anyway."

The three went on into the building and took a seat beside each other on one of the benches placed along the left side of the building. Lucas noticed that most of the women sat on the right side, but a few sat beside their husbands or boyfriends on one side or the other. He wondered if they were non-members. He saw that Abigail and Virginia's daughters were seated together in the fourth row back from the front as were many of the other young people.

There was a bench behind the lectern on the pulpit and four men in suits were seated with song books in their hands. When the congregation was settled, someone started a song and soon the house was filled with beautiful harmonized music, the kind that only perfectly tuned human voices can make. Lucas sat listening in amazement. He realized that Abigail and her nieces were singing, as was everyone else who wanted to sing.

He heard a beautiful soprano voice raised an octave higher than all the others, which seemed to emphasize the tune. He realized it was coming from a shriveled older woman who didn't look strong enough to move, but on closer scrutiny he saw a beatific glow radiating from her sweet wrinkled face. *She looks like an angel and is singing like an angel as well,* he thought and continued to stare.

Lucas suddenly felt completely at peace; as if he was surrounded by love. He'd never felt like this before and he wanted to hold onto it. However, when the singing stopped and the congregation bowed their heads in prayer the feeling left him as quickly as it had come. He didn't listen to the prayer, but sat pondering why the feeling had left so suddenly. Not finding a plausible answer, he concentrated on the preaching and the rest of the service. An older white-haired man called Elder Owens impressed Lucas by his humble appearance and clear deliverance, but even that didn't affect Lucas the way the singing had in the opening. He had thought by concentrating he would feel that sense of peace again, but hadn't.

Chapter 6

Lucas left the church building in a bemused state. "Who taught those people to sing?"

Kyle grinned. "I guess the Lord must have. They certainly haven't had any formal training."

Rob Baker came up behind them. "Well, young feller, what did you think of that preaching?"

Lucas shook his head slowly. "I don't know what that old white-haired man was talking about, but he had me convinced. All four of the preachers talked about how much God loves us, and didn't one time threaten us with the burning lake of fire. Don't they believe in it?"

Rob grinned. "They shore do. They believe in the fire that Jonah experienced in the belly of a fish. There was water all around him but his Hell was hot enough to make Jonah willing to do what the Lord had bid him to do."

By this time the churchyard was filled with departing members and visitors. When Lucas saw Abigail coming out with her mother, he stepped quickly to her side. "I'm ready whenever you are, Abigail," he said smiling.

"I thought Dad wanted the wood from those trimmed trees brought home," said Abigail, looking at Kyle.

Kyle raised his eyebrows. "He does. I forgot. Come on, you boys, let's get that wood loaded." He turned to Lucas. "You better pull the truck around back or we'll be here all night."

Abigail stood talking to some of her friends as did Marie, Kyle's wife, until the men came back with a truck load of wood.

Soon everyone was loaded and vehicles were pulling out into a long line on the highway. Lucas grinned. "I feel like I'm in a funeral procession. I don't know if I've ever seen this many cars leaving an ordinary church service."

"Doesn't your church have many members?" asked Abigail.

"Sure. I think Mom said they have seventy-five active members, but the Presbyterians have Sunday school, prayer breakfasts, youth worship, and choir practice. This means that people are always coming and going," explained Lucas.

Abigail sat silent as if deep in thought. Lucas turned his head to look at her. "What are you thinking? I can see the wheels spinning in that head of yours. I guess you don't approve. Am I right?"

"I have no right to approve or disapprove. Each organization has and does what they believe to be right, and I certainly don't feel that I should condemn them. It's kind of like the Bible says, 'one star differs from another in glory,' so we can't all be expected to act and believe alike, but we are supposed to love each other."

"That's a pretty tolerant view," said Lucas as if he was surprised.

Abigail looked narrowly. "I guess it is. I just never thought about it. I think that when one loves humanity they can't help but be tolerant or understanding of their differences. Our faith is based on God's love for his creation. So, yes, I think we are tolerant."

Lucas smiled. "You look like a very young girl, but you have a wise head. I can tell you that something happened to me when everyone was singing before the prayer. I don't think I'll ever forget it, but right now I want to know if you are willing to forget about our first meeting and go to a movie with me tonight."

"I can't. I have to go back to my job this evening," Abigail replied.

"Well, what about next Friday or Saturday night? I could come to where you work and bring you home first. Later we could go to a movie in Bradshaw."

"Don't you have to work? Most people don't get off work until five o'clock," said Abigail.

Lucas laughed. "I sort of set my own hours. I have a certain area to cover and I am always on the lookout for new boundaries of timber. If there are no immediate opportunities, I'm free to work whatever hours I need to."

They pulled up in Garson's driveway behind Virginia's station wagon before Abigail could respond to that information. Lucas shut off the engine and turned, expecting her answer, but Abigail jumped out of the truck. Before she could dash into the house, Lucas caught up with her. "Wait a minute, young lady. You haven't said whether you will take in a movie with me or not."

Abigail stood looking at him. She felt different around him, like she was on the edge of something, but she couldn't explain it. He was certainly handsome and now she didn't believe he meant to scare or harm her, but she told herself she didn't want to date. Deep inside she knew that she would really like to date Lucas, but she couldn't stand to be touched. "I'll go, but just as friends. I mean, I don't want to date anybody."

Lucas looked stunned. "Don't you date at all?"

"No, I don't."

"Why? I'm sure you are asked out a lot." Lucas couldn't understand her statement.

Abigail turned red. "I have my reasons. Now, if you still want to go to a movie just as friends, I guess I could go."

"I guess friends it will be then, but I still don't understand why."

Abigail shrugged and walked up the steps and into the house without replying.

After dinner Kyle, Damon, and Lucas walked down through the orchard to look at Garson's stand of walnut trees. "This will be worth a mint one of these days," said Lucas, walking around and feeling the bark on several of the trees.

"That's what Dad says," spoke up Damon. "He keeps telling me that they're my college money."

"That's better than working your way through like I did. You'd better be glad he's saving them for you. I doubt if you'll get scholarships like Abigail did," said Kyle.

When they returned to the house, Marie and their two boys were ready to leave. Sally, Garson, and the rest of the family followed them onto the porch.

Lucas looked around and didn't see Abigail. "Where's Abigail? I need to know if she wants me to drive her home from her job next Friday."

Every head turned and stared. Sally spoke up. "You mean she's agreed to go on a date?"

Lucas shook his head. "I don't think she wants to call it a date. She said she'd go as friends, though."

"Good, good," said Sally, looking toward the door. "Beatrice, run back inside and tell Abby to come out here."

Soon Abigail appeared, being tugged along by Beatrice. "What is it? I was packing my things for this week."

Lucas stepped toward her. "I just needed to know whether or not you wanted me to come to your job and drive you home next Friday."

Abigail turned red and looked around at the assembled group. "Well, what is everybody gawking at? A friend is taking another friend to see a movie." Then giving Lucas a disgruntled look, she said, "No, I don't want you to drive me home."

Lucas shrugged his shoulders. "Okay, friend, I was just trying to be helpful. I'll be here at five o'clock Friday evening. Is that all right?"

Abigail's face turned pale. "I . . . I guess." She turned quickly and went back inside.

Lucas stood there looking bewildered. Sally looked at Lucas, "I hope you are a patient man. It'll take that. This is that first step I've been praying for." Lucas was surprised when he saw tears in her eyes.

"You're welcome Mrs. Dawson, but I really didn't do anything. Abigail is a beautiful girl and very intelligent. But, she's also like an elusive butterfly. You can't catch her to pin her down. I'm just trying to get to know her." Lucas stood waiting, expecting he would be given some explanation, but Sally had turned away.

Marie and the others started walking toward the steps. "I guess we'd better get a move on. It's getting late."

Kyle yelled from the car. "Come on. I've been waiting out here for ten minutes."

Soon all the cars had pulled away. Sally and Garson stood on the porch waving until they went out of sight. "That Lucas is a fine young man, ain't he?" said Garson as he turned toward the door.

"Seems like he is. I'd hoped the Lord would send some decent young man who would take a liking to Abby. I've been worried since that happened to her. She changed so much. She's always been shy and quiet, but now she acts like a skittish doe. I pray God that this young feller can help her to get over that."

Garson gave her a disgruntled look. "You want one of your girls to find some decent man! I thought you said there weren't any decent men," he said with a sneer.

When he didn't get a barbed response, he turned away. "Aw, you worry too much anyway. She talks to me now. That's an improvement. Things usually work out if we leave them alone. I'd like for lots of things to get fixed differently, but we have to wait for everything and sometimes they never get fixed. Pap always said time had a way of fixin' things if we'd just get out of the way."

"Your pap was right. We do have to wait and the Lord will fix things, but I just don't have as much faith as I need," said Sally.

Garson grinned. "You don't have enough faith! What in the world are you always spoutin' off about then? I don't reckon I've got an ounce of faith, but I'm surprised at you. You don't show no feelings, but always seem able to pick up your load and go right on."

Sarah shook her head. "Everybody has some kind of burden, I reckon, and ain't nobody else going to carry it for us.

I figure there ain't no sense in complaining and carrying the burden too."

Garson guffawed. "You're the beatenest woman I ever seen. Once in a while you come out with something that makes sense."

Chapter 7

The friendship between Abigail and Lucas got off to a good start even though Abigail came home on the following Friday with a sense of dread. *What if I go with him and then after we get away from people, he starts to . . . Oh Lord no. I can't go with him. I wish to God Kyle had never brought him here.* Yet, Abigail knew if she didn't go with Lucas tonight her mother would be very upset. This surprised her since Sally was always cautioning her girls about the evilness of men. Now, however, Sally seemed worried and had been like that for the last three years. Abigail didn't want to give her further cause to worry.

Lately Sally had been saying, "Abby, every man ain't like that old man. Most men are decent towards women, I reckon. You know your daddy and your brothers are, and all of our neighbors seem to be decent men. I wish you'd just remember that and quit thinking about that nasty old man."

Abigail would scold herself and really try, but after one of Sally's talks, she'd have nightmares for several nights. She did well during the day unless some man touched her. If any man even acted like he was going to touch her, she hurriedly walked away. Virginia had told her that everybody thought she was 'stuck-up' because she wouldn't stop and talk to people.

"I do talk to people. I used to stop and talk to Mary Mullins, but I don't walk out of Collins Ridge anymore," insisted Abigail.

Virginia shook her head and grinned sadly. "Abby, you wouldn't even ride out of the ridge with her husband, Walter. Mary told Mom that she felt like you was afraid of Walter. Mom made up some story to keep from hurting her feelings."

When Abigail reached home on Friday, she had made up her mind to go with Lucas, even though she was scared. "Surely Kyle wouldn't have brought him to visit his family if he was a bad person," she told herself over and over.

Lucas came at five o'clock and Abigail was ready. She thought he would be in the old blue truck, but instead, he was in a gray Buick sedan that looked new.

He didn't help her into the car, but did open her door and closed it after she was seated. "We'll be back by eleven, Mrs. Dawson," he said as he got into the driver's seat and closed the door. Neither of them spoke until they were going up Cecil Kennedy Hill. Lucas sensed that she was very tense. Actually, it seemed as if she were terrified.

"When is your job over?" he asked. "By the way, what is your job? I mean what kind of work do you do?"

"I'm a glorified 'dogsbody.' In this area, it is called hired girl, a jack of all trades. I do a little of everything from cooking to chopping weeds in the garden. I carry in wood, I build all the fires, I cook, I sew, I clean house, and you name it and I do it," replied Abigail.

"Good God! You're too little to be doing all of that. Why are you working in a job like that? You've graduated from high school, haven't you?" Lucas asked.

"Yes, I graduated from high school and I'm working to earn enough money to go to college," replied Abigail.

Lucas looked at her with compassion. "You must really want to go to college."

"I do. I want to be a teacher. I think I can start next fall, but I need to save a little more," said Abigail.

"You've not even had a summer break, have you?"

"Yes, I have. Virginia's girls came to stay and we had a good time," said Abigail, smiling in remembrance.

"How long did they stay?"

"They stayed over the weekend and two extra days."

"You mean you didn't go anywhere? Are you saying that you and those two girls just stayed on the farm and that was all the vacation you had?"

Abigail had turned to look out the window without answering. Seeing her reaction, Lucas hurriedly got onto another topic.

"Kyle and your dad said you liked the orchard. Is it just the orchard or is it any kind of tree?" Lucas was being very cautious but thought trees would be a safe topic.

"I like all trees, even the locusts, but I like the trees in the orchard best. They are like old friends." Abigail was caught up in her love of nature and seemed to relax.

"You must like the outside more than you do the inside, I mean you'd rather garden than clean house, wouldn't you?" asked Lucas glancing toward her.

"I . . . no, I like to keep my room clean and I like to cook, but I like the orchard because I can go there and be by myself," Abigail replied thoughtfully.

"Don't you like people, Abigail?"

Her head jerked around. "Yes, I like people . . . well, not all people, but I like to be alone and just think about things."

"Don't you talk to your sisters and your mother?"

"Of course I talk to my sisters and my mother."

"I didn't mean there was anything wrong about it. I just meant that you seemed to have a good relationship in the family," replied Lucas.

"I do, but I can't talk and think about things that bother me at the same time. Can you? Don't you ever just want to be alone?" Abigail asked.

By this time they were going down Bradshaw Mountain and Abigail realized that Lucas hadn't offered to touch her or act in any way except like a friend or even a brother. She relaxed and smiled as he answered.

"Well, yes I suppose. You know, I've never thought about that before. In our family we sometimes sit around and really enjoy each other's company. I guess I'm out in the woods so much that I just enjoy wherever I am. I do love the woods, but I hadn't thought about it in terms of being alone."

"Do you have brothers and sisters that are close in age to you? I don't, except for Damon, and somehow he seems so much younger. He's four years younger than I am, but I think of him as being . . . I don't know. I don't talk about things to him. Maybe it's because he is the baby," said Abigail thoughtfully.

Lucas didn't reply for a few minutes. "You know, I'll bet that the baby or the youngest in the family gets treated that way a lot." Seeing Abigail's astonished look he quickly added. "I don't mean that you treat Damon bad or anything like that. You just made me think of my sister Charlene. She's the baby in our family and really we often don't include her or rather don't give her an opportunity to express herself."

They rode into town pondering the idea, but not commenting on it. They pulled into the parking space at the Bradshaw Bus Terminal. "Kyle said this was the only decent restaurant in town. Is that right?" asked Lucas.

"I don't really know. I've not been in Bradshaw much."

"Didn't you go through town to get to Iaeger High School?" asked Lucas.

"Yes, but passing through is not stopping and learning about the town," replied Abigail as they exited the car and walked toward the door.

When they were inside and seated in a booth in the back of the room, Lucas asked, "Abigail, did you mean that you never came to Bradshaw?"

Abigail's eyes looked thoughtful. "Yes, I came and got a permanent once, and my brother brought me to see a movie twice, and I travel on the bus when I visit Kyle and the bus stops here at the bus terminal."

Lucas' eyes widened in astonishment, "Your farm is only ten to twelve miles from the town. I would have thought you would come here to shop or something."

"Well, I didn't," said Abigail just as the waitress came to take their order. When the order was given, Lucas sat waiting. When Abigail made no further comment, Lucas asked, "Where did you shop?"

"Mom made most of my clothes until I started doing odd jobs for people when I was in high school. I bought most of the clothes I have now while I was doing that kind of work," replied Abigail.

49

"Do you mean that you lived all your life there on the mountain and never came to the nearest town but four or five times?" asked Lucas in amazement.

"What's wrong with that? I had no reason to come to town and had no way, even if I did. Do you have a problem with that?" asked Abigail, getting angry.

"No, I don't have a problem, but I don't think I've ever heard of a situation such as yours. I mean, most teenagers want to go to town and have fun," said Lucas.

"I had fun so don't look at me as if I'm some stupid, backwoods hillbilly. We had books to read, we listened to the radio, read the newspapers that Dad brought home, and lots of people visited. After Kyle bought Dad his television, we also watched it. So we were informed about the world and you don't have to go to a town to have fun."

Lucas reached out his hand, but suddenly remembered Kyle saying she didn't like to be touched and picked up a salt shaker instead. Moving it around and around he said, "I wasn't looking or thinking you were stupid or a hillbilly. You . . . Well your life has certainly been different."

The waitress came with their food and nothing else was said until everything was placed and she returned to the front. Abigail picked up her knife and fork to cut her fish. "I suppose you'll have a good laugh when you get with your friends. I can just hear you now telling them about this backwoods girl who didn't know anything about her own hometown."

"No, Abigail. I'd never laugh at you. I know you are intelligent. In fact you have a very intelligent family. It's just that I'm used to a more . . . no, not more, just a different way of living," said Lucas, who seemed to be having trouble articulating his thoughts.

Abigail laughed. "We're Scots-Irish, which means we live an isolated existence, at least from the big metropolis of Bradshaw."

"That explains a lot of it," said Lucas, also laughing. "I wouldn't call Bradshaw a metropolis though."

"You're right there, Lucas. Bradshaw is not a thriving city

by any means. It used to be more prosperous and bigger, but it seems to lose population every year."

"Didn't your Dad visit Bradshaw or was he an isolationist also?" asked Lucas.

Abigail sat thinking. "I don't guess Dad is an isolationist. He comes to town every Saturday and Sunday and I've never heard our way of life called isolationism before. We don't attend the established churches like Catholic, Methodist, Presbyterian, or Episcopalian. There's nothing wrong with those churches as far as I know, but they are located in the town and we just don't go to town that much. We don't trade at the company store either, but that's because we refuse to buy on credit, our men don't work in the mines, and we grow most of our food and make most of our clothes. We just don't have the need to come to town and don't feel that we miss much by not coming. "

By this time they had finished their dinner and Lucas looked at his watch. "I guess we'd better go if you're finished. The movie starts in ten minutes."

Abigail grinned. "Didn't you see me sitting there twiddling my thumbs?" She rose from her seat and walked to the front of the bus terminal and stood waiting until Lucas settled the bill.

Lucas followed her out the door. Suddenly, he grabbed her arm and jerked her backward just as a car barreled around the corner and almost flipped over. Abigail was so shocked that she didn't even notice that Lucas still held her against his chest. She shivered, and when Lucas saw her startled, wide-eyed stare, he slowly turned her toward him. "Abigail that man almost hit you. I'm sorry if I scared you. He must be drunk."

Abigail drew in a long breath. "You didn't scare me, but he did. Thank you, Lucas." She didn't jerk away and Lucas stood still with her there on the sidewalk.

His hand slid down her arm to clasp her hand in his. "Are you all right? Do you still want to go to the movie or do you want me to take you home?"

Abigail looked up at his concerned face and smiled. "I'm all right. Let's go on to the movie."

Still holding her hand, Lucas grinned. "Sounds like a winner to me."

Chapter 8

Lucas kept her hand in his as they crossed the busy street. Although there were two theaters in Bradshaw the much praised movie *Shane,* featuring Alan Ladd, was playing across the street at the Hatfield Theater, and people were flocking to see it. "That's probably the reason the town is full of cars," said Lucas as he explained about the movie.

After standing in line for twenty minutes, Lucas led Abigail into the lobby and stopped to buy popcorn and two sodas. As they started into the theater itself, Lucas said, "Abigail, hold onto my arm. It's dark until your eyes adjust and you may fall."

"I know. I've been to movies before, you know. Charles brought me down here once, and we went to movies when I visited Kyle," said Abigail as she cautiously took his arm.

They went about half-way down the middle aisle and found two seats near the end of the row. Abigail entered the aisle first and took her seat. Lucas passed the popcorn and one of the sodas to her until he was seated. He left the popcorn in Abigail's lap and picked up her hand but she pulled away and he let it go. They sat watching the previews and the cartoons while sampling the popcorn. When the main event came on, Abigail forgot about the popcorn altogether.

She was so engrossed that Lucas clasped her hand again and she acted as if she didn't even notice. *I'll act like I don't realize he's holding my hand. Maybe, by trying, I can overcome my fear or whatever it is,* she thought and again was caught up in the movie. She found herself with tears in her eyes near the end, but turned her head to swipe her hand across her eyes.

When the lights came on, Lucas looked at her and smiled. "That was kind of sad, wasn't it? She remained faithful to her husband, but there was an attraction between them that they just couldn't help."

Abigail didn't know how to reply to that. She had stayed away from all males and knew nothing about the attraction he was talking about. Then she remembered how she had reacted to Lucas the first time Kyle brought him to the farm. She was startled out of her musing by Lucas.

"Didn't you think they were attracted to each other?" he asked as they rose from their seats to leave.

The bustle of the crowd trying to exit kept her from replying and soon they were outside. Again Lucas took her hand and they walked across the street to his car. Soon they were on their way out of Bradshaw. Lucas looked over and seeing that she was relaxed, he asked, "Did you really enjoy the movie?"

"Yes. I thought it was very good. Alan Ladd played his part well."

"Why did you cry there at the end?" he asked.

"I felt sorry for her but I admired her also," said Abigail.

"I felt sorry for both of them. Didn't you feel sorry for him? I thought he acted as an honorable man should. Didn't you?" Lucas asked, glancing over to catch her reaction.

"He knew she was married. He shouldn't have stayed there like he did," Abigail replied.

"Now, be fair, Abigail. She knew she was married also. The truth is they were both attracted to each other and they both fought it. I think it was something they couldn't help. How do you see it?"

Abigail sat thinking about how she felt. Lucas said, "Abigail, haven't you ever seen someone that you were drawn to?"

"No, I have not," said Abigail in an abrupt voice.

"Well, don't get all upset? We're just discussing a movie, but I can drop it if you don't want to talk about it," said Lucas in a puzzled voice.

"I'm sorry, Lucas. I just don't know much about relationships between men and women. That's why I insisted on friendship only," replied Abigail.

"Abigail, I know you said friendship only and I respect that, but don't you ever think about having a permanent relationship, like a home and a family? I know you like children."

"Yes, I love children and I have thought about a home and a family, but I can't have those without a husband and I don't want a husband."

Lucas was bewildered. Finally he said, "You're right there, but why don't you want a husband? If a man loved you he would be gentle and kind. Men are just like women about the people they love."

Abigail thought about her grandfather and knew that Lucas was speaking the truth, but another image popped into her head and she shivered. "I could never trust a man enough to find out, I guess, and I don't like this conversation. Let's talk about something else, please."

Lucas shrugged. "Okay. What do we talk about? What kind of music do you like? Bluegrass and country seems to be the usual type for the mountains."

"I like any music that's played well. I'm not an Ernest Tubb or Lefty Frizzel fan and I really like piano, if that helps you any."

Lucas smiled. "You're prickly as a chestnut burr. I wasn't being nosey. I just wanted to know some of your likes and dislikes. After all, friends know a lot about each other, don't they?"

Abigail looked over at him and smiled. "I'm not really like a chestnut burr. I'm just wary, I guess."

"Abigail, I'd be lying if I said I wasn't attracted to you. You are a very pretty girl and you're intelligent as well, but you have nothing to be wary about from me. I promise that I will never do or say anything that would harm you or even upset you, if I knew it. However, I confess that I don't understand your desire to not be touched."

Abigail turned pale, but didn't make a comment. Instead she turned her head and looked out the window.

"You know that if something bothers you and you bury it inside you'll never get rid of it. Instead it will fester and become bigger than it is," said Lucas.

Abigail jerked around. "How do you know? Things don't happen to men. Men are base, evil creatures."

"What? Young lady I'll have you know that I'm neither base nor evil and I resent being classified as such. Where did you come up with that kind of nonsense," Lucas shot back.

Abigail dropped her head. She was mortified. Now, how was she going to apologize without explaining? "Lucas, I . . . I'm sorry. I didn't mean you. I don't think you are evil or base. I just mean most men are."

"That's unfair also. Most of the men I know are decent, honest, hardworking people who have no evilness about them. Who in your family is like that?"

"Nobody in my family! I didn't mean my family. Oh, I don't know how to explain," said Abigail. "Forgive me. Let's just hurry and get home. I don't guess we can be friends after all."

"Can't be friends! You mean that friends can't have a difference of opinion. I differ on many things from lots of my friends, but we're still friends," stated Lucas.

They were now going down Stateline Ridge and Lucas had to pull over to let a truck pass. When it had inched by, Lucas didn't pull out. "Abigail, don't you think you should seek help about your attitude toward men?"

"No, I don't. I'm working on it and I'm getting better," she said.

"It seems to me that you are trying on the surface, but hiding some deep rooted problem," challenged Lucas.

"Do you have a degree in psychology, Lucas Sutherland?"

Lucas shook his head and pulled back into the road. "No, but I have lived a little longer than you and I know a woman doesn't act the way you do without some reason. You're not willing to discuss the reason, so therefore you must have it buried and it's affecting your daily life."

"Not until I met you, it didn't," said Abigail stubbornly.

"Oh, I see. I started your problem. Well, explain that to me."

"No, you did not start my problem, but you certainly are harping on it. You won't have to worry with it any more. Take me home and forget you ever met me. It isn't your problem anyway," said Abigail in dejection.

By this time, Lucas was pulling into the parking place below the Dawson home. He shut off the engine and turned. "Are you saying you don't want to be friends after all? I still want to be friends with you, Abigail."

Abigail had cracked the car door open but now turned. "I enjoyed the movie and spending time with you except for the trip home. I'm not ready to discuss my personal life with you or anyone else. If we can't be friends without that then I think it's better if we call a halt right now."

Knowing he was letting himself in for a lot of frustration, Lucas still wanted to see Abigail again. "Well, I still want to be friends. We'll just not talk about your phobia."

"I don't have a phobia," spat Abigail.

"Okay, your fear or feelings or whatever you want to call it. We'll not talk about it. Now, how about it? Can we still be friends?" asked Lucas.

"You sure are a glutton for punishment, aren't you? All right. Friends it is. I hope you don't regret it. When you want to stop, just say the word and I'll not bother you."

Lucas wanted to shake her, but realized that she was very young, eighteen to his twenty-eight, and certainly didn't know much about the world. He shook his head in exasperation. "Abigail, I swear you would drive a wooden man to drink, but I'm made of stone. So, let's shake on it." He put out his hand and Abigail put hers into it. Lucas' grip was warm and firm. "I wouldn't ever hurt you, Abigail, and I hate to see you so troubled. If you ever feel like you can tell me what's happened to you, I promise I'll listen."

Abigail shivered. "Thanks Lucas, but I doubt if that will ever happen."

She opened the door wide and got out. "I had a good time,

Lucas, and none of this is your fault. I'll understand if you don't want to be friends."

Lucas smiled. "Well, I still do, so what about going skating with me on Wednesday night. That skating rink in Stringtown should get some use."

Abigail laughed. "Believe it or not, I can skate. I'd like to go, but I can't go on Wednesday. I work for these old people through the week and they go to bed at nine o'clock every night."

"Okay. What about Friday? Do you get home by five o'clock? I don't think the rink opens until seven and I can be here at five," said Lucas.

"If Damon comes after me on time, I can be here at five. Mom usually has supper ready by five thirty. Do you want to come for supper?" asked Abigail.

"Sure, if she doesn't mind. But, if you want to go out to eat we can do that. I think they serve hot dogs and other sandwiches there at the rink."

Abigail smiled. "Let's just eat here."

Lucas smiled in agreement and waved as Abigail turned toward the house. He revved the engine as he drove slowly up the hill and out of sight around the curve. Abigail stood on the porch until the sound of the car was carried away on the evening breeze.

Lord, please help me. Lucas is so nice and handsome and I don't think he will bother me. Please Lord. You know what I need.

Chapter 9

Abigail could hardly wait for Friday to arrive. She told herself that it was because she was so eager to get on skates again. However, she had to admit that she was so eager because she really did want to see Lucas Sutherland again.

Sally noticed the difference in her as soon as she came home on Friday. She had a ready smile and her eyes sparkled almost like they had before she had been assaulted. Suddenly, remembering her sweet little red-headed baby girl from so long ago, Sally shivered and jerked her mind away from those memories. *Thank you, Jesus, for letting her find happiness again,* she breathed silently.

Lucas arrived promptly. *Gosh he sure is handsome,* thought Abigail, looking out the window as he stepped from his car. His black hair was cut short and waved naturally. His eyes were a soft nut brown shade which seemed to twinkle when he laughed. He was dressed in jeans, a black T-shirt and a denim jacket that he took off and flung into the back seat of the car as he got out. Abigail couldn't help but admire his broad shoulders and lean hips. She suddenly realized she was staring and turned to open the door, not realizing how red her face was.

Lucas wondered why she was so red, but didn't say anything. He stepped up on the porch and smiled. "I wasn't sure what to wear, but I can skate better when I have on comfortable clothes. I see you had the same idea," he said as he looked at her jeans and green T-shirt.

Abigail grinned. "Jeans can be washed and I've never gone skating yet that someone didn't bump me and cause a spill."

"I hadn't thought about that since I don't do the laundry at home, but it does make sense." He followed Abigail through the living room and on into the kitchen. Sally was putting the bread on the table straight from the oven and Garson was already seated.

Garson didn't get up but said, "Hello, young feller. Grab a seat and find out why I've stayed with the same woman all these years. You know the old saying that 'the way to a man's heart is through his stomach' and I reckon it's the truth. Course Sally won me by her cookin' whether she won my heart or not."

Lucas smiled. "I'll bet she won you stomach and all." Sally mumbled something as she turned back toward the stove

Garson looked down at his stomach and then let out a loud guffaw. "You're right, good cookin' is a powerful incentive."

Sally shook her head. "When a man's got a big stomach and a little heart you can guess which incentive he took." She sounded bitter and Garson gave her a hateful glare that didn't go unnoticed by Lucas.

Throwing caution to the winds, Sally said, "My daddy always said that a body could catch more flies with honey than with vinegar, but I guess nobody ever said that in front of Garson. He don't know what honey is." Sally took her seat, but looked so sad that Lucas had trouble not saying something to comfort her.

Abigail and Lucas ate hurriedly and were soon rising from the table. "Well, pon-my-honor," said Garson. "I ain't never seen young'uns eat so fast in my life? Ain't you two going to get no pie?"

"I think we'd better get going since I don't know how late the rink will remain open," said Lucas, looking at Abigail, who had started out of the room.

Abigail turned and nodded her head in agreement. "You're right, Lucas, but you'll have to give me a few minutes. I have to brush my teeth."

When Sally heard the bathroom door close, she looked at Lucas. "She's acting different . . . like she is happy. I hope you two get along good. I like to see her happy."

"I hope so too, Mrs. Dawson. I'm trying," said Lucas.

"I know it and I appreciate it. Abigail is a good girl," said Sally.

"Okay, friend, I'm ready to roll," said Abigail, coming back through the door with a denim jacket over her arm.

Lucas followed her as she turned to go. "We'll see you folks before eleven. You did say she had to be in by eleven, didn't you?" Lucas looked at Garson, who nodded his head.

"You heared right. Eleven o'clock is late enough for working people to be out if they plan to do any work the next day."

"What would he do if we weren't here by eleven?" asked Lucas, laughing merrily as they hurried out to the car.

"You wouldn't be laughing when he followed us." Abigail raised her eyebrows as she replied.

"Was he like that with all the others?"

"He was worse with the girls, but the boys had to be home by eleven as well," said Abigail.

Lucas turned to look at Abigail in unbelief.

"You can look like that if you want to, but Daddy has always had that rule. He says that working people have to have enough sleep to do a good job. According to Dad only thieves and robbers need to be out and around in the night."

"Some people work the night shift. Did none of your brothers work on the night shift in the mines?" asked Lucas.

"None of my brothers were or are miners. They don't like unions," said Abigail.

"Well, I know that Kyle has always worked in the timber industry, but what about Charles?"

Abigail grinned. "He's a carpenter. I guess you could say all of my brothers are woodsmen."

"A carpenter! Does he build houses, or what branch of carpentry is he in?"

"He does build houses, but mainly he makes furniture. He's very good at it. People come from all over to buy furniture from him and put in orders for special pieces," stated Abigail proudly.

Lucas drove along thinking that Abigail had a very

prosperous family. Kyle now owned a lumber distribution center near Lewisburg, Charles had his own carpentry business, Garson still worked as a contractor and timber appraiser and even Wilson, the son-in-law, was a salesman for sawmill parts and other timber related supplies. He turned to Abigail, "Well, they all seem to be doing well. It's no wonder that you love trees so much."

Abigail laughed. "I loved trees before I knew how the men in my family made their living. Grandpa always talked to me about the brotherhood of creation and I got the idea that trees were related to me since they are part of God's creation."

Lucas chuckled. "I make my living in the woods, but I don't think I've ever thought about trees in that light. Hmm, I think your grandfather must have been a very wise man."

Abigail sat quietly thinking and then said, "He was a wise man and also a very gentle, kind man. I loved him dearly and could never see a fault in him. I think I must have assumed in my mind that all old men were the same way, but they aren't." She shivered and turned to look out the window.

They were coming into Stringtown and Lucas slowed down. As he pulled into the only parking space beside the road he said, "No, they're not. Granted, there are some really bad people in this world, even old ones. Yet, most are good, decent, God-fearing people. I don't know why some turn out bad. It just makes me appreciate the good ones that much more."

Abigail gasped as she realized that she had not thought about the many good people she had met. For the first time she was aware that she had only been thinking of the bad ones. Lucas heard her sharp intake of breath and said, "What is it? Is something wrong?"

Abigail opened her door. "No, nothing's wrong. You just gave me something to think about."

Lucas got out and locked the door, then came around to her side and took her arm. "I hope I made you think of something good. Did I?"

Abigail grinned as they started up the little hill that led to the skating rink. "I don't know. I'll have to think about it."

Lucas looked down and saw that she was grinning and he pushed against her side. "By the time I fall and knock you down several times I'll bet you'll do a lot more thinking, but bad thinking, about me."

They walked into the entrance and stood in line to get their tickets and their skates. Soon they were out on the floor. Abigail hadn't been on skates since she left high school and was a little uneasy until Lucas took her hand and said, "Come on, let's show these people how to skate."

After one turn they were gliding around the rink in perfectly synchronized motions and became caught up in how well they skated together. The music changed to a slow waltz and Lucas turned to take her in his arms and still they skated as easily as dancers. Abigail was entranced. Lucas looked down on her happy face and was pleased. Neither of them had noticed how much attention they were getting until the music stopped and everybody began to clap.

Abigail looked around in astonishment. Lucas was also surprised, but looked around laughing and then bowed. Abigail realized what he was doing and gave a curtsey before she followed Lucas off the floor. When they reached the benches around the side, she sat down and then looked up at Lucas, smiling. "Gosh! That was fun wasn't it?"

"Yes, it was. I didn't know I would be with an Olympic skater. You are really good," said Lucas, smiling proudly at her.

"Hey, you are really good as well. It made it easier for me since you were so sure of yourself," said Abigail.

"I'm thirsty, are you?" asked Lucas and Abigail told him to get her a bottle of water. "I should have brought a bottle from home. I used to take water when I went skating, but I forgot it this time."

"Don't you drink pop?"

"No. I don't like it. Damon loves it, but I just never learned to like it. We didn't have it when I was little and now I just don't like it."

"Well, you're probably better off not drinking it, but I like a cold Pepsi when I'm thirsty," said Lucas as he left to get their drinks.

They skated until the rink was ready to close at ten o'clock and then reluctantly sat down to take off their skates. The manager came over and sat down beside them. "You two are good for business. Are you from around here?"

"She is, but I'm not. I'm in the area a lot lately, though," said Lucas.

"I'd like to get your picture skating to do some advertising. Would you be willing to be photographed?" asked the manager. "By the way, my name is Brad Gregory."

Abigail was shaking her head vehemently. Lucas looked at her and turned to Mr. Gregory. "The lady says no, Mr. Gregory."

Mr. Gregory turned to Abigail. "Why? I could probably pay you about twenty-five dollars each for one good picture."

Lucas looked at Abigail but she still shook her head no. "I don't think she'll change her mind, sorry."

Mr. Gregory turned away. "I really can't see how one picture could hurt you. It wouldn't have to be a close- up of your faces. I just need a good shot of some of your fantastic moves."

Abigail didn't shake her head. She looked at Lucas and he looked at her. Abigail was thinking about how much twenty-five dollars would add to her savings. "I'll think about it. Can we let him know next Friday?" she asked, looking at Lucas.

They now had their skates off and their jackets on ready to leave. Lucas turned to Mr. Gregory. "We'll see you next Friday and give you our answer."

Mr. Gregory grasped his hand with a big grin. "I hope you decide to do it. I don't see how it could hurt anything and you would be making twenty-five dollars."

Chapter 10

Abigail and Lucas discussed the offer on the way back up Bradshaw Mountain. "I don't know, Lucas. I don't feel comfortable drawing attention to myself."

"I don't see how that would draw much attention, since he promised it would not be a close-up of our faces. If you don't want to do it, however, we'll just forget all about it."

"We were good, weren't we?" Abigail said confidently. "I mean it was like I knew exactly what you were going to do and I could follow it so easily. Of course, I was uneasy at first, but after we skated around one time it seemed as if we'd skated together all our lives."

"We're partners, woman. We're made for each other. Can't you see that? I knew there was something special about you the first time I saw you."

"You were drunk the first time you saw me. A drunk doesn't know what he saw," Abigail teased.

"I was not drunk. I'd had a couple of drinks, but when I saw a small red-headed girl walking, I just had to stop, and when a pair of wide green eyes looked up at me, I said to myself, 'That's her.'" Lucas was serious, but when he saw Abigail's startled gaze, he laughed and said. "Maybe, I was a little tipsy."

"You were more than a little tipsy if you thought that, but my eyes were probably wide. You scared me to death."

Lucas sobered. "You're not scared of me now are you, Abigail?" he asked.

Abigail looked at his serious face and realized he wanted to make sure she wasn't afraid of him anymore. "No, Lucas, I'm not afraid of you now and I hope I'll never be again."

He reached over and picked up her hand. "I promise that I'll never do anything to scare you or harm you." Then he grinned. "Well, not unless you are afraid to let me hold your hand or hug you."

Abigail looked at their clasped hands. "Hands don't bother me, but hugs I'm not so sure about."

They were now going down Stateline Ridge. "I had my arm around you when we did the skating waltz. That didn't bother you, did it?"

"No, but we were skating. That's not like . . . like other kinds of hugs," she stammered, not knowing how to explain.

"Abigail, has some man abused you?" asked Lucas and started to say something else but at Abigail's gasp, he stopped.

"Has Kyle been telling you things? He'd better not have. Let's drop this conversation right now. We're almost to the house anyway. Are we going to skate again next Friday?" asked Abigail hurriedly.

Lucas drew in a long breath and realized that whatever had happened to her, he had rushed his fences and now she had clammed up. "I promised the man I'd let him know about the picture, so whether we skate next Friday or not, I'll have to let him know our decision."

They pulled into the parking place below the house at ten forty-five and Lucas cut off the engine. "It's your decision. Do you still want to skate next Friday?"

Abigail sat studying. "I wish we had a telephone. I'll make up my mind about the picture before Friday. I guess we could skate whether we agreed to the picture or not, couldn't we?"

"Sure, as long as we buy a ticket, I don't see why not. I'll be here before five on Friday and we can either go or not. I'll leave it up to you. Is that all right?" asked Lucas.

"I guess so. I wish he hadn't asked that. I had such a good time and now I'm almost regretting going."

Lucas started to grasp her shoulders, but dropped his hands. "You're tougher than that. Make up your mind and then stick to your guns. It's not going to change a thing for me. I don't really care one way or the other."

"Well, I thought you wanted to by the way you talked to Mr. Gregory."

Lucas looked at her thoughtfully. "Oh, because I said that I didn't see how it could hurt. I still say that, but if we do, it's all right, and if we don't, it's still all right. Abigail, the only thing I care about is how you feel about it."

Abigail heard concern in his voice and it touched her. She reached out and patted his hand. "Thanks, Lucas. You are truly my friend, aren't you?"

"You bet I am, but right now I'd better get you in that house before Mr. Dawson comes out with his shotgun," said Lucas as he opened his door and got out. He walked beside her through the yard and up onto the porch just as the porch light was turned on.

The door opened and Garson Dawson stood silhouetted in the doorway. "You just barely made it. Of course, I know you two have been setting in that car for the last ten minutes. You'ns were sparkin' I reckon," he said with a laugh.

"We were not," spluttered Abigail as she rushed on in the house and into the kitchen.

Mr. Dawson looked at Lucas and raised his eyebrows. "Oops! I made a mistake, didn't I?"

Lucas shrugged his shoulders. "I do believe you did, Mr. Dawson."

Garson slapped him on the shoulder. "You can't josh with Abby. She don't want to be linked with no man in a sparkin' manner; not even in fun."

Lucas turned to go, but stopped. "Mr. Dawson, I think someone must have abused her at some time. Do you know if anything like that happened?"

"Well," began Garson, just as Sally came to the door. "Lucas, she said she had a good time and that you all are going again next Friday. She seems happy and there ain't much happiness in this life. Thank you."

Lucas looked at Sally and wondered if he should ask her,

but changed his mind. "I had a good time too, Mrs. Dawson, and I'll see you two again next Friday. Good night!"

"Nite! You drive careful. Sometimes drunks drive too fast along this road, especially on Friday nights," said Sally as both she and Garson stepped back into the room and closed the door. They left the porch light on until they heard Lucas start his car.

Lucas drove out of Stateline Ridge thinking about the various reactions he had noticed from Abigail where men were involved. "Something has happened that was very traumatic. Maybe she was raped. God, I hope not, but that would account for her fear of being touched," said Lucas aloud, since he was alone in the car.

He drove down Bradshaw Mountain and as he neared Stringtown he recalled how Abigail felt in his arms as they skated. She had lost herself in the rhythm of the music and the skates, but he had been aware of the feel and smell of the girl that had touched his heart. He hadn't mentioned to Abigail that he had to drive all the way back to Ronceverte. "If I had she would have refused to go skating and I certainly didn't want to miss a chance of being with her," said Lucas as he switched on the radio.

He wondered about Abigail all the way home. She was scared of men, but she acted as if she trusted him. "I'll bet she'd go wild if I tried to kiss her, though," he said as he pulled into the garage of his parent's home.

The next morning he told his mother about Abigail. "Mom, she is a beautiful little girl. She's shaped like a woman, but a very small one. She is already eighteen, but she looks about thirteen. She has the most amazing green eyes I've ever seen and long, shiny red hair."

"How long have you been dating her, Lucas?" asked Mrs. Sutherland.

"I'm not really dating her. Well, I am, but she calls it just being friends. I can't hug her, or do anything but hold her hand occasionally," replied Lucas.

Mrs. Sutherland looked shocked. "Why? You are a

handsome man and most girls that I've seen around you would be tickled to have you hug them, or more than that."

Lucas sighed. "Yep, I know, but looks don't seem to mean a thing to Abigail. She doesn't trust men. I nearly scared her to death the first time I saw her."

"Scared her to death? You? Why you wouldn't hurt a flea. How did you scare her?"

Lucas told her about first seeing Abigail walking out of Collins Ridge, in McDowell County. "I scared her so badly that she ran down and hid in the woods." Mrs. Sutherland listened in unbelief. "There must be something wrong with her. Is she slow? . . . You know . . . a mental problem or something like that."

"No, she's super intelligent. She's working in this awful job to save money to go to college next year. She has a full four-year scholarship, but I don't think her father intends to help her any. She does have a problem, though. She's afraid of men. Kyle said she hadn't ever dated anyone that he knew about," explained Lucas.

"Maybe she was attacked. Something had to cause her to feel like that, didn't it?"

Lucas got up from the sofa and, running his hand through his hair, he walked over to the window and looked out. "I don't know, but Sally, her mother, seemed to appreciate me being interested in her. The whole family seemed pleased that she would even go anywhere with me or any other man."

"So, she has she gone places with you. Weren't those dates? I thought you said she didn't date," said Mrs. Sutherland.

Lucas turned from the window and grinned down at his mother. "We've gone to a movie and we've gone skating, but only as friends. I guess I must have something special, since I'm the first man she's ever gone anywhere with at all."

Mrs. Sutherland rose from the sofa and patted him on the arm. "Something has happened to that girl. I'll bet money on it. You'd think some of them would tell you what it was unless she's done something really bad. Maybe she was pregnant and aborted her baby. They wouldn't want to tell something like that."

"Mom, you think of the worst things that could happen to a woman, don't you? I don't believe Abigail would abort a baby regardless of how she got pregnant. Mom, that girl is as pure as the driven snow. I'd almost stake my life on it." Lucas was so adamant in his defense that Mrs. Sutherland hurried to soothe him.

"I didn't mean to suppose the worst thing that could happen, but I thought it must be serious or the family wouldn't try so hard to keep it a secret." She reached up and patted Lucas on the shoulder. "You really like her don't you, Son?"

"Yes, Mom, I really do like her. I think I'd like to marry her, but unless there's some way to break down that barrier I don't think there's a chance for me."

"Didn't you say the whole family went to church?" asked Mrs. Sutherland.

"Yes, well her mother and Kyle's family went with us on Sunday. I don't think Mr. Dawson does, but Abigail talks freely about God. Abigail knows so much about the Bible that I thought she was a member. She isn't though. They believe you have to wait for a divine calling from God to become a member. Why did you ask that? How can going to church help the situation?" asked Lucas.

Mrs. Sutherland looked astonished. "I never heard of a belief like that. What's it called?"

"It's called Primitive Baptist. They don't preach so much about the burning in a lake of fire like Preacher Gilmore does. All I heard them talk about was love of people. You didn't answer my question, though. How would going to a church help Abigail's situation?"

"She needs prayer. We need to all pray that the Lord will look down on her in mercy. Maybe he'll put her with a good counselor. The cause of her being afraid needs to be brought out in the open and not kept locked up to grow."

Lucas hugged his mother. "You're right, Mom. She needs a counselor, that's for sure."

Chapter 11

All the next week Lucas wracked his brain trying to find a way to approach Abigail about seeing a counselor. He finally decided that he would talk it over with her parents. Once having made the decision, he could barely contain himself until Friday.

Had Lucas known, he wouldn't have to approach anybody; the approach came all by itself. He reached the Dawson home at four-thirty since he wanted a chance to talk to Sally and Garson.

Abigail came down the steps to meet him. She was smiling. "I've made up my mind, Lucas. We'll do the picture if Mr. Gregory assures us that it will not be a close-up of our faces."

Lucas wanted to enfold her in his arms, but instead smiled and clasped her hand. "Good! Now, we can put on a show that they won't forget for a long time, can't we?"

Abigail pulled her hand away, but still smiling, she turned toward the steps. "It'd be about my luck to fall flat on my face."

"If you do I'll fall with you. Remember we will be waltzing. I wish they'd play 'The Blue Danube.' It would be like a real holiday on ice, wouldn't it?" asked Lucas, following her up the steps.

Abigail turned with shining eyes and looked up at Lucas. "That would be wonderful. Music sets the tone of anything or rather gives it an atmosphere, I think."

"Gosh! You are so beautiful, Abigail. Did you know that your eyes are brilliant when you smile?"

"Now, Lucas, remember we are friends and friends don't try to butter each other up."

Lucas laughed. "Now, what if I said, 'Abigail, you look awful,' instead? How would that feel?"

Abigail stopped and stood looking at him thoughtfully. "I think it would hurt, but I don't want us to be anything except friends. I know you don't understand why, but maybe when we're really, really, good friends I'll talk to you about it."

Lucas looked down at her serious expression and answered just as seriously. "I hope so, Abigail. I'll listen and not say a word unless you want me to."

They went on into the house, to be met at the kitchen door by Sally. "Are you two goin' to eat before you leave?" she asked.

Lucas looked at Abigail. "Unless Abigail is too excited to eat, we will. I've taken a liking to your cooking, Mrs. Dawson."

Just then Garson came through the kitchen door. "So have I, son. First time I eat her cookin' I decided I'd marry her so nobody else would get the best cook in the county." Garson grinned and came on into the room. "How are you, Lucas? Have you found any more big boundaries of timber?"

"Well, yes I have. I found about thirty acres on the back side of Crane Ridge. I don't think there's even a road into it yet and it's full of rattlesnakes according to Ira Shortt."

"Well, you can catch and sell every snake you find to that Chafin feller down at Jolo. He's a snake-handler. He belongs to that Church of Jesus Only up in Three Forks," said Garson.

"Not me! I'll kill them, but I certainly won't try to catch them. Rattlesnakes are dangerous," said Lucas shivering. "Are you serious? I mean do people actually pick up those rattlers?"

"They certainly do," broke in Abigail. When everyone turned to look at her, she turned red. "Well, they do. I saw a documentary when I was in my senior year and that Chafin man was in it."

When Lucas still looked shocked, Garson said, "I swear it's the truth. They play that loud music and then pick up them snakes and twirl them around their heads and dance whilst they're speakin' in tongues."

"What do you mean 'speak in tongues?'" asked Lucas,

71

hunching his shoulders in revulsion still thinking of the snakes.

"I don't rightly know. They are in a trance or something and they start talking, but it sounds like nothing I've ever heard before. You can't understand what they say, or at least I can't. I don't mean to criticize no religion, but I only went that one time and I ain't never been back nor don't plan to go back neither," said Garson.

"You shouldn't have gone that time. It's a wonder you didn't get snake bit," scolded Sally as she set a bowl of creamed potatoes on the table.

"Well, I don't plan to attend, Mrs. Dawson. Somebody will be bitten and then the law will come in and close their doors," said Lucas.

"That ain't likely. One of them preachers' girls got bit and they prayed over her but wouldn't get a doctor and that poor girl died a painful death," said Sally sadly. "I don't want the law to get involved in people's religion but in my way of thinking that is plain dangerous."

Garson went on to tell how many times the Chafin man had been bitten. "His hands are drawed like somebody with real bad arthritis, but I reckon it is just where he's been bit so many times."

Sally got up to pour Garson another glass of milk. "Abby tells us that the manager of that skating rink wants to take a picture of you'uns skating. It makes me kinda proud. I didn't know Abby was that good. It must be you skating with her," she said as she sat back in her chair.

"No, Mrs. Dawson, it isn't me. You should see your daughter skate. She's like an Olympic Gold Medalist," said Lucas proudly as he smiled at Abigail.

"Both of you'uns must be good or that feller wouldn't have wanted a picture. I'm glad Abby is gettin' interested in something again," said Garson and Sally gave him a knowing look.

Abigail jumped up from the table. "We won't be able to skate at all if we don't get a move on."

Lucas looked at his watch and seeing that it wasn't yet five o'clock, he realized that Abigail wanted to change the subject. He rose to his feet. "You're right and besides, the longer I sit here the more I'll eat and that's not good to do before skating.

They were soon out the door and in Lucas's car. "You forgot your jacket Abigail. I'll go back and get it," said Lucas.

"It's that brown corduroy on the back of the sofa," yelled Abigail as he made it to the porch.

When Lucas came back, Abigail didn't put the jacket on but placed it across her lap. "I think it's warm enough without a jacket, but Mom thought the night air would be colder."

"I have one in the back too, but I don't think either of us will need them once we start skating, but we might when we leave," stated Lucas. They drove along talking about the litter along the highways and the condition of the roads, until they pulled into the parking lot at the skating rink. "This is the most cars I've ever seen here as I've driven past. There are certainly more than there were last Friday night."

"Well, they can't be here to see us, since Mr. Gregory doesn't have the picture yet," said Abigail as she opened her door and got out.

Lucas came over to her side, took her hand, and they entered the rink. When they stopped to buy their ticket, Mr. Gregory came out of a room on the side and smiled. "Well, what's your answer?"

"We'll do it if you put it in writing that it will not be a close-up of our faces," said Lucas. "I would have stopped and told you before if I had known, but I had no way of knowing how she felt until this evening."

Mr. Gregory looked at Abigail and smiled. "I think you'll be very glad you agreed, young lady. It's already brought a bigger crowd tonight. I guess the regulars have spread the word."

Lucas took their skates and walked with Abigail to the benches and knelt to help her get her skates anchored securely. When Abigail's skates were on she sat patiently waiting until he fastened his and looked around. She saw lots of people she hadn't noticed on the previous Friday night. Finally, Lucas was on his feet and pulled Abigail to her feet. They went onto the floor hand in hand. Mr. Gregory motioned for them to come over to the far side of the rink where he had set up a camera on a tripod.

"What I plan to do is let you skate around once and then I'll keep snapping shots as you skate past this spot. Some will be wide angle shots and some closer, but I won't take a full face shot," he explained, and both Lucas and Abigail nodded and then skated off.

As they finished one complete circle, the strains of "Tennessee Waltz" came floating through the air and from then on Abigail was off into some other world as she glided and swayed in Lucas's arms. Mr. Gregory was snapping away, but Abigail took no notice. She was off in a dream world like Cinderella at her first ball.

After four rounds, they skated to the benches and sat down. Both of them were perspiring and Lucas produced a large white handkerchief and offered it to Abigail. "Thanks Lucas! I usually don't perspire this much. It's a good thing we didn't wear our jackets, isn't it?"

Lucas smiled. "If I smell bad, don't say a word. I did take a shower before I left home."

Abigail laughed. "That goes for me as well. The lights were brighter while we were skating. I'll bet that's why we got so warm."

Lucas looked up and noticed that now the lights were dim. "That's right they were, but I was enjoying myself so much I didn't notice. I guess he did that to get good pictures."

Lucas took his skates off and looked at Abigail. "Do you want to take your skates off and go get something to drink?"

"You can get me a bottle of water while I take my skates off, if you don't mind," said Abigail.

Lucas stood up and then bowed over her hand. "Your wish is my command, fair lady."

Abigail laughed merrily. "Goof! Go on before you make a fool of both of us."

Lucas walked around the edge of the barrier and then

through the opening to the concession stand. Abigail bent over unfastening her skates. She was happy and Lucas made her feel so safe. *Lord, thank you for sending Lucas. I believe I'm on the road to recovery,* she thought, but jerked her head up when someone grasped her shoulder. Her vision was filled with the white-haired man from three years before who now had a patch over his left eye.

Chapter 12

"I've found you, girl, I'm . . . "He didn't get any further.

With her hands thrust out in front of her, Abigail jumped to her feet, shoving the man backwards, and her scream of terror turned every head in her direction.

Abigail hadn't seen anything but the man who had attacked her three years previously. When she shoved him the man stumbled back, but righted himself and started toward her again. He tried to grab her arms, but her frenzied attempts to ward him off kept him from getting a firm grasp. Her actions, however, didn't deter Lucas's fist that slammed into the man's jaw. The white head was sent backwards onto the floor. The man lay there stunned.

Lucas had turned with the drinks in his hand when he heard Abigail scream. The drinks went flying as he rushed into action. He reached down for the man to pummel him further, but two men grabbed his arms.

Meanwhile, the white-haired man slowly raised himself to sitting position and before anyone could stop him, a shot rang out. Lucas had just managed to break loose from the hands that held him. He stepped back to steady his balance and in so doing, was only grazed on his arm as the bullet whizzed past and landed in the wall of the concession stand. Abigail would have received the full force of the bullet if grazing Lucas hadn't caused the bullet's path to angle slightly to the left.

Lucas shook his arm and turned to Abigail, who was still screaming and flinging her arms in all directions. "Abigail, it's all right," said Lucas in a soothing voice, but she wouldn't stop screaming. Lucas looked frantically around for help, knowing he needed to get her home. Luckily, Dr. Henry Jackson, the local doctor, had stopped by to watch the skating and quickly made his way to Lucas's side.

Abigail was still screaming, striking out, and shaking, and Lucas feared touching her would make it worse. She was staring in horror as if something awful was just before her as she continued to fight. Her struggles were still going on when the doctor stepped up. He took in the situation quickly and turned to Lucas. "Put your arms around her and don't let her loose. I'm going to have to give her something to knock her out."

Lucas, whose arm was bleeding freely, pulled Abigail into his arms, but not without a struggle. She scratched, kicked, and tried to bite him, but he held on. Once the doctor had given her the injection, she began to move more slowly and then finally stopped.

Lucas picked her up in his arms and started for the door, to be stopped by the doctor. "Here, let me see to that arm before you bleed to death." Someone pushed a chair forward and Lucas sat with Abigail on his lap until the doctor had cleaned and bandaged his arm. Then he walked out of the skating rink with Abigail in his arms. The doctor followed him to the car and opened the door.

"She needs to go to the hospital. Is that where you are taking her?" asked Dr. Jackson.

"I've got to take her home first. Her parents will have to make that decision, but I'll try to get them to. I'll take her to the hospital if they'll let me."

"There's a very good doctor who is trained in emotional problems at Doctors Memorial Hospital. His name is Dr. Alan Fischer and he'll know how to treat her. Has she done this before?" asked Dr. Jackson.

Lucas grimaced. "I don't know. I've only known her for about a month but she works all week long for an elderly couple and surely they wouldn't have hired her if she was prone to this kind of behavior."

By this time, Lucas had Abigail lying in the back seat and

went to get in the driver's seat. "Wait," said Dr. Jackson as he pulled out a note pad and wrote on it before tearing the sheet out. "Here, take this with you to the hospital and give it to Dr. Fischer so he'll know what I've given her."

Lucas took the paper folded it and placed it in his shirt pocket. "Thanks, Doctor. I don't know what I would have done if you hadn't been here."

"You're most welcome, young man. Good luck," called Dr. Jackson as Lucas backed up to turn and went speeding back up Route 83.

Everybody crowded around the doctor wanting to know what had happened. "Your guess is as good as mine, but I think that girl must have had some experience with that feller before. What did he do before he started shooting?"

"This white-haired feller did it, Doc," spoke up Brad Gregory pushing a white-haired man with a patch over his left eye, in front of him.

The man was struggling to get away, but Brad held him. "What did you do to that girl before you tried to shoot her? You must have done something since she started screaming as soon as she saw you. Who are you anyway?" asked Dr. Jackson.

"I didn't do nothing to her, but look what she's done to me," said the man, jerking down his patch to reveal a horrible sight. "I wanted her to see what she'd done, but when she saw me she started screaming and acting wild," snarled the man, jerking out of Brad Gregory's hold.

"You're pretty ugly, but that's the first time I've known someone to get scared that bad just by looking at somebody," said the doctor solemnly.

"Get out of my way. I'm getting out of this place," said the man, shoving at a young man who had his way blocked.

"Hold on, here. You ain't going nowhere. You came in my place and started shooting at my customers," spoke up Brad Gregory, grabbing his arms again and forcing them behind him. The man struggled to get away and started cursing. Just then Deputy Sheriff Buck Jones stepped into the fray.

"What's going on here, Doc?" asked Deputy Jones.

Dr. Jackson told him what had happened and the deputy turned to the man with white hair. "What's your name and where are you from?"

"William Jeffers from Wytheville, Virginia," replied the man sullenly.

"What are you doing in this part of the country?"

"I've a right to travel wherever I want to go. I'm just passing through."

Just then Jimmy Puckett pushed through the crowd. "I know you. You're the man that was in Gus's Place earlier this evening. A bunch of us was talking about this little red-headed girl who was going to skate tonight and you was asking where the skating rink was."

"Well, Mr. Jeffers, if that's really your name, I'm taking you in for questioning. Deputy Jones pulled out his handcuffs, but suddenly the man jerked loose from Mr. Gregory and turned with a gun in his hand. Nobody had taken the gun from him after the first shot and now it was pointed straight at Deputy Jones.

"Get back all of you. I don't want to shoot your deputy, but I will if I have to," he stated grimly as he backed through the crowd. He was nearly to his car when a young boy grabbed at his legs. His gun went off and then another shot rang out, but this time it was from the deputy's gun. The man slumped to the ground. His shot had whistled past the deputy's ear and plowed into a tree just before the entrance to the skating rink.

Everything stopped for a moment. "I think he'll need more than a patch over his eye, don't you, Doc?" asked Brad Gregory as he, Dr. Jackson, and Deputy Jones knelt beside the fallen man. Deputy Jones picked up his weapon and told some of the young men to put him in the back of the police car.

"I'll have to take him to the hospital. Can you come along with me, Doc?" asked the deputy.

"No, I can't, Buck. I've promised to check on Albert Payne this evening." Just then the police radio came on and Deputy

Jones pulled out saying that Deputy Ira Mullins was going with him to Welch.

"That stranger's other eye will be black in the morning I'll bet," said Brad, rubbing his own cheek. "That Lucas feller knocked him for a loop. That man must have done something to that girl before. He claimed she blinded him and she wouldn't have done that for no reason. Me and her daddy are the best of friends, but I hadn't seen her in three or four years, maybe more. When she first started coming here, I didn't know who she was. I didn't see that man until she started screaming, but I did see his hand on her shoulder. She was screaming and fighting like she had gone plum wild," said Mr. Gregory in an astonished voice.

"Alice is going to quit letting you out at night, Brad. It's a wonder you didn't end up with a black eye since you was manhandling that feller pretty rough." Dr. Jackson laughed and slapped Mr. Gregory on the shoulder.

"When I tell her what happened, she's going to be as shocked as I am. I don't know what to make of it myself. I don't believe that girl knew she was in this world. She was scared plum out of her mind. I hope her folks take her to see a good doctor." Then suddenly realizing he was talking to Dr. Jackson, he was embarrassed. "Not that you ain't a good doctor, but you know what I mean."

Meanwhile, Lucas drove up Bradshaw Mountain much faster than he had made it down. He pulled to a stop before the gate at the Dawson residence and blew the horn. Garson Dawson turned on the porch light and came out on the porch. Lucas jumped out of the car, after looking back at Abigail, and said, "Mr. Dawson, you and Mrs. Dawson need to come with me to take Abigail to the hospital."

Sally had now come to the door and hearing this, she stepped out on the porch and rushed toward the car. "Take her to the hospital! What's wrong? Did she fall and get hurt?" Sally asked as both she and Garson arrived at the car.

Lucas opened the back door to reveal Abigail lying asleep,

but covered by both her jacket and his. "Dr. Jackson gave her a shot to knock her out," he explained.

"Why? I mean what was wrong that he needed to do that?" asked Garson angrily, while Sally felt of Abigail's head and hands as tears crept silently down her cheeks.

"That's the way she was before. Did she scream and fight?" asked Sally as she straightened up.

"Yes, Ma'am, she did. I had to hold her arms and still she kicked and screamed until the medicine calmed her. Dr. Jackson said to tell you she needs to go to the hospital tonight. He said there is a Dr. Fischer there at Doctors Memorial that is very good with emotional problems. I'll drive if you all will take her and I really think you should," said Lucas in a pleading voice.

"Did some man bother her?" asked Garson angrily.

"I don't think so. I'd gone to get us something to drink when I heard her scream. I ran back and this old man with a patch over his eye and a head full of white hair was trying to get to her, but she was fighting and screaming. I knocked him down."

Sally gasped and looked at Garson. "That man again! Oh Lord!"

Lucas was so disturbed that he didn't hear Sally's comment. "I didn't know what to do. She was fighting as if she was in a battle or some kind of struggle. I was afraid to touch her since she doesn't like to be touched, but when Dr. Jackson came up and told me to hold her I did. She still struggled and kicked and even tried to bite me until the doctor gave her the medicine."

"What's your arm doing all bandaged up?" asked Garson.

"That man had a gun and his bullet grazed my arm, but nobody else got hurt. I think he intended to shoot Abigail." Lucas shook his head and let out a long sigh. "When she comes out of this, she'll never speak to me again."

Sally and Garson both gasped in shock. "Did the police arrest him?" they asked in unison.

"He was knocked out and I got out of there with Abigail.

I don't know what happened but if I know those people, they won't let that man get away."

Garson and Sally were looking at each other and then Sally said, "We'd best go, Garson. That's what we should have done before. The Lord gives doctors gifts to heal and we should have remembered that."

She turned and went into the house, saying over her shoulder. "I'm going to get my coat and pocketbook. Do you want to get anything before we start?"

Garson went back up the walk. "We'll be back in a minute, Lucas," he said and hurried on into the house.

Lucas slumped against the car. *Thank you, Lord. I prayed all the way up the mountain that they would agree to take her. Thank you for listening to me.* He looked up into the starry sky and then wondered why. *I've never tried to pray before, but Mom said that's what we need to do.*

Sally got in the back and eased Abigail's head onto her lap. Garson closed her door and eased himself into the front seat. Soon they were out of Stateline Ridge and speeding back down Bradshaw Mountain.

"Slow down, son. Ain't no use trying to kill us all. Abby'll probably sleep 'til morning. Sally took her to the doctor the other time and he give her some kind of shot. She slept the rest of that day and all of the next day," said Garson, who had been pressing the brake pedal, or acting as if he was, all the way down the mountain.

Lucas turned to glance at Garson. "You said, 'the other time,' Mr. Dawson. Has she been like this before?"

Sally spoke from the back seat. "She never wanted us to tell anybody, but after tonight I think you ort to know. What do you think, Garson?"

"Yeah. Just go ahead and tell him. I can tell you're worried to death, ain't you, son?" asked Garson.

"Yes, I am. I think I'm in love with your daughter and seeing her like this is really tearing me up."

Sally swallowed and began. "Abby wrote to me from Kyle's where she was visiting about three years ago, saying she was coming home and would be home before Thanksgiving. I told Garson and he was going to meet her in Bradshaw, but he got held up and didn't get there on time. She started walking and this old man with white hair stopped to ask her to ride." Sally stopped to wipe the tears from her eyes. "You tell him, Garson."

"Sally had always told her never to ride with strangers and several people had offered her rides, but she wouldn't ride. Then this old man came along and Abigail loved older people and trusted them. I guess it was 'cause she loved Sally's daddy so much. She thought there was nobody like her grandpa. Anyway, this old man reminded her of her grandpa and so she got in the car with him. He was nice until they reached the top of the mountain and then he started just flying around the road. He was going so fast that Abby couldn't jump out. Then he cut off the road and took a lane back in the woods and stopped. Abby opened the door to jump out, but got her foot tangled on her suitcase and the man caught her," Garson said, then he also stopped.

"Did he rape her?" asked Lucas fearfully.

Sarah spoke up. "No, thanks be to God. I don't know exactly how she got away but he tore most of her clothes off and beat her in the face. She had bruises and scratches all over her when Charles met her trying to run out the road."

"She thinks she poked him in the eye with her finger. She had blood on her hands and under her finger nails. Charles said she was so tore up she didn't even know she was nearly naked. When she saw Charles she just dropped to the ground screaming and crying," said Garson, taking a deep breath.

"This man had a patch over his eye. Did Charles go look for him?" asked Lucas angrily.

"Yes he did, but that devil had drove right on out that lane and down the other side. We didn't have no tag number or no kind of description and besides there ain't many telephones on the mountain. By the time we could of got to Bradshaw for a deputy he'd have been long gone anyway," explained Garson.

"What happened with Abigail? I mean, what happened at the doctor's office?" asked Lucas.

Abigail stirred and groaned. "Sh-h, I believe she is waking up," whispered Sally and there was complete silence. After a few minutes they each breathed a sigh of relief.

"The doctor give her some medicine that we had to wean her off of slow like. She went for over a year not talking to any men and she wouldn't even let her daddy or brothers touch her. Abby changed from a shy but happy girl to a quiet, silent ghost. She lost weight and wouldn't go anywhere for six months. She didn't go back to school that year but they passed her anyway so she could graduate the next year," said Sally.

"I thought she was all right, 'til you scared her when she was walking out of Collins Ridge. But, she seemed to have got over that and was doing the best I've seen her in three years 'til tonight," said Garson.

They were now going over Caretta Mountain and everybody got quiet as Lucas swung around first one curve and then another. When he reached the bottom of the hill, Garson turned his head to look back at Sally. "You ain't car sick are you? I'm about to be sick and I figured with you being back there you might be."

"No, I'm too worried about Abby to get sick. She seems to be breathing to fast," said Sarah anxiously.

"Put your hand over her heart, Mrs. Dawson. Is her heart beating fast?" asked Lucas, turning his head to glance at Sally.

"Here, son, you just keep your eyes on the road and me and Sally will take care of Abby," ordered Garson. Lucas speeded up as they came into the level roadway, but didn't glance back anymore.

Chapter 13

When they pulled into the emergency parking space at Doctors Memorial Hospital, Lucas jumped out of the car and ran inside. Soon a gurney was placed beside the car door and Abigail was loaded onto it. Lucas, Sally, and Garson followed the gurney into the service bay.

A nurse came over and started taking information. An orderly came by and said to Lucas. "You'll need to pull your car over to one of the parking spaces."

"I will, but I don't want to leave her until the doctor has seen her," said Lucas.

"The nurses will have to do a lot before they call the doctor, so you'll have plenty of time," replied the orderly and Lucas hurried out.

When he came back in the doctor had just come on the floor. The nurse gave her report of all that she knew and the doctor turned to Sally. Before he could ask a question Lucas said, "Wait!" He fished in his pocket and brought out the paper that Dr. Jackson had given him. "I was told to give this to Dr. Fischer. Are you Dr. Fischer?"

The doctor unfolded the paper and read it. "No, I'm not Dr. Fischer, but I'm going to call him." He left the cubicle and picked up the phone on the counter behind which several nurses and doctors were working. He put the phone down and came back into the cubicle. "Dr. Fischer will be here in about fifteen minutes."

He motioned for the nurse to bring two more chairs. "You people can sit down and try to relax until he gets here. You've done all you can. Dr. Fischer is very good. You've brought her to the right place, I assure you." He smiled at Sally, patted her on the shoulder and started out, but stopped. "We have coffee here, would you like a cup?"

Garson spoke up. "I think that's a good idea, Doc. We'll probably be up here purt near all night. Coffee'll keep us awake."

Soon Sally, Garson, and Lucas were seated and sipping coffee. Garson leaned over and whispered to Lucas, "This'ud be a lot better with a piece of Sally's homemade cake, wouldn't it?"

Lucas grinned. "Why don't you go get us a slice, Mr. Dawson?"

Garson looked at Sally. "I'd spill it wouldn't I? She says I'm the clumsiest feller around the house that ever was."

"It's just your way of gettin' out of doing anything, Garson Dawson," Sally scolded.

Soon a door at the side of the Emergency Station opened and a short, spectacled man, with a receding hairline walked through the door. He had a stethoscope curled around his neck as he came into the cubicle where they were seated. "I'm Dr. Alan Fischer. I'm a medical doctor but also a trained psychologist."

Garson got to his feet and put out his hand. "I'm Garson Dawson, Abby's father, and this is Sally, her mother." Then he turned to Lucas and said, "This is Lucas Sutherland, her boyfriend or friend."

"What brought this on?" Dr. Fischer asked as he listened to Abigail's heart, checked her carotid arteries, her pulse rate, and lifted her eyelids to look in her eyes. Abigail moved her head and moaned and Sally quickly jumped to her feet. Dr. Fischer shook his head and motioned her back to her seat, and then he turned and stood waiting.

"Lucas you were with her, so I guess you'd better tell him," said Garson.

Lucas told him everything that had occurred at the skating rink, making sure he left nothing out. Dr. Fischer sat down on the foot of the bed deep in thought, and then turned to Sally, "Had that man molested her?"

Sally turned pale and shivered, but told him about the episode that had happened three years before with the same man. When she said, 'white-headed man' Dr. Fischer spoke up. "Did she know or have someone in the family who was white-headed?"

"Yes, my daddy was silver headed and she loved him dearly," said Sally.

"Are you sure she wasn't raped three years ago?" asked Dr. Fischer.

"She said she wouldn't and she still had her underpants on. The doctor also told us she hadn't been raped. She said she jabbed that man in the eye with her finger and this man tonight had a patch over one eye. I reckon it might be the same man," replied Sally.

The doctor turned to Lucas. "What happened to the man?"

"I don't know. I put Abigail in the car and took her home so her parents could decide what to do."

Dr. Fischer turned to the nurse and said, "Call the sheriff's office and tell them to send a deputy over here. Then he turned back to Abigail and asked if anything else had happened except having her clothes torn off.

"She was beat up pretty bad and had bruises that lasted a long time," said Garson.

"Did she receive counseling after that incident?"

Garson dropped his head. "No, and it's my fault she didn't. We didn't have much money and since she wouldn't raped, I thought time would take care of the counseling. She was better until this happened."

Dr. Fischer grimaced. "She wasn't healed. It was just covered up. You see, she undoubtedly didn't want to worry her family and she just buried it deep inside and wouldn't do anything that might bring it up."

"I thought that when we first met, but nobody said anything

and I hated to bring it up," said Lucas. "She doesn't like to be touched and she told me she had never been on a date."

Dr. Fischer looked at Sally and Garson. "Didn't you think that was unusual behavior? She's a very pretty girl and I'm sure boys were attracted to her."

"She wouldn't go nowhere except to church meeting with me and she wouldn't do that for a long, long time after that happened," said Sally.

Dr. Fischer rose from the bed. "Well, I wish she had seen a counselor then, but she didn't, so we have to work from here. I'm going to put her in a private room for tonight and after I see her in the morning I'll know more how to treat her. I suggest that all of you go home tonight. This is Friday, so you can come back on Sunday, but wait until about one o'clock. That will give me more time to decide the best approach. It may be that she can go home and come here once or twice a week for counseling or she may have to stay here for a while. I'll know more Sunday."

"Can't I stay with her, Doc? She'll be scared when she wakes up. She'll start screaming if she's anything like she was the other time. I slept with her for six months and she had nightmares every night," said Sally.

"I'll put a nurse on duty in her room who will know what to do if that happens. Mrs. Dawson, we treat people like Abigail all the time and we will take good care of her," said Dr. Fischer as he motioned to the nurse.

"Get her assigned to a room and I want you to stay with her the rest of the night, he ordered. "I'll assign Judy Fletcher to take the other shift."

Reluctantly, Garson, Sally, and Lucas rose from their seats to go to Abigail's bedside. Sally started to kiss her forehead, but instead patted her hand, Garson patted her shoulder, and Lucas bent and kissed her forehead.

Lucas and Sally spoke at the same time. "We'll be back, Sunday." Then Sally patted her hand again and turned away. Lucas bent close and whispered, "I love you, my friend," and this time kissed her cheek.

Dr. Fischer had waited patiently and now said, "Well, good night and I hope you have a safe trip home." Seeing Sally's grief-stricken face, Dr. Fisher patted her shoulder. "I feel she will eventually be all right. Try not to worry."

Garson put his hand on Sally's shoulder and she gasped in astonishment, but made no comment. They walked out with Lucas following close behind. Nobody spoke until they were outside. "I thought I couldn't bear it to leave her there like that, but I did," said Sally and then clamped her lips together.

Lucas looked at Sally and smiled gently. "I know what you mean, Mrs. Dawson. It sure is hard to leave her, but I think he is a good doctor."

Garson had walked on ahead and was now at the car. "It's hard for us, but I spect it'll be harder for Abby. She don't know nothing about it, though. I think she's goin' to need a lot of help."

Riding back over the mountains they talked about who that man was and wondered what had happened to him. Since they had no way of knowing, they started talking about what to tell the family and friends. "We'll have to go around and tell Harve and Matty. They'll have to get one of their girls to come and stay 'til Abby gets better, won't they?" asked Sally.

"Yeah, I'll have to go out Collins Ridge since they ain't got no telephone either. That's what we need, Sally, a telephone, and I'm going to get us one too. That Wagner man wouldn't let the lines come across his land, or I would have already had one," said Garson.

"I'd be right glad if you would, Garson, but these people that bought the Wagner place may be of the same mind," Sally responded.

"I don't know, but it won't hurt to ask. I'd be willing to pay him something if he'd agree," said Garson.

Lucas had been driving and not saying anything, but now he said, "Telephones are really useful even if you have a party line. Just think we could have had Abigail to the hospital much sooner if I hadn't had to bring her home first."

"Yeah, I know and it's made up my mind for me. I'll check on getting a telephone just as soon as I can," said Garson.

They rode for miles each involved with their own thoughts until they came into Bradshaw. As they passed Pete Francisco's service station, which had a large clock above the outside door, Garson said, "Well, pon-my-honor if it ain't three o'clock. I don't know how long it's been since I've stayed up this late. We go to bed early, don't we Sally?"

When there was no answer, Garson said, "Well that's a first. I do believe she's nodded off." As they passed the skating rink a large crowd was still gathered.

"How late does that place stay open? I thought you said it closed at eleven," said Garson.

Lucas shrugged as he told Garson that it had always closed at eleven. "Maybe the police caught that feller and they're all waiting around to talk about it. I hope they did catch him."

Lucas had driven slower since he remembered Garson saying he had gotten car sick on the way. "You'll have to wake her to get her inside when we get to your place. Of course, I could carry her if you want me to."

"She'd wake up anyway as quick as her feet left the ground. I'm surprised she went to sleep, but I guess she was just plum tuckered out," said Garson just as they pulled into the parking spot below the house.

When the car stopped Sally did wake up. "Well, bless my soul we're already home. I must have dozed off."

Garson laughed. "You did. You snored like a freight train."

"I did not. I don't snore, Garson Dawson. You're the one that saws logs all night," retorted Sally as she opened her door and got out.

Just as they reached the door, Sally turned. "Lucas, you keep a check on that arm. You don't want it to get infected."

Lucas waved. "I'll take care of it. I don't want you worrying about anything else."

Chapter 14

Lucas picked up Garson and Sally at ten o'clock on Sunday morning and they once again made the long, snaky ride down Bradshaw Mountain, over Caretta and Coalwood Mountains, and arrived in Welch at twelve noon. Just before they got into Welch, Lucas asked, "We need to eat. How about me taking you two down to the Mountaineer Grill for lunch?"

"The doctor said we shouldn't come before one o'clock and it's just now twelve so I think that will be just fine. Don't you, Sally?" asked Garson.

"Yes, it will be fine, but I don't aim for Lucas to pay. He's done enough already. You can't run a car back and forth like he has for nothing," said Sally.

"Well, I'll just buy his dinner, then." Garson said as if that settled it.

They pulled in beside a parking meter on Main Street just down the street from the restaurant.

Lucas killed the engine and turned. "Now listen, you two have accepted me into the family and treated me like a son. You'll never know how much that means to me, so I don't want any more protests, I'm buying your lunches."

Sally and Garson sat very still for a minute and then Garson said, "Well he couldn't a put it no plainer than that, could he, Sally?"

Sally smiled. "All right, son, we'll gladly accept your invitation."

They finished their meal by twelve-forty-five and were back in the car headed for Doctor's Memorial Hospital. As they pulled into the hospital parking lot Sally said, "I'm nervous as I can be. I don't know what to expect when we get in there. What if she don't want to see none of us?"

"I think she'll want to see you two, but I doubt if she'll want to see me," said Lucas worriedly. He heaved a sigh. "It doesn't matter as long as she gets better. I'm not saying I don't want to see her for I do, but I want her better and if her not seeing me will help then that's all right."

"Now let's not cross our bridges 'til we get to them. You're both guessing and if I said anything I'd be guessing too. Let's just wait 'til we get in there before we lose all hope," said Garson just as they arrived at the reception desk.

When they inquired about Abigail Dawson they were told she was on the third floor, but they would have to ask the nurse at the third floor station about her room number.

Lucas thanked the receptionist, and taking Sally's arm, walked with her and Garson to the elevators. They were soon on the third floor at the nurse's station. Lucas asked if they could see Abigail Dawson.

A nurse with mingled gray hair looked up and smiled. "I'm glad you all came. She's been asking for her mother." The nurse came around the corner of the station and took Sally's arm. "I think it would be a good idea if only her mother went in first. When we get her reaction we'll know more how to proceed about you men visiting her."

She started to lead Sally away, but turned and said, "There's a waiting area at the end of this hall. You two can go in there and we'll come back and let you know one way or the other."

Sally walked away with the nurse as Garson and Lucas walked down the hall to the waiting area. They took seats on the side of the room next to the windows and neither of them spoke for several minutes. Finally Lucas asked, "Do you think the doctor would come and talk to us? I'd like to know what he thinks, wouldn't you."

"I aim to ask the nurse that very question when she brings Sally back. We need to know what we are lookin' at, down the road," said Garson, getting up and looking out the window.

Lucas had taken a seat and idly picked up a newspaper

lying on a table and turned to the front page. "Well! They arrested that man, Mr. Dawson."

Garson turned. "What does it say?"

Lucas began to read and when he came to the part where Deputy Buck Jones had shot him, Garson interrupted. "Did he kill him? I hope he did."

"No, he's alive but in intensive care. He told what he tried to do to Abigail three years ago, but he is still angry because she messed up his eye," replied Lucas.

"He'll go to the pen if he lives, because he went there planning to kill Abby. That's called premeditation. I hope they give him life," said Garson. The two men sat waiting, deep in thought.

When Sally hadn't returned in twenty minutes, they both became anxious. After reading all the newspaper, Lucas picked up one magazine after the other. He turned the newspaper over to Garson who had already made several trips to the door, cracked it open, and looked down the hall. They had both gone to the windows and were staring down in the street below when the door opened. Dr. Fischer held the door and Sally preceded him into the room.

Both men turned from the window in eager anticipation of some kind of news. "Hello, Doc. I hope you've got some good news for us," said Garson.

Dr. Fischer took Sally to a seat and now turned to face the men. "Abigail is much better than she was when she came in here. She has been asking about her mother and she's mentioned somebody named Lucas a few times," said Dr. Fischer with a twinkle in his eyes.

Lucas looked as if he was fighting tears. "Did she really mention me? I was afraid she'd never want to see me again." He looked over at Sally and asked, "Did she seem all right to you, Mrs. Dawson?"

"She's better than she was Friday night, but she's not well, I don't think, but she did ask if you were all right, Lucas," said Sally, hoping to make him feel better.

"Will she want to see her daddy, I wonder?" asked Garson.

Dr. Fischer turned to Sally. I've not been in to see her since eight o'clock this morning. What do you think, Mrs. Dawson? Should we let her father in to see her?"

"I don't rightly know, Doctor. She seemed like she was half asleep all while I was in there. I didn't ask her about seeing her daddy. I just let her talk," said Sally.

Dr. Fischer stood deep in thought and looked as if he was studying a picture on the wall. "I may have to try her on another medicine. Let me go in and talk to her and I'll come back to get you if she is ready."

"That's fine, Doc. I'm glad her mother got to see her even if I don't, but I want to see her if I can," said Garson.

Dr. Fischer opened the door and went out. Garson and Lucas eagerly turned to Sally. "What did she talk about? Did she make any sense?" asked Garson.

Sally gaped at him. "She ain't crazy, Garson, her nerves is just all wrecked. She talked as sensible as she ever did, but it was just so slow like somebody about to fall asleep."

"Did she ask if anyone had notified the people she works for that she was in the hospital?" asked Lucas.

Sally smiled. "Yes she did. She told the doctor that she needed to let Harve and Matty know she couldn't come to work for a few days." Sally turned to Lucas. "I told her you had took good care of her and had brought her to the hospital."

"What did she say?" asked Lucas.

"She said you were a good friend and to tell you she really appreciated what you did, but Lucas, I don't think she is going to want to see you for a little while. She believes you think she is crazy. I wanted to tell her different, but didn't know what was best until I had seen the doctor," said Sally.

Lucas' face fell, but he said, "That's all right, Mrs. Dawson. I certainly don't think she is a mental case. I'd like to let her know how I feel, but that can wait. I'll just have to pray that the Lord will change her mind."

"That's right, son. The Lord has his way in a whirlwind and he can change things when we think there ain't no hope a'tall," said Sally. Garson's eyes opened wide as she actually patted Lucas's shoulder. Sally seldom displayed any feelings, not even to her children.

Dr. Fischer opened the door and motioned to Garson. When Garson went out into the hall, Dr. Fisher closed the door and stood looking at him. "She would have allowed you to come in, but I sensed that she would rather not have any men visit her right now. She said, 'Tell Daddy that I'm not mad at him' and I told her I would. There's just something that I have to try to get her to talk about that is at the root of the problem. I think it would be wise if you'd wait a few days and then we'll see about a visit from you."

"All right, Doc. You know best, but I hope you can find out why she turns against me when something happens. She wouldn't like that a'tall until after that old man done her like that three years ago. She never was one to hug on me, but she used to run and meet me in the evenings and was real glad to see me," said Garson sadly.

"It's probably not anything related to you in any way, but just some fixation she has about men," said Dr. Fisher. "We'll take it slow and I feel she'll come out of this more like her old self. I'm going to try her on another medication that has been very effective with similar cases."

Garson turned back toward the door and stopped. "Do you reckon she'll ever want to see that young feller in there again? He's crazy about her and he is a good young man. I hate to see him so hurt."

"She mentioned Lucas several times this morning, but seems to think people will believe she is having a mental breakdown. I tried to convince her otherwise, but she's not quite ready for that yet. I think she cares for Lucas as well. She is fighting it awfully hard because she is afraid of men," said Dr. Fischer and turned to go. "Tell that young man to not give up hope."

Dr. Fischer walked a few steps and turned. "Did you see the paper this morning? That man is in Stevens Clinic Hospital in

Intensive Care. I guess he and the deputy shot at each other and the deputy won."

Garson told him he'd seen the paper, and then went back inside. "I can't see her today. Doc said to give her two or three more days. She did tell him to tell me that she wasn't mad at me. That's a good sign, I think, don't you, Sally?"

"It is, Garson. She is just so mixed up. If I could find that old man that done that to her, I'd black both his eyes, if Abby didn't blind him herself," said Sally harshly.

"That old man is out at Stevens Clinic Hospital in Intensive Care. The paper didn't give much hope of him surviving. I don't want to see him again. I wanted to kill him when I heard Abigail screaming," said Lucas.

"You shouldn't want to kill anybody, Lucas. Life belongs to God and we have no right to try to take it," said Sally.

Garson frowned. "I'd have felt the same way in his shoes. A man that would bother a young girl ain't much of a man anyway."

"Mrs. Dawson is right and I'm ashamed of my feelings, but right then I was so angry I wasn't thinking straight," said Lucas and dropped his head.

Sally and Garson looked at his woebegone face and felt so sorry for him. "The Doc said to tell you not to give up hope, that Abby had talked to him and mentioned your name several times this morning. He says she is just so afraid of men and feels that people will think she's a mental case," said Garson.

Lucas squared his shoulders. "I'm not giving up. Mom told me that we all had to pray. I don't know much about praying, but I've certainly been trying. I hope the Lord hears a beggar."

"He does, son. He certainly does," said Sally with a gentle smile. "I think we should just go home. I think Charles will bring us back over here tomorrow don't you, Garson?"

"Doc, said I needed to wait a few days before she would see me, so I don't see the sense of me coming over here every day," replied Garson.

"I can come back over tomorrow and bring you over here, Mrs. Dawson," Lucas offered.

"No you can't. I ain't never been to Ronceverte, but I know it's a good distance from here. You come back next Tuesday and we'll let you bring us then," said Sally.

Lucas looked so worried that Sally felt such compassion. They were now in the car heading out of Welch. "Lucas, if you will leave your telephone number I'll get Charles to call you tomorrow so you'll know how she is doin'," said Garson.

"That would be great. I was going to ask you if there was any way you could let me know," said Lucas. "Mrs. Dawson, didn't you say the doctor said in two or three days she might allow me to see her?"

"That's what he said, Lucas."

"Today is Sunday, so two days from now will be Tuesday. Do you think that's too soon? I'd call the hospital, but they probably wouldn't tell me anything, since I'm not family, would they?" asked Lucas.

"I don't know, Lucas, but I guess it wouldn't hurt to try," replied Sally.

That's how they left it and quietly rode back to the top of Bradshaw Mountain each caught up in their own reflections and praying silent prayers.

Chapter 15

Abigail had been brought to the hospital on Friday night. She did not wake from her drug induced sleep until seven o'clock on Saturday evening. She looked around in amazement and wondered why she was in what looked like a hospital room. She sat up in the bed just as a nurse came through the door.

"Good evening! How do you feel?" asked the nurse. Abigail was looking around wildly as if she was scared.

"Where am I?" She started trembling. The nurse quickly came to her side. "Miss Dawson, you are in the hospital. Don't be afraid. We'll take care of you," she said in a soft, pleading voice.

"Hospital! How did I get here? I mean who brought me?" asked Abigail.

"Your parents and a Lucas Sutherland brought you here Friday night around twelve o'clock. You were asleep and you've been asleep until now," said the nurse. "My name is Mavis Hatcher and I'll be caring for you today and Judy Fletcher will be on night duty."

Abigail wanted to ask a lot of questions, but didn't know where to start. The last thing she remembered was the white-headed man grabbing her shoulder, but she didn't want to tell anyone about that. She sat looking at the nurse as she put a pitcher of water and some plastic glasses on her bedside table.

"May I go to the bathroom?" asked Abigail, still trembling but not as badly. The nurse stopped arranging things on the bedside table.

"Sure, honey. I'll have to go with you, though," she said

and Abigail frowned. She didn't like people to see her doing personal things.

"I can go by myself. I don't want you to go to the bathroom with me," said Abigail.

Seeing that Abigail was upset, the nurse said, "I won't stay in the room with you, but I have to make sure that you don't fall. Once you are in there I can step back outside the door."

Abigail relaxed and started to get out of the bed. The nurse took her arm and held onto it as she started to walk toward the bathroom. Abigail was still trembling. "Do you think you're strong enough to walk? I can get a bedpan."

"No. Oh no, I don't want a bedpan. Just hold onto me and let me go to the bathroom, please."

After she used the bathroom she felt much better. She wanted to wash her face, but felt so weak and nauseous that she was glad the nurse put her head through the door. When she saw Abigail's face, she grasped her arm.

"Come on, honey. You need to get back in the bed. I probably shouldn't have let you go," said the nurse anxiously.

Abigail made it back to the bed, but didn't get in it. "I feel sick," whispered Abigail and the nurse held a receptacle in front of her just as she began to vomit.

She was still gagging as Dr. Fischer came through the door. He stopped and waited until the nurse had washed Abigail's face and given her some water and then came on into the room. When Abigail saw him, she said, "No, no." and began shaking again. "Please, don't let him touch me," she begged, turning to the nurse with tear drenched eyes.

Mavis Hatcher's heart wrenched with compassion as she looked at the tortured expression in the eyes of this beautiful young girl. "Don't be afraid dear. This is Dr. Fischer. He is a very good doctor. I will stay right here with you. I won't leave you alone," she said as she put her arm around Abigail. "Let's get you back in bed and I'll stand right here beside you while Dr. Fischer talks to you."

Dr. Fischer stayed near the door while all this was going on and when Mavis had Abigail back in bed, he walked on into the room. "Good evening, Abigail, or would you rather I called you Miss Dawson?"

Abigail was trembling, but she tried to fight it. "Abigail is all right. Please don't touch me. I . . . I don't want to be touched."

"Why don't you want me to touch you?" asked Dr. Fischer quietly.

"You're a man," said Abigail as she started crying and shaking violently.

Mavis cuddled her close. "Hold on, dear. I won't let him touch you. See, I won't let him come any closer. Please try to calm down."

Abigail tried but couldn't stop the shaking. She wouldn't raise her head to look at the doctor. She clung to Mavis' arm as if she feared she'd leave her in this man's presence.

Dr. Fischer quietly said, "Abigail, I am a doctor trained to help people who have suffered as you have. I'm going to have Mavis give you a shot, then I want you to eat some breakfast. Is that all right with you?"

Abigail nodded. Dr. Fischer turned to leave. "I'm leaving now, Abigail, and Mavis has to come out to get the medicine I want you to have. She will be right back. You won't be left alone." He went out the door and Mavis followed. Abigail sat fearfully, watching every move that was made.

Mavis came back in and right behind her was a young black girl with a tray of food. The girl smiled at Abigail and said, "Good evening! I brought you a good supper."

"Thank you," said Abigail through shaking lips.

As soon as the girl left, Mavis came over and said, "Do you want the shot in your arm or in your hip?" Abigail put out her arm and Mavis had the needle in and out so fast that Abigail hardly felt it.

Mavis uncovered her tray to reveal scrambled eggs, two pieces of bacon, jam, a biscuit and several sections of orange. "Do you drink coffee or do you want this milk?" asked Mavis.

Abigail pointed to the milk. Mavis opened it and put it beside her plate. "Here's your fork. Try to eat something. You can't get better without feeding your body."

Abigail took the fork and picked up a bite of the egg. She ate that and waited. Then she took a bite of the biscuit, but when she picked up the milk and took a sip, she quickly put it down and grabbed the receptacle she'd used before. Mavis moved her food back away from her. "I don't believe you should try the milk right now. Wait until your stomach settles again and then eat some of the egg and biscuit if you can."

Abigail sat for a few minutes and when she had stopped feeling so nauseous, she picked up the water in the glass on the tray and took a sip of water. She waited and it stayed down.

"Well, that stayed down. Do you feel like trying a bite of egg?" asked Mavis, and Abigail picked up her fork and took a bite. She chewed slowly and swallowed. They both waited with bated breath and when she wasn't sick they smiled at each other. Abigail ate all of the egg and two bites of the biscuit.

"That's all I can eat. I'm sleepy," she said and lay down and was instantly asleep. Mavis wiped her face and moved the tray out of the way just as the door cracked open and Dr. Fisher looked in. Seeing that Abigail was asleep, he walked on into the room.

"Did she eat anything? I hoped she would before the shot put her to sleep. She needs nourishment to help her body fight off the effects of her trauma," said Dr. Fisher.

"I don't know how you're going to be able to treat her since she is petrified that a man will touch her. What happened to get her in this condition?" asked Mavis.

"Did you see this morning's paper? An old man had tried to rape her three years ago and she put his eye out with her finger. Yesterday evening he came back to kill her, but was again thwarted. In a shoot-out Deputy Buck Jones shot him and he is now over at Stevens Clinic hospital in Intensive Care. Anyway, Miss Dawson was at a skating rink and he went there looking for her. When he grabbed her shoulder, she went into a panic," said Dr. Fischer thoughtfully. "The attack three years ago so traumatized her that it was still in her system. A local doctor gave her nerve medicine and she was taken to a faith healer. I think she never really talked about that incident to anyone. She only told her mother what happened, but she didn't talk about her reactions or her inner turmoil."

"Didn't a boyfriend bring her to the hospital?" asked Mavis, thinking that indicated that she had gotten back to normal.

Dr. Fischer shrugged his shoulders. "A young man brought her and her parents here and he said that he and Abigail had gone skating, but only as friends. She has never dated anybody."

"Isn't it strange, how some girls can even be raped and seem to come through that and not be traumatized. Then here she is in terrible shape, but they say she wasn't raped. What makes the difference?" asked Mavis.

Dr. Fischer busily checked Abigail's pulse, listened to her heart, and felt her lymph glands. "I don't know for sure, but I have some ideas. I think she has held some belief or something that made these attacks take on enormous proportions. That's what I expect to discover."

"I'll come back in an hour from now. The shot shouldn't keep her asleep any longer than that. You know, of course, that you will have to be present at every session until there is a big improvement," said Dr. Fischer as he went out of the room.

The next thing Abigail knew was hearing a noise in the hall. She jerked awake trembling in fear. She listened and then realized that someone was running a vacuum cleaner or floor polisher. She breathed a sigh of relief and relaxed. She lay thinking about the dream she had just had. She and Lucas were skating and she felt so wonderful. She wasn't afraid. Lucas had his arm around her, but he wasn't tearing at her clothes. He was so gentle and she felt so safe, then she'd heard that noise and awoke to panic again. She closed her eyes and could see Lucas's face. He was so handsome. Abigail smiled.

The door opened and Mavis came through. "You're smiling. That's good. What are you smiling about?"

Abigail sat up. "I dreamed about skating with Lucas. We were waltzing to the 'Tennessee Waltz.' It was . . . so beautiful."

102

Abigail swung her legs over the edge of the bed. "I'd like to get up, please."

Mavis hurried to help her. "I need some house shoes, but I don't know when Mom will be over here," said Abigail as Mavis helped her into a chair.

"Is Lucas your boyfriend?" asked Mavis.

"No. He's just a good friend. We went to a movie once and we've gone skating twice. I don't have a boyfriend, though. I don't want a boyfriend, but I like Lucas. He's nice."

Abigail got up and walked to the dresser across the room and looked in the mirror. "Gosh, I look awful. I don't even have a comb and my hair is a tangled mess."

"Just hang on to the dresser a minute and I'll get a comb," said Mavis.

She came back with a comb and Abigail started trying to comb her hair, but she was too weak. "What is wrong with me? I don't have enough strength to comb my own hair."

"Let me comb it," said Mavis, taking the comb. "It's probably the medicine. The weakness won't last after it gets into your system." Mavis was combing one strand at a time. "Your hair is gorgeous, Abigail. It's so silky. What kind of shampoo do you use?"

"Coconut oil. I buy it from Mom. She sells supplies for Zanol Products. I tried the shampoo and really liked it, so I've been using it ever since.

Mavis finished and Abigail went into the bathroom and washed her face before turning back into the bedroom. "Are you hungry now? I'm going to bring you a piece of toast. Do you want butter and jelly on it?" asked Mavis.

"Do you have any strawberry jelly? I like toast and jelly."

"When you have finished eating, I'm going to sit down beside you and Dr. Fischer wants to come in and talk to you. Are you willing to talk to him? He can't help you if he can't talk to you."

Abigail shivered, but slowly nodded in agreement. "I'll stay right with you. I promise," said Mavis and left the room.

Chapter 16

This time Abigail ate all the toast and drank a full glass of water then wiped her mouth with the napkin. "That was good. I guess I must have been hungry."

Mavis smiled and looked at her watch. "I guess so, since you've had very little food from around five-thirty on Friday until now. It's almost ten o'clock Saturday night. Did you know that?"

"No, but I know I've been doing a lot of sleeping. My mouth feels like fur. I need to brush my teeth."

"I can take care of that. You have toothpaste and a toothbrush right here in this drawer," said Mavis, pulling out the drawer. Abigail's eyes lit up.

"May I go to the bathroom and brush my teeth?"

"I don't see why not. Do you need any help?" asked Mavis. Abigail shook her head and went into the bathroom and closed the door.

Soon Abigail was back in the room and feeling much better. Mavis told her to sit in the chair by the bed while she changed and made her bed. Soon everything was just as Mavis wanted it. "Now, you can get back into bed."

"I'd like to sit in the chair. May I?" asked Abigail.

"Yes, but Dr. Fischer will soon be coming in to talk to you. Do you want to be in bed or sitting there?" Seeing the wild look come into Abigail's eyes, Mavis hurriedly said, "I'll be right here. I won't leave."

"I . . . I believe I'll get back into bed," said Abigail uneasily and Mavis assisted her.

Soon the door opened and Dr. Fischer stepped inside the

room. He closed the door and stood looking at Abigail. Mavis moved to her side and put her hand on Abigail's shoulder. She could feel the tension in Abigail's shoulder.

"Relax, Abigail. I'll be right here beside you. You do want to get better, don't you?" Mavis asked.

Abigail nodded and Dr. Fischer advanced a few steps into the room. "Will it bother you if I take a seat?" he asked.

"No," Abigail whispered.

Dr. Fischer walked over to a chair located about three feet away from the bed and sat down. "Have you eaten anything today?"

"Yes sir. I ate toast and drank a glass of water."

"Do you feel nauseous?" he asked and when Abigail shook her head, he continued. "Your parents and Lucas Sutherland will be in after one o'clock tomorrow."

Abigail's face brightened. "Good. Maybe Mom will bring me some clothes."

Sensing that Abigail was more relaxed, Dr. Fischer asked. "Do you know why you are in the hospital?"

Abigail looked up and sat thinking. "That white-headed man grabbed me and I fought him, but . . . he didn't get to hurt me, did he?"

"No. According to Lucas's story and the newspaper this morning, that man didn't have a chance. Lucas knocked him down and then carried you out and brought you to the hospital. The man and the deputy had a shoot-out. That man is in the hospital and not expected to live," said Dr. Fischer.

"It was his white hair. That's all I saw. He . . ." Abigail stopped. "It was the white hair."

"Did you know the man?"

Abigail hesitated and then repeated, "I didn't see anything but the white hair and felt his hand on my shoulder." Abigail shivered convulsively.

"Abigail, do you realize that your behavior or reaction toward men is not normal?" Dr. Fischer sat waiting and watching Abigail as she pleated the quilt with her fingers nervously.

"I can't help it. Do we have to talk anymore? I don't want to talk anymore," said Abigail as she began to tremble.

Dr. Fisher looked at her calmly, and then said, "Are you upset with Lucas Sutherland?"

"No, but he . . . he, I know he thinks I'm a mental case," said Abigail as she not only trembled but became teary-eyed as well.

"How do you know Lucas thinks that way? Did you ask him?"

"People think like that. If anyone has a nerve problem everyone says they are crazy," said Abigail sadly. "I'm not crazy am I, Doctor?"

"No, Abigail, you are not crazy. You have been traumatized and it was not treated properly. Had you been taken to a counselor three years ago you probably would not be here now."

Abigail's eyes grew large. "How did you know about three years ago?"

"Your mother told me, Abigail. I asked her," he replied. Abigail didn't make any reply and Dr. Fischer sat looking at her calmly for a moment.

Then he rose to his feet. "When your parents and Lucas arrive, do you want to see only your mother? I know that both Lucas and your father want to see you."

Abigail wiped her eyes and gripped her hands together. "I know I have to fight this and it is not Lucas's or Dad's fault, but will you ask them not to touch me. Please explain that I will keep forcing myself until it will be all right, but not right now."

"Yes, Abigail, I'll explain your feelings. Don't get yourself agitated. They'll understand," said Dr. Fischer, turning toward the door. "I'll be visiting you again around eight o'clock in the morning and we'll have another talk."

Abigail nodded and Dr. Fischer went on out the door, closing it behind him. "See, honey, that wasn't too bad, was it?" Mavis asked.

Abigail breathed a long sigh. "No. I know the doctor has to come in and after he leaves I feel so silly to have acted the way I do, but, Mavis, physical touches from men have made me feel bad as far back as I can remember."

Mavis's eyes blared. "You mean you had those feelings even before that happened three years ago?"

"Sometimes I did, but only with men outside the family. I never felt like that around Grandpa, though. He saved me."

Abigail stopped as if startled and Mavis quickly asked, "Saved you from what?"

"I guess I meant . . . I don't know what I meant. I just felt safe with Grandpa," said Abigail in a puzzled voice.

At eight o'clock the next morning, the door was pushed open and a jolly, laughing woman came in carrying a tray. She stopped as she entered the door. "Well, you are the prettiest little thing I've seen in a long time. That hair makes you look like a store-bought doll." She came to the bedside table and began moving things to make a place for the tray. She set it just as she wanted it and then pulled the table across Abigail's lap.

"There you are, pretty girl," she said as she removed the covers from the dishes and stepped back. "Is your hair naturally curly? I ain't never seen a head of hair like that."

Abigail smiled. "Yes Ma'am, it is naturally curly. I thank you and I'm glad you think it's pretty. It's easy to get tangled if I don't use a conditioner on it."

The woman reached out her hand and picked up a tress of Abigail's hair. "My, it's like silk. I bet you get a lot of attention from the men, don't you?"

Abigail's eyes blared. "No." She looked imploringly at Mavis who immediately cut in. "She'll have to hurry and eat, Josephine. She's expecting her parents," and Mavis stepped between the woman and the bed.

"Oh! I'm sorry. I have to get the other lunches ready anyway," she said and left the room, but at the door she looked back and smiled.

"Do you think you should try the milk today?" asked Mavis in an attempt to get Abigail's mind away from any thought of a man.

"I don't think I want it. In fact I don't really want anything, but

I'm sure I should eat. Is loss of appetite one of the side effects of whatever medicine the doctor has me on?"

Mavis looked at her chart. "I don't think so, but then medicines act differently with each individual. You couldn't take the first one Dr. Fischer tried, but if you feel the same tonight I'll discuss it with him."

Abigail forced herself to eat a few bites of everything on the plate and drank two glasses of water. Then she pushed the table away. "Please don't ask me to eat anymore. I'll be sick if I do."

"Well, we don't want that. Let me move all this out of the way and you can get up for a while. Do you want to do that?" asked Mavis.

"It's a long time until one o'clock isn't it?" You did say my folks were coming about that time, didn't you?"

"That's what Dr. Fischer said, so we'd better get you prettied up, hadn't we?" Mavis said laughing as she held to Abigail's arm until she was seated in the chair beside the bed.

Abigail took the chair the doctor had occupied. She sat there for a while, leafing through a magazine Mavis had brought in until Mavis said it was almost one o'clock. "I wish you could have eaten lunch, but we don't want you vomiting again.

"I'm going to get back in the bed, since this gown doesn't cover me very well," said Abigail just as someone knocked on the door.

She scrambled into the bed and pulled the covers up to her shoulders as Mavis opened the door.

Sally came in first. She had Abigail's new small suitcase which she'd bought to keep for college. "I hope you don't mind me bringing your things in your new suitcase, Abby. I didn't have nothing else to put them in besides a paper poke."

Abigail smiled and unexpectedly reached her arms up to her mother. Sally hesitated a moment and then enfolded Abigail in her arms. "Oh Abby, I've been so worried," she said, dropping her arms and stepping back as if embarrassed.

Sally busied herself taking out the things she had brought in the suitcase. "I figured you'd want pajamas since that's what you wear at home and you only had these house shoes. Abby, I didn't bring that old ragged lookin' robe. I told Garson that we should go buy you a new robe after we got here. We'll do that before we leave."

"Thanks, Mom and I'm so sorry about this. I didn't mean to worry you. I just got scared and couldn't help it."

"I know that, girl. You never was one to worry anybody, but sometimes things just happen, I reckon," said Sally and then moved down to the end of the bed. "Do you think you could talk to your daddy and Lucas today? They've been mighty anxious about you."

"Yes I'll talk to them. Where are they?"

"They're out in the waiting room. I told them I'd ask if it was all right for them to come in," said Sally with a relieved look on her face.

Mavis said, "I'll go tell them they can come in, then I'll take a little break while you're visiting with your family. You may want to talk about family matters." Mavis looked at Sally. "Don't try to tempt her with food. She's been vomiting and we don't want that." She smiled at Sally and went out the door.

"She seems like a nice person. Does she stay in here all the time?" asked Sally.

"She's the day shift nurse, but there's another one who will come on about eight-thirty. I've always been asleep and haven't met her yet. I don't know if she'll stay all the time or not. I don't imagine she will since I'll probably be asleep."

Sally looked at Abigail closely. "How are you really feeling, Abby? I mean, are you eating, and why are you vomiting?"

Abigail kept her eyes on the door, but said, "I ate some breakfast, but I can't drink milk without it coming back up. Mavis says it might be the medicine."

They both were hesitant about what to say to each other. Sally feared she would say the wrong thing and Abigail didn't say anything because she was so anxious. She sat hoping that she wouldn't start trembling when Lucas came in. She didn't want him to see her shake, cry, or vomit like she had been doing. There was a knock on the door and Dr. Fischer poked his head in. "Abigail, you have two men who are anxious to see you. May we come in?"

Abigail clamped her teeth together and clasped her hands in front of her, willing herself to be calm and said, "Yes, doctor, come on in."

Chapter 17

Dr. Fischer stepped back and Garson came in first, followed closely by Lucas Sutherland. They stood stiffly just inside the door looking half scared.

"I'm not insane, Daddy. You and Lucas can come on in and sit down," said Abigail in a shaky voice.

"I know you're not crazy, Abby, but I didn't want to disturb you," replied Garson.

Lucas smiled as he took a chair that Dr. Fischer pushed toward him. "I wanted to see for myself that my skating partner was still able to skate."

A happy smile lit up Abigail's face. "You still want to skate with me?"

"What man wouldn't want to skate with an Olympic style skater? You should see that woman skate, Dr. Fischer. She has Sonja Henie beat by a mile," bragged Lucas, still smiling at Abigail.

"She didn't tell me about that," said Dr. Fischer, also smiling.

Abigail turned red and then looked Garson. "Did you wear a hole in the floorboard on the way over the mountains, Dad?"

"No I didn't. But when we brung you over here I told this young feller to slow down or let me out. I couldn't see no sense in all of us being in the hospital," stated Garson with a satisfied smirk.

Dr. Fischer had been observing while all this was going on. Now he said, "Abigail is much better than she was that night. She slept most of the time she's been here. I've only had one session with her and we're trying out different medicines to make sure we have the one that will be right for her."

"How long do you think she'll have to stay, Doc?" asked Garson.

"I don't know right now. Let's give it a week and then we'll talk again," he moved back toward the door. "I'll be having two sessions a day with her. I'll do another one this evening. I felt this morning's session was good. What did you think, Abigail?" he asked looking at her.

"It made me nervous, but I guess it was all right." Abigail felt agitated, but looked at Lucas and somehow felt easier.

Dr. Fischer smiled and turned back to the door. "I'll leave you to visit with your family." He went on out the door, closing it quietly.

"Are they feedin' you good?" asked Garson as soon as the door closed.

"That nurse said she'd been vomiting, so I'll bet she's not eatin' much," said Sally.

"I think the medicine caused that, Mom. I ate breakfast this morning."

"Well that nurse told me a lie then," blurted Sally.

"No. She didn't lie. I did vomit the first few times that I tried to eat, but I didn't at breakfast," said Abigail.

"That's a good sign. Maybe they just had to find out the things you didn't like," said Garson in a kidding voice.

"They should have brought you some fish, shouldn't they, Abigail?" asked Lucas. He turned to Garson. "I learned that the first time we went out. They had several things on the menu at the Bus Terminal in Bradshaw, but Abigail looked at the menu and didn't want anything on it until she found fish."

"That's right! You don't care much for meat, do you Abby," said Sally sitting down on the foot of the bed.

Abigail smiled. "No, I'd really rather have vegetables, but I do like fish."

"Well, you hurry and get out of here and I'll buy you all the fish you can eat," said Lucas.

Sally was busy putting the other things from the suitcase into the drawer by the bed. She said over her shoulder. "Garson, we need to go out and buy Abby a robe before we leave. The one she has is threadbare in places."

"Can I buy her a robe? I started to bring a box of candy, but didn't know whether she could have it, or really whether she would want it or not," said Lucas, looking at Abigail with pleading eyes.

When nobody spoke up, Sally said, "I don't see nothing wrong with you buying her a robe if Abby don't care. What do you think, Garson?"

"A fool and his money is easy parted, so I say let him buy it if he's that anxious to get rid of his money." Garson laughed and fake punched Lucas's shoulder.

Abigail sat listening to her parents agreeing as if she were a marionette. "Do I have a say in this?" she asked rebelliously.

Lucas stood up. "Abigail, don't you buy things for your friends? I'm your friend so please let me do this for you."

She looked up at Lucas. He made her feel safe just like her grandfather had. She felt tears welling up and batted her eyes to stop them from flowing down her cheeks. She smiled. "It touches me, Lucas, that you want to buy me something, but you don't have to. I'll be your friend anyway."

"That's good to hear. Abigail, I was afraid that you would somehow blame me for what happened at the skating rink. You don't, do you?" he asked.

"No, Lucas. I know it wasn't your fault," and then she could hold the tears no longer and soon her face was flooded in tears.

Lucas started toward the bed and stopped. Sally rushed to her side. "Abby, what is wrong? Here, take hold of yourself, girl."

Garson jumped up. "I'll get that nurse." He rushed through the door and Lucas stood like a statue, thinking he had caused this upset. Sally grabbed some tissues and said, "Here, Abby, wipe your face. The nurse will think we've done something to you."

Mavis came hurrying into the room with Garson behind her. "Abigail, what happened to upset you?" She looked around at Lucas and Sally suspiciously.

"I don't know what we did. We were just talking and she suddenly started crying," said Lucas uneasily.

Abigail wiped her eyes and said, "They didn't do anything. Lucas reminded me of Grandpa and for some reason I started to cry." She started crying again and scooted down in the bed and turned her back to the room.

Mavis motioned for them to go outside and wait. When everyone was gone, Mavis turned Abigail to face her. "They've left. Can you tell me what happened?"

"Nothing happened. Lucas wanted to buy me a robe since mine is worn so badly. There was just that kind look in his eyes that made me think of Grandpa." She started crying again. Grandpa was so kind and he saved me," she mumbled.

Mavis stored that comment in her memory and stood holding Abigail's hand until she stopped crying. "It's all right now. I don't guess you want to see your folks anymore today, do you?"

"Yes, I do. I want to apologize to Lucas and to Mom and Dad. Will it be all right if I change into my pajamas before they come back in," asked Abigail, wiping her face vigorously.

"Sure. Let me tell them to wait and then I'll come and help you to the bathroom. You'll want to wash your face," said Mavis as she went to the door.

Mavis came back in to tell Abigail that her parents and Lucas had gone out to buy her a robe. "Let's get you bathed and prettied up before they get back. I know you'll feel more comfortable in pajamas than you do in that hospital gown."

About twenty minutes later there was a knock at the door and Mavis admitted Sally, Garson, and Lucas, who had a vase of yellow roses in his hand. "My goodness, Abigail, look at these flowers. They're already in a vase, too," said Mavis with a broad smile.

Abigail stared in awe. "They're beautiful. Who bought them?" When she looked at Lucas and saw his wary anxious look she knew who had bought them.

"Lucas Sutherland, what are you trying to do? Mom, you shouldn't have allowed him to spend so much money," chided Abigail.

"Now, Abby, how did you expect your mammy to stop a

grown man," said Garson with a grin. "I did think about robbing him, since he seemed to have so much money, but after I seen how much he'd spent I just felt sorry for him."

"Do you really like them, Abigail?" asked Lucas.

"Who wouldn't like them? Of course, I like them and I thank you very much," said Abigail and smiled. She saw that Sally, Garson, and Lucas were uneasy since they didn't know what had caused her crying jag and said, "I want to apologize for my actions and none of you did anything to cause me to act that way. It may be the medicine or it may be that I haven't gotten over the trauma, or whatever it was, but believe me, none of you did or said anything that caused it."

Mavis smiled widely. "That's what she told me. I think she really just wanted to get you people out so she could deck out in her pajamas. Was that it, Abigail?"

Abigail laughed. "No, but I sure do feel better." She looked at Sally still standing there holding a package. "Is that my robe, Mom?"

Sally hurried to the bed. "Lucas picked it out and paid for it. I hope you like it." She opened the bag and pulled out a soft pale green silky robe. It had a lace trimmed collar and long sleeves also trimmed in lace.

Abigail's eyes widened and her mouth opened in an awed gape. She put out her hand and touched the tail of the robe, which Sally had spread out on the foot of the bed. "It's so soft and I love that soft green color." She turned to Lucas. "My friend you're just bent on making me cry, aren't you?"

"No. I'm just a friend who wanted to do something nice for you," said Lucas, looking her right in the eyes.

"Well, you two can say friends all you'uns want to, but if them ain't sparkin' looks I ain't never seen none before," chortled Garson.

Sally gave him a malevolent glare. "What would you know about what looks mean, Garson Dawson? You should keep your thoughts to yourself."

Garson started to come back at her, but realized that Mavis was in the room and backed down. Sally walked over to Abigail and said, "Here, Abby, let me help you get this on so we can see if it fits or not."

Abigail soon had the robe on and buttoned down the front. "Can you get out on the floor to see if it's too long?" asked Sally. Abigail swung her feet over the side of the bed and Mavis hurried to her side as she stepped down to the floor.

"It's a perfect fit except it's a little too long, but it'll be a little better when you get your house shoes on," said Sally.

Lucas couldn't take his eyes from Abigail. *The green robe highlights her hair and makes her look like a small fairy . . . no, an angel,* thought Lucas as he stood gazing, transfixed.

"It's beautiful, Abigail. If I had a robe like that, I'd never get dressed again. I'd just wear it all day long," said Mavis, laughing merrily.

Abigail grinned. "Well, I guess I'll do that especially while I'm in the hospital." She looked at Lucas. "Thanks Lucas. You shouldn't have spent so much though."

"I wanted to buy it, but I was afraid we couldn't find your size. That was the only one they had in that size. I wanted that color, but I would have had to take it regardless, since it was the only one I could find. We went in three stores before I found that one," said Lucas.

Garson walked a little closer. "Since we done something that got you smiling I reckon we ort to go. I'd rather leave you smiling as crying any time." He grinned and stepped back. Soon Sally and Lucas said their good-byes and all three left.

Mavis closed the door and walked back to the chair vacated by Lucas. "That is a very nice friend you have, Abigail. Not many men would have taken the time to bring your parents over here and then go out and buy you flowers and a beautiful robe."

Abigail rubbed her hand down the sleeve of the robe. "It is nice, isn't it? I haven't known Lucas long, but he seems nice. I feel safe with him."

Mavis looked at her shrewdly, but made no comment.

Chapter 18

Dr. Fischer came twice every day and Abigail felt she was slowly getting better, but there was still a deep fear of men. However, she could think of the episode of three years before without panicking or having nightmares, which she felt was a big improvement. Also, she now knew that the white-headed man would never bother her again; the morning paper had given the information that he had died. He had confessed to attacking Abigail and several other young girls in three states.

Sally and Garson had come back to visit on the following Tuesday, but Lucas had not visited again. He had sent candy, flowers, cards, and had called the nurses to check on her. Now her room was overrun with his gifts. He had written a note on his last card saying he'd had to make a trip into North Carolina to inspect a boundary of timber. From his note Abigail knew that he would be gone a week or more.

I wish Lucas would come to see me. I miss him. I've never missed a man before and I don't know why I'm missing him, but I am, thought Abigail.

I miss him, but I know I don't want him as a boyfriend. I can't stand to be hugged, kissed, or anything to do with intimacy, thought Abigail and shivered convulsively. She knew that she shouldn't feel this way and wondered why, since she felt that Lucas would never hurt her.

Abigail had now been in the hospital six days and had seen Dr. Fischer twelve times. He usually didn't work on Sunday, which was a relief to Abigail. Each session seemed to get her more agitated, but she wasn't afraid of Dr. Fischer now. Mavis still stayed in the room when he visited, but Abigail felt she would be all right if she wasn't. She didn't tell Mavis that, however, since she still didn't know what had brought on that crying spell when Lucas bought her robe.

Mavis checked in on her several times each day, but didn't stay in the room with her. Mavis or someone had left a Bible in the room and Abigail found herself wanting to read it. She'd never gotten past the begats in the Old Testament in her previous attempts to read. When she picked it up this time, for some unknown reason, she turned to the New Testament and began reading in Matthew. She read for a short while and then put the Bible down and lay back, thinking of one special time. She remembered walking around the road from the farm. It was in the spring time and the birds were singing, bees humming, and the sky was such a clear blue that she felt she could look into heaven. *I wish I could see Jesus,* she had thought and stood still, looking up. Abigail remembered thinking *Jesus wouldn't think I'm nasty and filthy. He loves me. Grandpa said he loved me and Grandpa doesn't lie.* Abigail was startled and sat straight up in bed. *Why would I think that? Where does that come from? Am I thinking I'm filthy because that old man attacked me?*

She became very agitated and got off the bed to pace back and forth. A prayer began to form in her head and soon she was whispering, "Jesus, please help me. I don't want to be like this. I'm so miserable and I don't belong anywhere. I know you can help me and sweet Jesus, I'm begging you to please give me some peace. I don't know who I am anymore. This is such torment . . . It's like I'm tied to a heavy load that I just can't carry anymore."

Abigail dropped to her knees beside a chair and first laid her head in the seat, but that didn't seem low enough and she dropped her head down to the floor and murmured as she cried. "Oh, Jesus, please hear my cry." She remained in this position until she heard the door open. She lifted her head to see Mavis standing just inside the door.

"What's wrong, Abigail? Are you sick?" asked Mavis, coming on into the room.

Abigail got to her feet, red with embarrassment, but smiled. "No, I'm not sick. I thought I saw something on the floor and I was down trying to find it." She felt shocked. The lie had come out so easily and she knew that her excuse didn't make sense. Still red in the face, she wondered why she didn't just say, *I was praying.*

Mavis laughed. "It must have been an awfully small something if you had to get that low to find it."

Abigail grimaced. "Some things are very hard to find, especially if we don't have eyes to see them with." As soon as the words were out of her mouth she knew she didn't make sense to Mavis, but she knew what she had been referring to. *Peace is so hard to find unless Jesus gives one new eyes to see with,* she thought, but quickly smiled at Mavis.

"I don't think I know what you are talking about. Do you know?" asked Mavis with a questioning look.

"That's what comes when I try to read the Bible. It gets me so tangled up that I don't realize what I'm saying. I think I meant that the really important things are hard to see sometimes," replied Abigail.

Mavis laughed and slapped her on the back. "Now, that makes sense, so I guess you haven't flipped." Mavis walked over to her bedside table and then to the dresser before turning. "Where would you want a phone placed?"

"Where would I want a phone placed? I don't have a phone and I can't pay for one anyway. Why do you ask?"

Mavis' eyes were gleaming brightly. "Your b . . . uh, friend, Lucas, wants to put a phone in your room. I was just looking for the best place to put it."

"I don't want him to do that, Mavis. I'll never get him paid for what he's already done. Just tell him that I refused," said Abigail.

"You'll have to tell him yourself. He's going to call back at five o'clock," said Mavis as she went back out the door. "Do you want to talk to him?"

"Yes, I'd like to talk to him, but I don't like to be indebted to anyone. I'll talk to him when he calls and tell him that," said

Abigail. She had written him several short thank-you notes when he had sent flowers or candy, but she didn't want to be indebted to him any more than she already was.

Mavis left and Abigail sat down in the chair she had knelt beside and thought about Lucas. *I'm not a fool. Lucas likes me as more than a friend, but he hasn't tried to touch me except when we skated. I didn't mind him holding my hand nor putting his arm around me while we skated. Does that mean that I like him as more than a friend as well?*

She sat there pondering her own thoughts and feelings and trying to be very objective. *I have wondered what it would be like if Lucas kissed me, but then I get afraid. When I think like that, I feel like I've done something wrong and I don't know why. All my friends talk about hugging and kissing boys, and some say they do more than that. I always leave before they say too much though. That kind of talk really bothers me, but my friends Mary and Cecilly think it's funny*, thought Abigail getting restless.

She walked to the window and looked outside. It was a beautiful day and Abigail wished she was home on the farm. She knew that there she would be wandering through the orchard. She could almost feel the wind blowing through her hair and hear the birds singing. The loud ringing of a telephone halted her in mid-thought and she stood waiting. She knew it was Lucas.

Someone knocked on the door and Abigail opened it. "You've got a phone call. Mavis said to ask you to come to the nurse's desk," said a girl dressed in a candy striped uniform.

Abigail followed her out to the nurse's desk. Mavis handed her the receiver. "Hello! Oh, how are you, Lucas? Where in North Carolina? No, I don't know where Winston Salem is, but I've heard of it. Yes, I liked the yellow roses, and I ate some of the chocolates, but I also shared them with the nurses. You must want me to get fat," Abigail stood laughing, but then listened raptly. "That's so strange, Lucas. Well, I . . . I don't know why, but I had a desire to read today. I thank you very much. Yes, I know you are right and I do want to get better.

No, I'm not upset. I'm glad you did, but listen, Mavis told me that you wanted to put a phone in my room and I don't want you to do that."

Abigail argued with Lucas about the phone and then said, "Now, listen, you think you'll be home next week. So, I promise that I'll work really hard at getting better and then we can talk. I'd rather be able to see you when I talk to you. Yes, please do. I'll need all the help I can get. Bye, Lucas."

Abigail thanked Mavis and walked quietly back to her room. *Lucas said he had prayed that I would start reading the Bible and I had a desire to read. Does that mean that Jesus is going to help me get better? I hope so, Oh, I hope so,* thought Abigail as she entered her room and closed the door behind her.

That night when Dr. Fischer came in he was alone. He stopped in front of her and stood for a moment then put out his hand. Abigail looked solemnly up at him and then put her hand in his. His grip was firm yet gentle and he put his other hand over the top of hers and smiled. "Well, now that wasn't too bad, was it?"

"No. I trust you, Dr. Fischer," said Abigail, smiling.

"That's the best news I've heard all day. I think we are making progress, don't you?" he asked.

"I hope we are. I can't really remember a time when I felt free and safe." Abigail sat thinking pensively. "I think . . . at one time I did feel like that, but I don't know why I think that. I'm not making much sense, but it's just a feeling or something . . . like a long forgotten memory." She looked at Dr. Fischer and shrugged. "It may be that I just want to feel like that so badly. I do know that I do want to get better."

"Did you not feel safe before that episode three years ago?" asked Dr. Fischer, who had released her hand and pulled up the other chair to sit facing her.

Abigail bit her lip and sat thinking. "No. That's what I've been thinking about today. That's why that memory or something has been niggling at me. Today I got this feeling that at one time I was happy. I could see myself like a butterfly flitting here and there, free as a breeze. Why would I feel like that? Do you think it is because I've been trying so hard to understand what is wrong with me?"

Dr. Fischer sat deep in thought and then abruptly asked. "Abigail, were your brothers and sisters good to you?"

Abigail gasped. "Yes. . . Well, I'm sure they got tired of tending to me since I was the youngest girl, but they all were good to me."

"What about your parents . . . were they good to you?"

"Of course, they were. I mean they didn't have a lot of time to play with me, but they didn't beat me or anything like that . . . or at least I don't think they did."

Dr. Fischer rambled on, asking about relatives that visited, and friends in the community. Then he started asking who she felt closest to in the family.

"I loved Grandpa better than anybody on earth, but he died," said Abigail, tearing up.

"Are you saying you liked your grandfather better than you did your parents?" asked Dr. Fischer.

"Yes," erupted from Abigail before she even thought about it. Then she said, "You see, he was really old and he tended to me. Everybody else worked in the garden and fields and Grandpa took care of me and Damon, my youngest brother."

"Does or did Damon feel the same way about your grandfather that you did?"

"I don't know, but I know he really liked Grandpa. I don't think he was as close to him as I was, though. Grandpa saved me." Abigail stopped as if she'd done something wrong.

"What did your grandfather save you from, Abigail?" asked Dr. Fischer.

Abigail jumped up and went over to the window. She was trembling as she turned. "I don't know. I don't know. Please, let's stop," she pleaded; now crying.

Dr. Fischer stood. He put out his hand and stood waiting. Abigail finally placed her trembling hand into his. "It's all right, Abigail. We'll stop today, but I want you to know that often opening the lid on something that's been buried a long time is hard. However, it may be that very thing that will make you whole."

Dr. Fischer patted her hand with his other hand and then released her. "I hear you received a phone call today. Is that right?" asked Dr. Fischer.

Abigail smiled. "Yes, Lucas called me from North Carolina. He's been praying for me."

"How does that make you feel?"

"Good. Really good. I've been trying to pray also. I feel so lost," mumbled Abigail.

Dr. Fischer smiled. "I think Jesus is very glad you called on him. He loves you."

"That's what Grandpa said. He said, 'Child, Jesus don't love the wrongs we do, but he does love us. We belong to him,' and Grandpa never, ever told lies," whispered Abigail and now tears were creeping down her face.

Dr. Fischer put his hand on her arm. "I think you're headed for a much brighter future, Abigail. You keep on praying and then don't doubt."

Chapter 19

Lucas Sutherland hung up the phone after talking with Abigail feeling light-hearted. He went into the bathroom and when he returned he picked up the phone again. When it was answered he said, "Hello, Mom. No, I'm in a hotel room in Winston-Salem, North Carolina. I'll be finished by Thursday or Friday, I think."

They went on to talk about affairs at home and his work in North Carolina and then his mother said, "Lucas, have you heard from Abigail?"

"I talked to her on the phone just before I called you. Yes, there is a big improvement, but Mom; I had the strangest dream about Abigail. I dreamed that she was reading the Bible and then she got on her knees and prayed. No, I didn't tell her all of it. I told her that I had prayed for her and I have been, but then she told me that she suddenly had an urge to read the Bible. I know that Jesus heard my prayers. I've felt all day long that she will be better soon." Lucas let out a long sigh and his mother cautioned him to not put time on the Lord.

"The Lord doesn't deal with time, Lucas. Our months could be seconds to him, so don't expect Abigail to be better overnight," cautioned Mrs. Sutherland.

"I won't, but I feel like something is about to happen. You keep praying, Mom. I knew the first time I saw Abigail that the Lord had meant her for me, but when everything got so mixed up I was full of doubt."

Mrs. Sutherland drew in a long breath, which Lucas heard? "I know, I know . . . she's young and doesn't know much about the world, but Mom, she is very intelligent. She is also ambitious and a very honest person," stated Lucas as if he needed to convince his mother.

"Lucas, I hope you're right and I have no problem with you loving or liking Abigail. I don't know her, but from what you say she is a fine girl. But, son, you can't make somebody love you just because you love them. I'm just afraid you're going to be hurt.

"I'll take my chances, Mom. As soon as she gets better, I'll try to bring her over to meet you," said Lucas, adding in a hesitant voice, "Well, it won't be right after she gets better. She still just wants to be friends."

They went on to talk of his dad's health and Mrs. Sutherland gave the news that his middle sister was expecting a baby. Then they hung up.

Lucas sat down with his Bible and read for a while and then he dropped to his knees beside the bed. *Lord, I don't know how to pray, but if you hear a beggar will you please visit Abigail and heal her troubled mind and heart. I know she prays to you also or she may just plead the way I am, but you made us both and you know our hearts. Lord, I love her and I ask that you please let her know that I'll always be good to her and keep her safe.* After a mumbled "Amen," Lucas rose to his feet and climbed into bed.

Soon he was asleep and dreaming about Abigail. They were skating and he was holding her close in his arms. She was not afraid because she put her head on his shoulder. Lucas woke up smiling and lay there in a pleasant daydream until he drifted back to sleep.

Abigail, however, had been so troubled after her session with Dr. Fischer that she couldn't relax. She turned on the television anchored above her bed, but didn't like the program. She didn't know how to find other channels and just turned it off. Finally she got out of bed and went out to the nurse's station. Judy Fletcher, the night shift nurse, saw her and turned from the charts she was working on.

"Abigail, is anything wrong? You've never come out here before at night," said Judy.

"Does warm milk really make a person sleep?" Abigail asked, turning red in the face.

"A lot of people swear by it, but I haven't tried it. Why, are you having trouble going to sleep?" asked Judy and looked suddenly alert. "You've not had your nerve medicine tonight, have you?"

"I've not been taking it at night, for three nights. I was hoping to gradually stop taking it," said Abigail.

"I'll get you some warm milk, but I'm going to call Dr. Fischer and see what he thinks. After I call him, I'll know whether you should take it or not," said Judy and rose from her seat. "Wait and I'll fix you a glass of warm milk. We'll see if it works for you."

Soon Abigail was going back to her room with a glass of warm milk with a paper towel wrapped around the bottom. In her room she turned the milk up and drank it down, shivered in disgust, and climbed back into her bed. "I'll not think about Dr. Fischer," she said and lay thinking about skating with Lucas.

She drifted off to sleep while thinking of Lucas' arms holding her close and she felt so relaxed and comfortable. Judy came into the room an hour later and Abigail was sound asleep with a smile on her face.

"Well, that warm milk sure worked for her. She's sleeping like a log and has a smile on her face," said Judy, looking at the young student nurse who had fixed the warm milk. "You didn't slip some whiskey or anything in that milk did you?"

The young student's eyes blared in alarm. "Oh, Lord no. I wouldn't do anything like that."

Judy went off in gales of laughter. "I wish I had a camera. You look so outraged, but I was only kidding. We don't have a stash of whiskey on the premises anyway."

The student relaxed. "Did it really put her to sleep? I thought that was just an 'old wives tale' like Mommy is always telling me about."

"I don't know if it put her to sleep, but she is asleep. Let's hope she sleeps the night through. Dr. Fischer thought she might have a restless night, but didn't want to give her the nerve medication unless she became too restless," explained Judy.

The ward had settled down for the night and Judy was writing up her reports on all the patients when an earth-shattering scream broke the silence. Realizing that it was coming from Abigail's room, Judy jumped to her feet and literally ran to her room.

Abigail was thrashing about and seemed to be in some kind of combat. Judy went to the bed and said, "Abigail, wake up." The thrashing continued as well as the screams, so Judy put her hand on Abigail's arm only to be nearly shoved off her feet. She caught onto the railing around the lower half of the bed to keep from hitting the floor.

By this time another nurse had opened the door. "What's wrong with her? Has she gone wild?" she asked as she stared in astonishment.

Judy picked up a glass containing a small amount of water and threw the contents into Abigail's face. Abigail gulped and opened her eyes. "I didn't want to do that, Abigail, but I didn't want to be beaten up either. You were having a terrible nightmare," said Judy.

Abigail sat staring unseeingly as if she was still in the nightmare. "Abigail, are you awake? Look at me," Judy ordered and stood waiting. Finally Abigail stopped staring and dropped her face into her hands. She began crying convulsively.

Judy hurriedly left the room. "I think she will have to be knocked out, but I have to clear it with Dr. Fischer," she told the other nurse who had also exited the room.

When the sleepy voice of Dr. Fischer answered, Judy told him what was happening and he said, "Stay with her for twenty minutes and try to calm her down. If in that time she hasn't gotten calmer give her a shot of the medicine she is on, but increase it a half a centimeter. If she does calm down, give her a regular dose of her medicine. She hasn't been taking it at night, has she?"

"No sir, she hasn't for three nights in a row," said Judy, and after listening for another minute, she said "Good night!" and hung up the phone.

Judy returned to the room to find Abigail still crying. "Abigail

I've just spoken to Dr. Fischer and he said you need to take your nerve medication."

Abigail raised her head and looked at Judy. She had such a woebegone look on her face that Judy could have cried. "It'll be all right, dear. Things like this happen on the road to recovery. It will pass. I'm going to give your medicine in a shot. It will get into your system quicker."

Abigail didn't say anything, but put out her arm as if she didn't care what happened to her. Judy expertly administered the shot and pulled down Abigail's sleeve. "Do you want some water or anything else before you lie down?" Judy asked.

Abigail shook her head no and, still sitting up in the bed, pulled her knees up toward her chest. "Do you know what you dreamed?" asked Judy.

"No, not really. I just know that someone was trying to hurt me. I was fighting," said Abigail, beginning to cry again.

Judy handed her a tissue. "Now, don't start crying again, dear. It was just a bad dream. You'll feel much better in the morning." Abigail lay back and Judy pulled the blanket up over her arms and patted her shoulder. She dimmed the lights in the room but left the bathroom light on with the door cracked in case Abigail had to get up. She then walked back to the bed to see a much calmer Abigail lying quietly on the pillow. Abigail wasn't asleep, but she looked sleepy, so Judy walked quietly to the door.

"Goodnight, Abigail. I'll see you in the morning." Judy said and went through the door, closing it softly behind her.

Abigail lay thinking about that awful nightmare. She couldn't remember most of it, but she knew that someone was trying to get her to do nasty stuff. *Mommy called me nasty, filthy,* thought Abigail and then was startled. *I must be going crazy. Mommy wasn't in that dream . . . I don't think she was.*

Abigail, worried about why she had thought her mother was in her dream or nightmare, but her thoughts grew fuzzy and like a mist until finally, she knew nothing more until morning.

Chapter 20

Abigail awoke when she heard noises in the hallway. She sat up in bed and looked around. *I guess I must have dreamed all that stuff,* she thought since nothing was torn up or moved. She swung her feet over the edge of the bed and stepped to the rug in front of it. Her mother had brought the rug on her last visit saying, "Steppin' out of a warm bed onto that cold tile is enough to shock anyone's nerves. This rug will stop that."

Abigail stood up and stretched, then padded into the bathroom. When she looked into the mirror she gasped. *I look like I've been fighting. I must have had the nightmare I thought I had.*

Abigail went back into the room after taking a shower and brushing her teeth. *Tomorrow I'll wash my hair. I'm too edgy to do anything right now. I felt like I was going to smother in the shower. I'll have to ask Dr. Fischer why I would be like that,* thought Abigail as she sat down on a chair in front of the mirror on the dresser. She picked up a wide bristle brush and managed to get her hair back into some kind of order just as Dr. Fischer knocked on the door and walked in.

"I'm early this morning. Do you mind?" he asked, looking at Abigail with a penetrating gaze.

"No, I don't mind. In fact I'm glad you're here."

"Why are you glad I'm here? Did something happen?"

Abigail turned back from the dresser and pulled her chair toward the middle of the room and sat down. She waited until Dr. Fischer moved his chair to a position facing her. "I had a nightmare last night. I guess Judy told you, but also, I couldn't wash my hair this morning because in the shower I felt as if I was smothering."

"How do you feel right now? Are you still feeling that way?"

"Yes, but not as much as I did in the shower. I feel like something is about to happen and I'm afraid. Is that caused by the medicine?" asked Abigail.

Dr. Fischer didn't answer. He crossed his legs and leaned back with his fingers making a steeple in front of him. Finally he sat forward again and picked up both of Abigail's hands. "What was your nightmare about?"

Abigail started shivering. "I can't talk about it."

Abigail, have you ever heard of hypnosis? It's a therapy in which you go to sleep and you are so relaxed that you can handle things that you can't without the hypnosis. I'd like to try it because I think it is the only way to unlock this demon that has you bound," said Dr. Fischer with such a compassionate look that Abigail felt sorry for him.

"Will it hurt or have any side effects. I mean what if I don't come out of it once I'm hypnotized?" asked Abigail fearfully.

"I'll be with you and there are no side effects. I'm confident that you'll feel better by doing this," stated Dr. Fischer.

Abigail sat thinking how much she wanted to get better. Then she looked up at Dr. Fischer with wide anxious eyes. "If you're sure it won't hurt me, but I really don't care anyway. My life is miserable the way it is, so let's do it."

Dr. Fischer moved his chair a littler nearer to her and pulled a gold watch on a chain from his pocket. The watch had colors that constantly moved in a rhythmic pattern. He held the watch up in front of Abigail. "Have you ever seen a watch like this?" he asked, swinging it slowly. "Just watch the watch while I count to six. When I snap my fingers three times like so, you will wake up, but you won't remember any of this, okay?"

Abigail nodded her head, her gaze fixed on the changing colors. Dr. Fischer started counting, "One, two, three, four, five . . . Abigail can you hear me? Open your eyes please."

Abigail opened her eyes but Dr. Fischer knew she didn't see him. He waited a few seconds and then said, "Abigail you are a little girl and something happened, but your grandpa saved you. How did he save you?"

Abigail's mouth gaped open. "Mommy, don't hit me. Don't hurt me. Ow! Ow! Mommy, don't shake me. I not, I not filfy. I not nasty. I not bad. Please, Mommy." Abigail began shaking and crying, but she clung to Dr. Fischer's hands.

Dr. Fischer was stunned, but he didn't say anything. He kept soothingly rubbing her hands and watching her. "How old are you, Abigail?"

Abigail started crying and Dr. Fischer just let her cry for a moment. "How old are you, Abigail?"

Abigail dropped her head, but held up three fingers. "I'm free. A big boy has gum. I want the gum, but he won't give it to me. If I play a game he'll give it to me." Abigail shivered. "Grandpa saved me. He hit the boy with his cane. The boy ran away. Grandpa ran after him."

"What happened then, Abigail?" Dr. Fischer was watching her closely.

"I not like the game. The boy took my clothes off. Mommy grabbed my clothes. She hit me with a stick and hit me . . . every step she hit me. I bleed . . . on my legs." Abigail's eyes were wide and filled with pain. "Mommy is crying. She said I dirty, nasty, and filfy."

"I not dirty, Mommy. See."Abigail held out her hands. "I sorry, Mommy. I sorry."

"Did your mommy think the boy made you dirty?" asked Dr. Fischer.

Abigail was yelling, "Ow, Ow Mommy, you hurt me. I not filfy. I not nasty. Ow! Ow! Don't hit me, Mommy. I sorry, I sorry."

Abigail was shaking so badly that Dr. Fischer feared she would fall out of her chair, but she said, "Mommy, please, I sorry. Grandpa run to me. He slapped Mommy's face. She don't hit me now."

Dr. Fischer straightened up. "Abigail, when I snap my fingers three times you will wake up and you will feel tired but happy." Dr. Fischer snapped his fingers and Abigail opened her eyes.

"Is it over?" she asked, smiling tiredly.

Dr. Fischer picked up her hands again. "Yes, it's over. How do you feel?"

"I feel fine, but I am tired."

Dr. Fischer rose from his chair. "We'll talk again in the morning, but tonight I want you to think about something. In my opinion, each of us has the potential for good and for evil. The two sides are always warring, but I feel the one that wins is the one you feed. That is to say, people who do bad things have catered to that side of humanity, but then the major portion of the people I have met try to do the best they can. An old Indian once said, 'If you put a wolf cub and a baby lamb in a pen the one that grows is the one you feed.' So tonight I want you to think about which side you've tried to feed."

Abigail was now on her feet and listening carefully to what Dr. Fischer was saying. "That sounds like a verse in the Bible which says to choose each day whom you will serve; either God or Satan. I think the writer went on to say, 'As for me and my house, we will serve the Lord.'"

Dr. Fischer walked back and put both his hands on Abigail's shoulders. "That's exactly what I meant. You are a very intelligent girl, Abigail." Dr. Fischer dropped his hands and stood watching her.

Abigail turned red. "Thanks, Dr. Fischer." She turned away with a smile on her face, but stopped. "Do you want me to take that nerve medicine tonight?"

"Yes, I do. I think you should take it as you have been. Let's see, today is Friday. Take it two more days and then we may talk about cutting it into half a dose each time," said Dr. Fischer and then turned to the door.

Left alone, Abigail went into the bathroom. She soon came out dressed for bed. She drank a glass of water and then climbed wearily into bed. She lay back thinking about Dr. Fischer's story. "Lord, which part have I been feeding?" she asked aloud. She slowing slid out of bed again and prepared to get on her knees when Judy opened the door and came in.

"I got here just in time with your medicine. You're ready to go to dreamland, aren't you?" Judy said handing Abigail the little cup with her pill inside. Abigail popped the pill into her mouth and swallowed it down. Then she poured another glass of water and drained it also. Judy gave her a questioning look and Abigail said, "That pill makes my mouth so dry. I drink water all night long."

Judy tossed the cup in the trash, smiled back at Abigail, and walked briskly out the door. "Sweet dreams."

Soon Abigail was on her knees beside the bed. *Lord, I don't even know why people get on their knees, but I wanted to. I want to honor you, but I don't know how. Jesus, when Lucas called he said he had prayed for me and I know he has. I'm begging you now, Lord, to help me get rid of this awful burden that I've carried for so many years. I'm cowardly, Lord, but I honestly think I'd rather die than to have to live out my life . . . tied and bound by fear. Please, Lord, help me. I want to be whatever you want me to be, but I feel like I've been living in a cage and couldn't get out. I'm not making sense Lord, but you know what I need. Please, please help me. In Jesus' sweet name I pray. Amen.*

Chapter 21

Abigail went to sleep almost as soon as her head hit the pillow. Sometime along in the morning she began dreaming. In her dream she saw a little girl who was dancing along a dirt road. She met a boy who she thought was so pretty. He had yellow curly hair. He smiled at her and they began playing together. She was having so much fun, but then the boy stopped and as he stood there another boy came right out of that boy and he wasn't all golden haired. The little girl was afraid, but then he said he wanted to play a game. The girl was happy again. She liked to play games.

"Let's take off our clothes and go swimming in the flowers," said the boy.

"No, I don't want to play that game. Mommy will be mad," said the girl, but the boy laughed. "Your mommy is not here, and besides if you will play I'll give you this pack of gum."

The little girl had never had a pack of gum. She wanted the gum very much and she knew her Mommy took off her clothes when she put her in the washtub for her bath. She agreed and the boy started helping her take off her clothes.

"No. I'll do it. Mommy says not to let boys touch me." The boy won't stop and the little girl begins to cry and the boy gets angry. He yanks at her clothes and she screams for her Grandpa. Grandpa comes and hits the boy with his cane.

Abigail awoke with a start. She knew she had been dreaming, but all that had actually happened to her. The entire episode flashed through her mind and she sat up in bed. Like Dr. Fischer said, that boy was good at first, but then his evil side took over. Her Grandpa had saved her from the boy. He didn't save her from her Mommy though.

Abigail didn't want to think about that so she got out of bed and went to the bathroom and stopped to look out the window. From somewhere came the words, *I will lift up my eyes unto the hills from whence cometh my help. My help cometh from the Lord.* Abigail stood looking up into the hills behind the hospital. *Lord, help me to pray to you. Help me to believe without doubting, and Lord, if you have a purpose in me and Lucas being together please give me some sign. I'm so afraid.* She turned back into the room and looked at the clock. It was seven thirty. She put on her robe and went out to the nurse's desk. The dayshift was just arriving and when Mavis walked in, she stopped and stared.

"What are you doing up at this time in the morning? Have you had a bad night?" Mavis asked.

Abigail smiled. "No. I had a good night. I just woke up early. Do you have any coffee made?"

"This is a first, isn't it?" asked Mavis.

"I guess it is, but I could smell coffee and decided I'd like to have some. May I have a cup with cream, please?"

Mavis went into their little alcove and came back with a creamy cup of steaming coffee. "Does that look creamy enough?"

"Yes, thanks," said Abigail and went back to her room. She sat down with her Bible and began reading the story of Jesus's birth in the book of Luke. She became so engrossed that she didn't even notice the door opening for the girl bringing her breakfast.

"You sure must like reading the Bible. I was halfway in the room before you heard me," said the girl.

Abigail looked up and smiled. "What do you have for me to eat? I'm hungry." She got up and began lifting lids from the food placed on the bedside table. "Bacon, eggs, toast, cereal, and jelly, oh my! I'll eat all of that as soon as I wash my hands."

The girl grinned. "You don't look like you've been eating much, so I don't reckon it will hurt you. Have a good day."

"Thank you," said Abigail as the girl left and she headed for the bathroom.

Abigail was dressed and sitting in a chair when Dr. Fischer came in. "How are you, Abigail? You look different."

Abigail smiled and said thoughtfully. "I think I am different. Do you remember what you said last night about which side we feed?"

Dr. Fischer said, "Yes, I do, Abigail."

"I had a dream that I need to tell you about." Dr. Fischer pulled up a chair in front of her and said, "I'd like to hear it."

Abigail proceeded to tell him what she'd dreamed and then said, "The events in that dream actually happened, Dr. Fischer."

"I know. You told me about it when you were hypnotized. You told me up to the point where your grandpa slapped your mother. What happened then?"

"Mommy fainted. I thought she was dead and I ran to her and put my arms around her and kept saying, 'Mommy, I'm sorry, I'm sorry. I won't be nasty no more. Wake up, Mommy."

"Do you remember what happened next?" asked Dr. Fischer.

Abigail shook her head. "I don't know if I fainted too, or what happened after that. I don't remember any of this ever being mentioned again. I guess I forgot it."

"Did your mother act differently around you after that?"

Abigail sat thinking. "She never did hug me after that. Of course, she didn't hug the other children either, but I can remember sitting on her lap sometime, which must have been before that."

Dr. Fischer sat back in his chair. "Abigail, do you think men are bad, filthy, or nasty?"

"Grandpa wasn't, but I must have thought all other men were. I was always afraid that Mommy would whip me and call me nasty, dirty, and filthy. Mommy told all of her girls what bad things men would do if we let them. I didn't want anything to do with any men or boys, but I did trust old men like Grandpa. Now, I know they're all the same, young or old," said Abigail grimly.

"You're wrong, Abigail. Most men are nice, gentle, and kind.

The percentage of men that molest girls and women is really rather low compared to the population. You just happened to meet up with one of those few men three years ago," explained Dr. Fischer, rising to his feet.

Abigail didn't get up nor look up. "I've always thought I must have done something for Mommy to call me those names and whip me so hard. I was afraid to be around boys for fear I might do whatever I did the first time."

Dr. Fischer walked over and put his hand on Abigail's shoulder and with his other hand he lifted her face to look at him. "Abigail, you are none of those things. You were an innocent little child not knowing good or evil. There's good and bad in each of us, but we all work to make the good overcome the bad. In your case, you've always fought something that wasn't there."

Dr. Fischer smiled. "I think you are a very good, moral, young woman and I think you have reached a milestone this morning. Now, I'm going and I want you to try to eat breakfast and then take a nap. I believe you will feel better when you do. I know you must be tired; baring one's soul is very hard."

Abigail smiled. "It sure is. I thank you Dr. Fischer. I'll try to eat, but not right now."

"Don't force yourself to eat. I want you to take your medicine, but not on an empty stomach so eat a bite or two anyway," said Dr. Fischer, patting her shoulder before he left the room.

Abigail only ate enough breakfast to take her medicine then climbed back into bed. She felt drained as if part of her had been removed and she lay trying to understand what had happened. Soon she was fast asleep.

Mavis came in and stood looking at her sleeping so peacefully and wondered why she was asleep in the daytime. She didn't wake her then, but thought she'd come back at lunch time. "She needs to eat. She's far too thin," she muttered as she softly closed the door behind her.

Abigail awoke at eleven o'clock and stretched luxuriously before throwing the covers back and getting nimbly from the bed. She even did a few dance steps across the room to the bathroom. *Lord, I feel good. I can't ever remember feeling this good.* Then some long forgotten memory came to the forefront of her mind. She was walking along the road with her grandfather and he lifted her up to peep into a bird's nest. The nest was in a honeysuckle bush and the smells, the little birds, and the safety she felt in her grandfather's arms flooded over her. It was such a poignant memory that tears sprang to her eyes. "Jesus, thank you for that precious memory," she said aloud.

When she was back in the room she still felt really good, but she was hungry. *I wish I had a watch,* she thought just as the door opened and Mavis came in.

"Well you look all bright and chipper. How do you feel?"

Abigail smiled. "I feel just like I look, Mavis. I am bright and chipper. I woke up feeling like that. I'm hungry too. Is it time for lunch?"

Mavis looked at her watch. "In ten more minutes, if you can wait that long."

Abigail whirled around in the room. "Mavis, I feel full of sunshine; you know that easy, joyful feeling that a new day brings."

"A new day means I have to crawl out of bed and go to work so a new day doesn't give me an easy, joyful feeling," Mavis grumbled.

Still feeling like nothing could dim her joy, Abigail pranced over and flung her arms around Mavis. "But, you get to see me when you come to work. Doesn't that give you joy?"

Mavis stepped back and took a good look at Abigail. "To see you like this gives me joy, that's for sure. Did you have a good dream?"

Abigail shrugged. "Not that I know of, but I sure do feel good . . . as if there's not a care in the world."

Mavis put her arms around Abigail. "Here, let me hug you so some of that can rub off on me." They both hugged and laughed.

Just then someone knocked on the door and it was pushed open by the nice black girl that usually brought lunch. Abigail ran to take it from her arms and helped her arrange it on the table. "What's your name?" asked Abigail, smiling cheerfully.

"It's Natasha Collins. What's your name?"

"Abigail Dawson. I've wanted to ask your name every time you've been in here, but thought that would be too nosey."

Natasha rolled her eyes and then laughed. "Be nosey if you want to. How else you going to learn anything?"

Abigail giggled. "That's the truth. The Bible says, 'Ask and ye shall receive,' so I asked your name and now I know it. You're sharp, Natasha, and I'm glad I asked."

Natasha laughed and picked up the empty tray to leave. "I'm glad you asked too, Abigail."

Mavis had stood listening to this conversation in amazement. It was almost like one Abigail had been here yesterday and a new Abigail was here today. "Dr. Fischer is going to be really pleased when he makes his visit tonight," she said.

"I hope he is pleased enough to let me go home. I've been in here eight or nine days and I need to be back at work," said Abigail.

"If you stay like this I have no doubt that Dr. Fischer will release you. You act and sound like a different person. I don't mean there was anything wrong with you before, but you weren't happy. You sure seem happy now, though."

Abigail picked up the covers on her food and said, "I'm going to eat every bite of this, then maybe he will let me go home."

"I'll leave so you'll settle down and eat," said Mavis and walked quickly out the door.

Chapter 22

Abigail ate everything on her plate and drank a full glass of water. "I'd love to try a glass of milk, but I'd better ask Dr. Fischer first."

She had just finished brushing her hair when Mavis put her head in the door and said, "You're wanted on the telephone."

Abigail put down the brush and made sure her robe was buttoned all the way down before following Mavis to the nurse's desk. A nurse behind the desk said, "Here she is," in the receiver and then passed the phone to Abigail.

"Hello! Lucas. Where are you? You are! I sound good because I feel wonderful. No, I . . . well, I'll tell you about it when I see you. Sure, I want to see you. We have some skating to do, my friend. Why don't you wait until tomorrow to come? I think Dr. Fischer may let me go home. Just tell Mommy to bring me some clothes to wear home. Thanks! He must have heard you, for I truly feel wonderful. No, I took a nap after Dr. Fischer saw me this morning and when I woke up I felt like this. Okay, that sounds great. Thanks my friend. I owe you. Bye, Lucas."

Abigail turned with a broad smile on her face. Mavis looked at her with raised eyebrows. Abigail giggled. "Mavis, I think I have a boyfriend."

"Who would have thought that? It couldn't be because he's sent flowers, candy, gifts, and made phone calls. I mean all friends do that, don't they, girls?" asked Mavis mischievously, looking at the other nurses.

"Yeah, I got dozens of friends that spend all kinds of money on me," said one of the younger nurses and laughed at Abigail's red face. "She really does have a boyfriend. Look how red she is."

Abigail went back into her room and sat down to read a magazine, but soon the magazine was forgotten. *I think I would like for Lucas to be my boyfriend, but I don't want to feel like I'm doing something wrong if he touches me.* Abigail sat up straighter in her chair. *I've been afraid of Mommy . . . afraid she'll call me filthy and nasty again all these years. I wonder why she did that. I wasn't even three years old when that happened.*

Abigail sat puzzling over her mother's reaction. *I've never known her to act like that since then. I'm going to ask Virginia if she knows anything about that episode.*

She went in the bathroom, showered and washed her hair. *Whew! That feels so good. My hair felt heavy, but then I've been heavy all over for so long,* she thought and walked back into the room.

She walked over to the window and looked up into the hills. Soon she was praying. *Lord, I thank you so much. I thank you for sending Lucas to me. He said he hadn't prayed before, but he's been praying for me. When he told me he prayed I started trying to pray again. I hadn't been trying to pray as I should have until I met Lucas. You do move in mysterious ways and you do perform miracles. It was a miracle that I should come to this hospital and get Dr. Fischer as a doctor. If he hadn't hypnotized me I would have carried that awful secret around for the rest of my life. Oh God! How good you've been to me. Thank you! Thank you!*

Abigail felt so peaceful looking up into the hills and tears of thankfulness crept down her cheeks. She turned when the door opened and Natasha walked in bearing a vase filled with pink roses. "Girl, you got some man who's plum crazy about you."

When she got closer she stopped and exclaimed, "Whats' you crying about? I thought you'd be happy. I know I'd be if somebody sent me pretty flowers."

"I am happy, Natasha. These are tears of joy. I've just been going over how much the good . . . how much everyone has done for me and I'm so thankful." She had started to say 'the good Lord' and had changed it.

Now she was ashamed for not owning her Lord. She looked at Natasha. "Natasha, I've been praying and Lucas has been praying and the good Lord heard our prayers. I'm better. I know I'm better, but I may have to take medicine for a while. That's all right though, because the Lord has healed my heart."

Natasha had put the roses on her dresser and now turned. Her eyes were shining brightly. "You ain't the only one that's been praying, girl. I have too."

Abigail ran to her and threw both arms around her. "Thank you, Natasha. It's so good to know that people care about me. That shows love, you know when somebody does things for you that you don't expect and them not expecting anything in return. That kind of love touches hearts. Thank you."

Abigail stepped back and smiled at Natasha. "The next time Lucas sends me candy I'm going to save half of it for you."

"No you're not. Just look at me. Do I look like somebody that needs a half box of candy?" They both started laughing and then hugged each other again before Natasha said, "I better get out of here before the boss lady comes looking for me."

Left alone, Abigail put her face down to the roses and sniffed and then sneezed. She backed away and sneezed again, and again. "I must be allergic to roses," she thought and sneezed again. She picked up the entire vase and holding it out in front of her she carried it from the room and out to the nurse's station.

"I'm sneezing my head off and I wasn't until Natasha brought these flowers. Will you please give them to her when comes back. She can't be allergic to them since she carried them in to me and she wasn't sneezing," said Abigail and sneezed three times in a row.

One of the nurses came over just as Mavis came around the side of the station. "What is it? Whose flowers are these?"

Abigail had backed completely away from the desk, but was still sneezing every few minutes and her eyes were watering.

The nurse pointed to Abigail. "They were sent to her, but she must be allergic to them. When she started sneezing she brought them out here and wants Natasha to have them."

Mavis went into the nurse's alcove and came back with a pink and white capsule. "Here, take this Benadryl capsule. It will stop the sneezing, but tell your boyfriend not to send anymore pink roses." Mavis handed Abigail the capsule and a plastic cup of water.

"He's sent me yellow roses, and white roses, and red carnations, but those are the first ones which have caused me to sneeze," said Abigail.

"It may be whatever the florist sprayed them with to keep them fresh. Do you have roses at home?" asked Mavis.

Abigail nodded and sneezed again. "There's roses blooming in Mommy's yard from May through August and I'm around them all the time."

"That's it, then, but you'd better go back to your room. That Benadryl may make you sleepy," advised Mavis and took the offending roses away to another room.

Abigail did get drowsy and sat dozing in her chair until her dinner came. She straightened up, awake. "Gosh! That Benadryl sent me off into dreamland."

The girl putting her tray down on her bedside table, turned to look at her. "My daddy would say that you look like a wild jack rabbit with your eyes big like that. Did that Benadryl do that to you?"

Abigail jumped up and went to the dresser so she could look in the mirror. She studied herself and turned from the mirror smiling. "Your daddy would have been right. My pupils are certainly dilated. I must have gotten a reaction to the Benadryl."

The girl turned to leave. "You'd best tell the doctor about that. You probably shouldn't take Benadryl." She went on out and closed the door.

Abigail pulled the bed side table close to her chair and lowered it to a sitting level. Unconsciously she opened the carton of milk on her tray and drank from it, before she remembered that she hadn't been drinking milk. It tasted good and she still felt all right so she ate some of her other food and took another drink of milk. She still didn't feel nauseous and breathed a sigh of relief, but that was premature for suddenly she made a rush to the bathroom and lost all her dinner.

Dr. Fischer walked in while she was still retching and walked hurriedly to her side. "What brought this on? You've been doing so well."

Abigail turned to the washbasin and washed her face and rinsed out her mouth. "I drank milk with my dinner. I was hoping that I could drink it again, but I guess not." She dried her hands and looked up at Dr. Fischer with a smile.

He grasped her shoulders and turned her to the light. "Your pupils are dilated. Have you eaten something else?"

"Oh! That's the Benadryl. I got a reaction to some roses that Lucas sent and started sneezing. Mavis gave me a Benadryl. It put me to sleep, but I stopped sneezing. I didn't know my pupils were dilated until the girl brought my dinner. I wasn't nauseous though until I drank the milk," explained Abigail.

Dr. Fischer wrote on his notebook that he always carried with him. "I think the Benadryl and your other medicine together may have given you the reaction to the milk. We'll wait and see. How do you feel, otherwise?"

Abigail put her hands out palms up. "I feel wonderful. I awoke feeling like a new person and I've been that way all day until the roses came. I still didn't feel gloomy or down. I just couldn't stop sneezing and then lost all my dinner. I feel all right, though."

"You look different, Abigail, and not just big-eyed either. Your expression is different. Do you know what happened?" asked Dr. Fischer.

Abigail bit her lip deep in thought. "I've accepted that I've carried around a feeling of unworthiness and guilt since I was three years old. I know it was brought about by Mommy's reaction because the boy didn't really do anything but help me take my clothes off. I just can't understand why my mother reacted like that?"

Dr. Fischer sat looking at Abigail intently. "What kind of

relationship do your mother and father have? Do they show love, one for the other?"

Abigail looked solemn. "I guess I never thought about it, but they don't hug or kiss, if that's what you mean."

"You mean you have never seen them hug or kiss, but surely they have. Some people just don't do that where others can see them," said Dr. Fischer.

Abigail knew that was true, but now thinking about it she felt that for some reason her dad acted hateful to her mother. He didn't curse her or call her names, but said little snide things that must hurt her feelings. She told Dr. Fischer some of the ways in which her father was unkind and he nodded his head as if he had some insight.

"I think I'm going to ask Virginia if she remembers what happened when Mommy fainted that time. She's a lot older than I am, but she was home so maybe she'll remember what happened," said Abigail.

"That's probably a good idea. I think something similar must have happened to your mother and she, like you, kept it buried. She may not have told it yet," surmised Dr. Fischer.

"I believe I am well enough to go home and I'd like to get back to my job. The first semester of college starts in two more months and I don't have enough money saved."

"Can't your dad help you any?"

"He won't. He says girls just want to get away from home to see boys. That's why I'm being a hired girl. He said if I could get a decent job and pay my way, I could go to college. I have a four-year scholarship, but I need general living expenses. That's why I need to work. I'm going to go to college some way because I want to be a teacher," stated Abigail with assurance.

Dr. Fischer smiled. "Yes, I do believe you are ready to go home, but you'll have to come and see me once a week at first and then we'll gradually cut back. How does that sound?"

Abigail jumped from her seat. "That's wonderful. I told Lucas to wait and come tomorrow since I felt you would let me go home." Abigail twirled around, throwing her arms wide, with a big smile on her face.

Chapter 23

Abigail couldn't sleep that night. She was so excited that she kept getting up and cracking her door to see the clock at the nurse's station. She made sure she eased her door open quietly because she didn't want to let the nurses know she wasn't asleep.

They'd come in with a dose of nerve medicine and then Dr. Fischer wouldn't let me go home, thought Abigail as she climbed back into bed. She finally dropped off to sleep and dreamed of skating with Lucas. He was holding her close and she wasn't afraid.

The aide bringing in breakfast woke her. "Oh! I'm sorry. I didn't know you were still asleep."

Abigail sat up in bed and smiled. "I'm glad you did. I need to get a shower and get dressed before Dr. Fischer makes his round."

When Dr. Fischer walked in at nine-thirty, Abigail had showered, dressed, eaten her breakfast and brushed her teeth. She welcomed him with a beaming smile. "Good Morning! How are you this morning?" she asked.

Dr. Fischer's eyebrows lifted and he smiled his appreciation. "That's my line, Abigail. I don't have to ask how you are, though. You look on top of the world."

"You've described exactly how I feel this morning. You are going to let me go home today, aren't you?"

"I'll have to make sure you will be able to keep an appointment once each week, if I do," replied Dr. Fischer.

Abigail's face fell. She knew she had to work and she didn't know if her dad would bring her once a week. "Dad only drives around home. I don't know if he'd feel comfortable driving in Welch," she said worriedly.

"Do you have a neighbor or what about your boy . . . uh friend, Lucas? Could he bring you?"

"He lives in Ronceverte and I couldn't ask him to come all that way every week just to bring me over here."

Dr. Fischer looked around at the flowers and teddy bears and grinned. "If all these gifts are any indication of whether he will or not then I think you don't have to worry."

"I want to go back to work. I have to earn another one hundred and fifty dollars before college classes start in August. You don't see patients on Saturday, do you?" asked Abigail anxiously.

"I haven't been, but since I want to help you get to college I'll make an exception in your case," said Dr. Fischer thoughtfully.

Abigail wanted to get up and hug him, and was shocked that she would feel like that about any man. *I guess he reminded me of Grandpa's kindness,* she thought as she turned a smiling face to Dr. Fischer. She swallowed to combat the tears that threatened to spill.

"Why are you about to cry? I have children of my own, you know. I appreciate young people having a goal and you definitely have that," said Dr. Fischer, handing her a tissue.

Abigail dropped her head. "I don't get much encouragement in my family to go to college. My brother Kyle did tell me he was very proud of me when he learned about my scholarship."

"They should all be proud, but then each family is different. I'll bet they will end up being very proud of you. They'll have something to brag about," said Dr. Fischer with a smile.

Abigail thought her mother would be proud of her, but didn't think she would ever tell her if she was. As for her dad, she doubted if he would ever mention it, much less brag. Her sister Virginia had said, "Abby, I wanted to finish high school so badly, but Daddy wouldn't let me. That's why I left home."

She knew that both Virginia and Alice had been pregnant when they married. She'd never forget the cursing Garson had aimed at her mother when he'd found out. She could see her mother cringe as his foulmouthed abuse went on and on. Sally had only dropped her head sadly and crimped her mouth closed. Abigail knew that at times like that she didn't like her father.

She jerked her mind back to Dr. Fischer and smiled. "If you'll let me go home, I'll get over here some way. I might even hire a neighbor, since I think I wouldn't be afraid, now. I think I'll always be wary around men, but I don't feel like I did, that's for sure."

"That's great, Abigail. I think at one time you were a happy, vivacious little girl, but after that episode with your mother, you were afraid to be happy lest she would call you filthy, nasty, and dirty. You now know that none of those adjectives describe you, don't you?" asked Dr. Fischer.

Abigail narrowed her eyes in retrospection. "I know I have the potential to be all those things, but I don't choose to do or be any of those things and so I'm not. I've learned from you, Dr. Fischer, and as long as I'm in my right mind I'll never feed the bad side of me."

Dr. Fischer put his hands on her shoulders and looked her steadily in the eyes. "You'll do, Abigail Dawson. I have all the confidence in the world that you will overcome the evil in humanity because you will choose the good. That's who you are. It shines through in your eyes."

Abigail smiled. "Thanks! That means more to me than anything you could have said to me. So, having said all that, may I pack my clothes so I can go home?"

Dr. Fischer stepped back, smiling. "You just can't wait to get away from me, can you? I won't promise until I have assurance from somebody that you will be back here every Saturday morning at eleven o'clock."

Abigail smiled. "I'll twist somebody's arm because I need to get back to work."

"I'll see you when your folks come," said Dr. Fischer as he went out the door.

Even though Dr. Fischer hadn't actually said she could

go home, Abigail felt confident that she could. She pulled her suitcase from the closet and started putting everything in it. One of the nurses brought her a white plastic bag to put her dirty clothes in. This left her gifts, flowers, fruit, and candy to do something with. Since all the flowers had wilted except one vase, she packed the empty vases in the bag containing her dirty clothes and decided to give the candy and fruit to the nurses. She would wait until she was ready to leave to do that. Now she picked up a magazine and idly leafed through it as she waited for one o'clock, the time her parents had always arrived.

Suddenly she found herself praying, *Oh Lord, please let me not be afraid of Lucas. I want to let him know how much I appreciate all he's done for me, but I don't know how to do that.* She thought she might just smile and then she did smile. *He'd fall over in a dead faint if I ran and hugged him, but I couldn't do that. Besides Mommy would be thunderstruck if I did something like that.*

She was still trying to decide what approach to take when Natasha came in with her lunch. "What you been up to, girl? Where's all them flowers and teddy bears you had all over this room?" She was smiling as she said it and Abigail knew someone had told Natasha that she was going home.

Abigail picked one box of candy and the vase of flowers. "I saved these for you. I want you to have something to remember me by." Abigail smiled and pushed the gifts into her arms.

"I ain't going to forget you noway, girl. Are you sure you want to part with this stuff?" asked Natasha.

Abigail threw her arms around Natasha. "I'm sure I want you to have them. You've been a good friend, Natasha, and I wish you the best. Why don't you train to be a nurse?"

"I didn't get to finish high school. I quit in the eleventh grade and went to work, but I would like to be a nurse," said Natasha with a longing look in her eyes.

"Ask about the GED program? You could go to classes one night a week and then take the test. I don't think you'd have any trouble. You want me to ask Dr. Fischer to see what he can do for you?" asked Abigail, still keeping her arm around Natasha's shoulders.

"You think he would do that?"

"He's really nice and caring. I believe he would and besides all he can do is say no. You wouldn't be any worse off than you are now, but you'll never know unless you try," said Abigail.

Natasha slapped her lightly on the arm. "Go ahead and ask. If you can work to get something then I can to." She picked up the empty containers and turned to go. "Don't you forget me."

"I'll be coming over here every Saturday. I'll try to get with you and we'll go eat lunch together. I'd like that. Would you?" asked Abigail, smiling brightly.

"Sounds good to me. I hope I can get off from work at that time. Anyway, thanks again for all this stuff. I'll hide the candy here for if I take it home I'll not get one bite." She walked on out the door and Abigail closed it softly behind her. She stood thinking about how many nice people she had met while here in the hospital. They were, as Dr. Fischer had said, mostly good, honest, hardworking people who were kind to others. Of course, Natasha had said that every young man who had seen Abigail in the hall had asked a lot of questions about her. "They grabbed every excuse they could find to come out to the nurses desk, thinking they might get to see you. It's that pretty red hair, I think," Natasha had said, laughing merrily at Abigail's red face.

Abigail ate her lunch hurriedly so that she wouldn't have to wait when her parents came. She wondered if Lucas had told them that she was expecting to go home today. *He must not have or they would have come earlier,* she thought, jumping up once more to look down in the parking lot.

Chapter 24

Two o'clock rolled around and her family had not yet arrived. Abigail just knew they'd had a wreck or something. *Maybe Mommy is sick, or maybe Lucas couldn't make it,* she thought anxiously, walking back to look out the window the fifth time in the last hour.

She studied every car in the parking lot and still did not see Lucas's silvery gray Buick sedan. Dejectedly she turned back into the room just as there was a knock and then the door opened. Sally walked through the door, followed by Garson and Lucas.

"It's almost two-thirty. Why are you so late? I've been thinking everything in the world," cried Abigail.

"We got stopped in Bradshaw," said Garson, grinning from ear to ear. I ran into an old friend of mine. Do you remember Adam Hagerman?"

"Adam Hagerman! You mean that man that used to come to the house all the time? He gave me a quarter every time he came," said Abigail in wide-eyed wonder.

"He looks the same as he always did. He said he was at the skating rink the night all that happened. How come you didn't recognize him?" asked Sally curiously.

Abigail shook her head. "I don't know. I was enjoying myself so much until I saw that white-headed man, that I think I didn't see anybody else."

"Well now, the lighting in the skating rink is always dim," Lucas commented. "I'm sure that's why you didn't recognize him. Don't start browbeating yourself."

Abigail realized he was trying to help her out and turned to him with a smile. "Well, just as long as all of you are all right and are here it doesn't matter. How are you, Lucas?"

A pleased grin spread over his handsome face. "I'm fine. You're looking well. How are you?"

"I'm fine and I think I'll get to go home today. Mommy, did you bring my clothes? If you didn't, I'll just wear what I have on," said Abigail firmly.

Sally shook her head. "I didn't bring anything. I was afraid you wouldn't get to go home and would be upset. Lucas did tell me that you thought you'd get to come home, but I was still afraid."

"Your mam is the worst woman to believe the worst about everything," said Garson. "I swear if somebody give her a bar of gold she'd want it cut in half to make sure."

Abigail pushed some chairs around and said, "Well, sit down and I'm going to the nurse's station and see if Dr. Fischer is on the floor. If he is, I'll ask him if I can go home."

Lucas looked at her eagerly. "Do you want me to go with you?"

"No, it won't take a minute. I'll be right back," said Abigail, hurrying through the door. She soon came back saying, "He's on the floor and Mavis paged him. He'll stop by here at the end of his round."

Abigail sat down on her bed and turned to Lucas. "Thanks for all you've done for me. I gave one bunch of flowers and some of the candy to the girl who brings my meals on the day shift. Her name is Natasha and we are the same age. She had to quit high school to help her family."

"You don't need to explain to me what you did with what I sent. They were gifts. That means they were yours to do whatever you wanted with them," explained Lucas with a smile.

Lucas's chair was near the bed and Abigail suddenly reached out her hand to him. He was shocked at this spontaneous gesture, but quickly took her hand and held it. He looked at her and smiled as he gently squeezed her hand.

"Well, pon-my-honor if that ain't a big improvement, Abby.

I don't reckon I can remember when you ever reached out to any man except your grandpa," said Garson.

Sally had been sitting quietly watching, but suddenly blurted out, "She did before . . . well before all this happened."

"You've seen something . . ." Garson stopped because Dr. Fischer walked through the door. He noticed Lucas holding Abigail's hand but pretended he didn't.

"Good afternoon, folks. Have you come to take Abigail home?" he asked, smiling widely.

"We did, Doc. At least we were hoping to take her home, but her mother just couldn't believe it so she didn't bring her no clothes," answered Garson.

Fearing Dr. Fischer would change his mind, Lucas said, "There's nothing wrong with what she's wearing now. She can still go home, can't she?

Abigail pulled her hand away and stood up. "Dr. Fischer, I told you last night that I needed to get back to work. I hope Harve and Mattie still want me."

Dr. Fischer sat down on the end of the bed and patted the place beside him. "Sit down, Abigail. We need to have a talk. You and your family need to know the terms if I release you. I've gone over your file thoroughly before making these decisions and terms."

Abigail kept her eyes glued to his face. Sally was pleating the edge of the cardigan worn over her dress. Lucas was also listening raptly, and Garson said, "Okay, let's hear these terms."

Dr. Fischer looked at Abigail solemnly. "Abigail, please believe me when I say this is all for your own good." Abigail's face clouded over in dread and she sat forward.

"Abigail, one of the terms is that you are not to go back to work. I know you plan to attend college this fall, but if you don't rest and relax, I fear you won't be able to handle college. Another is that I have to be sure that you will be here every Friday for a one hour session for the next two or three months," said Dr. Fischer quietly.

Abigail dropped her head and when she raised it she

looked stonily at Dr. Fischer. "You know that I have to work in order to go to college. I told you why and now you're saying I can't work." Tears were running down her cheeks.

Lucas jumped to his feet. "Yes, you will go to college, Abigail, and I'll bring you over here every Friday. Dr. Fischer just wants you to get well and I do too."

Abigail looked at Lucas angrily. "How do you suppose I can go to college without a cent of money? I couldn't save enough. I only have a hundred and eighty dollars and I need at least two hundred and fifty, so how can you say I can go?"

"I'll give you the money, that's how," said Lucas.

Sally, Garson, and Abigail gasped. "No. I can't take money from you. I couldn't pay you back for four years."

"That's right, son. We Dawson's don't take charity," said Garson adamantly. "If Abby is that set on going to college, I can sell some timber and get the rest of what she needs, I reckon."

"I'd be pleased if you would, Garson. Working for Harve and Mattie was too much for somebody as little as Abigail. She was so tired when she come home on Friday evenings that she could barely make it," said Sally. "I didn't say nothing because I knew you . . ." She stopped when she realized she would be revealing too much about her family problems.

Dr. Fischer had been watching this exchange and now turned to Abigail. "It seems that your family is willing to help you, and Lucas has promised to bring you in for your sessions, so I guess you can go home. How does that sound?"

Abigail rose from her seat and walked over to Garson and leaned down and hugged him. "Thanks Dad. I'll pay you back when I start teaching."

Garson was too stunned to speak for a second. He looked up at Abigail with tears in his eyes and got to his fee. "You just paid me, Abby," and he pulled her into his embrace.

"Oh Daddy. I do love you," Abigail whispered from trembling lips.

She turned and looked at her mother. "Mommy, Dr. Fischer has helped me so much. Anybody with a problem should have the chance to talk to him." She broke away from Garson and went to Dr. Fischer and stopped in front of him. She looked up at him for a moment and then put her arms around him and hugged him also. Dr. Fischer hugged her back and looked over her head toward Lucas and winked.

"I spent three days trying to be in the room with Abigail, and a week with my nurse in attendance every time I came in the room. This reaction is what I had hoped for from the first time I saw her. Your daughter is almost a well girl, Mrs. Dawson."

Sally had been standing as stiff as a statue. They all turned to look at her and suddenly her face crumbled and she began weeping, but she covered her face with her hands. "Lord be praised. I never thought I'd live to see her happy again," she mumbled.

Abigail went to her and put her arms around her mother. "It's all right Mommy. I remember all about it and it's all right."

Sally's head jerked up and Garson sucked in his breath. They looked steadily at each other and then both dropped their heads. Abigail, sensing that some unspoken message had taken place between her parents, turned to smile at Lucas.

"What are we waiting for? I've had my things packed since ten this morning. Are you ready, Lucas?"

"Just tell me what you want me to carry and we'll bid Dr. Fischer good-bye. What time do you want her here on Friday, doctor?" asked Lucas.

"The latest I can see her is four-forty-five. Can you make it by then?"

Lucas thought a minute. "Yes, I can most of the time. If my work gets in the way some week, can she come another day in the week?"

"You'll need to give me a call at least two days prior to the date you want to come, but this is unusual for me to do so don't do it very often," Dr. Fischer cautioned.

Chapter 25

Soon they were in the car driving out of Welch. Sally and Garson had gotten into the back seat before Abigail had her things positioned in the trunk and, therefore, she found herself beside Lucas.

"Gosh, everything looks so green and pretty. I could see out my window, but it isn't the same as being outside." Abigail looked over at Lucas and grinned. "Your skating friend has certainly put you through a lot of trouble. All I can say is that you're not very good at picking friends."

Lucas grinned. "You just let me be the judge of that, my friend. You don't hear me complaining do you?"

Garson spoke from the back seat. "You keep your mind and eyes on your driving, young feller. We want to get Abby home in one piece."

Lucas looked at Abigail and raised his eyebrows. "You may have to let your dad ride in the front, Abigail. He got car sick when we first brought you over here."

"Pull over, Lucas. I'll ride the back. We can't have Daddy getting sick, can we?" Abigail smiled at Lucas and he pulled over in the next curve. Abigail and Garson traded places leaving her and Sally to talk about Lucas's offer to take her for her counseling sessions. They were also pleased about Garson's offer to sell some of his trees to help Abigail, but didn't dare talk about it lest Garson should hear them and change his mind.

They were almost in Bradshaw at four o'clock and Lucas said, "Would you folks like to stop at the Bus Terminal and get something to eat? By the time we get home, Mrs. Dawson will be too tired to cook."

"No, I won't be too tired and besides you've already spent a fortune on my family," spoke up Sally.

Garson craned his neck around. "He didn't say he was going to pay for it, woman. He just asked if we'd like to and I would. If you remember you just give me a bowl of cornbread and milk for my noon meal and now I'm hungry."

Lucas quickly pulled into the Bus Terminal parking area. "Let's go eat. We can settle who pays later. I'm like Mr. Dawson. I'm hungry." He stepped out and opened the back door for Abigail and Sally. Soon they were all in the restaurant and seated at a booth in the back. Garson and Sally on one side and Lucas and Abigail facing them.

Abigail couldn't ever remember eating in a restaurant with her parents and now she looked across at them and smiled. "This is the first time we've done this, isn't it, Mom?"

Sally looked across at her. "It is, Abby. In fact it's about the fourth time I've ever eaten in a restaurant, but your dad has many times."

Garson glared. "It's because I get out and go more than you do. You could go more if you wanted to."

The waitress came then and Abigail breathed a sigh of relief. She knew this strange relationship existed between her parents, but until now she had just accepted it. As the waitress took their drinks order, Abigail looked at her dad, wondering why he seemed to resent her mother. *They don't actually quarrel and have never fought, but there is something that I don't understand,* she thought as she told the waitress she wanted water to drink.

As soon as the waitress left, Lucas quickly jumped in. "Well, this is a celebration! Abigail is better and is now eating out with her parents for the first time. Also, I get to be a part of the celebration. I wish I had a camera, don't you, Abigail?"

"Gosh! That would be a treasured picture wouldn't it? Why don't you keep a camera in your car, Lucas?"

Lucas jumped up. "I do have a camera in my car. I took a camera with me last week when I went to Lewisburg and I haven't taken it out of the car yet. I'll go get it and get you a memory, my friend." He grinned broadly and walked hurriedly from the room.

"That feller shore does beat all. You can call him friend all you want to, Abby, but if that feller ain't trying to court you I ain't never seen nobody try," said Garson.

Abigail turned really red and looked at her mother. "I guess he is more than a friend, Daddy, but I don't really want to date anybody."

"How're you ever going to get married if you don't date?"

"I don't want to get married and please hush. Here comes Lucas!" whispered Abigail with a pleading look at her father.

Garson shrugged his shoulders and raised his eyebrows, but didn't say anything else. Lucas came through the restaurant waving the camera. "Sit over on the side with your parents Abigail and I'll take the picture."

Just then the waitress came back with their drinks and everyone sat down to look at the menu. When they had given their orders and the waitress turned back toward the kitchen, Lucas arose from his seat with his camera in his hand. He walked back a few feet and put the camera to his eye.

"I can get a shot of you three as you are and then I'll take another with Abigail between her parents. How does that sound?" he asked, looking at Sally.

Sally looked at Garson. "That would make a good family picture . . . I mean it would show how close we are or . . ." She dropped her head and said, "But if Garson and Abby wants it some other way it'll be all right."

At Sally's words, Garson's head jerked around and he gave her a level look, pursed his lips, and then said, "Yeah that would suit me just fine. In fact it would please me," he said, still looking at Sally, who was also looking at him.

Lucas took the first picture and then Abigail moved to sit between her parents, and behind her back she felt their two hands coming together. She didn't say anything, but had trouble keeping her tears back. She'd never, that she could recall, ever seen her parents touching, hugging, or anything that showed caring.

"Now smile! This is a happy occasion and I want a picture of a happy family," said Lucas, who stood waiting. Both Garson and Sally looked toward Abigail and smiled. That's the shot Lucas snapped.

He came back to his seat. "That was a good shot. I think you're going to be really proud to have it."

They all turned as the waitress came with the tray of food. "Well, pon-my-honor, you was quick. Did you have it already cooked?" asked Garson, smiling.

"We cook a big batch of everything every hour and it is fresh cooked, if that's what you are worried about," said the waitress.

"No, no, I wouldn't worried about nothing. I was just bragging on you for being so quick to bring the food," explained Garson.

They had all ordered fried chicken, mashed potatoes, green beans, coleslaw and biscuits, since that was the special. No talking went on for a few minutes as salt, pepper, butter, and jam was passed around. After a few minutes, Garson looked at Sally. "This is good chicken, but you've got them beat all to pieces."

Lucas and Abigail looked at Sally, who had turned red in the face. Lucas looked at her and smiled. "He's telling the truth, Mrs. Dawson. You are a really good cook."

She didn't look at Lucas but instead looked at Garson. "I try to do the best I can."

Garson was looking at her steadily. "I believe you do, Sally. I truly believe you do."

Abigail felt that something was being communicated between her parents. She looked at Lucas and realized he felt the same. Her hand was on the table between them and Lucas put his hand over hers. She didn't move her hand for a few minutes and Lucas looked at her from smiling eyes.

Soon the meal was over, but it was still in Lucas's thoughts as they drove up Bradshaw Mountain. *Lord, let Abigail's recovery be an opening for breaking down the barrier or whatever it is between her parents,* he silently prayed.

Before Lucas had met Abigail he had never even thought about praying. If he skidded in the car his first thought was *Lord have mercy,* but as far as actually saying words or giving it much thought he hadn't. After the talk he'd had with his mother, he had certainly been praying. He looked through the rearview mirror at Abigail and smiled when he found her looking at him. Abigail was better and was going home, so the Lord had heard his or somebody's prayers.

"Mr. Dawson, how long will it take you to sell that timber you were talking about? You know the trees you promised to sell to help Abigail," said Lucas.

"I don't know. I'll not sell them cheap, that's for certain. I'm thinking I can get fifty dollars a tree for some of my walnuts. I'll not sell them no cheaper than that."

Abigail's heart felt like it had dropped into her shoes. *He'll not be able to get that much for one tree, so I can't go to college after all,* she thought, but felt cheered when Lucas said, "I may know somebody who would buy them. If you want me to, I'll check next week. I could let you know next Friday when I come to take Abigail for her appointment."

Garson sat silent for a moment. "I'll not have some greenhorn cutting the trees. They'll ruin every tree around the ones they cut."

"Do you want to cut them yourself?" asked Lucas.

"I can, but they'd have to pay me extra. I don't work for nothing."

Lucas drove along in silence. "I don't know if I can get fifty dollars a tree for you and still pay you for cutting them. That's a pretty steep price."

"Walnut is hard to come by in this part of the country, too," retorted Garson firmly.

Realizing that Abigail may not get the money promised by her father, Lucas asked, "Would you let me cut the trees, Mr. Dawson?"

"Why would you do that? You'd be working for nothing 'cause I wouldn't pay you," said Garson.

"No sir. I would be working to help Abigail," replied Lucas.

160

"I'm willing to sell my trees to help Abigail too, but I ain't willing to give them away. If you think giving two-day's work will help her then go right ahead. You're not going to make me feel bad, if that's what you're trying to do." Garson glared angrily at Lucas.

They had pulled into Garson's driveway and Lucas stopped. He turned to Garson and stared for a moment. Abigail and Sally sat in stunned silence, fearful of a fight between Lucas and Garson.

Then Lucas said softly. "No, Mr. Dawson, I wasn't trying to make you feel bad, but I do feel that when someone has worked as hard as Abigail has to go to school, she deserves help. It isn't like she was going off on some spree. She's trying to prepare herself to help little children have a better life."

"Humph! Education didn't help her mother none. She still got married and raised a family. She ain't done too bad."

"Mr. Dawson, my purpose is to help Abigail and if you'll let me cut those trees, I think I can sell them. So, what's your answer?" Lucas hadn't opened his door and neither had Garson.

He turned and looked at Lucas. "I swear, I believe you're as stubborn as I am. Abby, you'd better grab up this feller 'fore some other girl grabs him. He ain't no quitter. He'll stand his ground in a fight, that's for certain."

Lucas opened his door. "I guess that means I'll be cutting those trees."

Chapter 26

Abigail spent Saturday lolling around the house, since Sally wouldn't let her do any work. "Mommy, my problem has been my nerves. It doesn't affect my arms. I can still wash dishes, sweep, and make beds."

"You can start helping Monday, but today just lay around. Tomorrow we'll go to meeting," said Sally.

Abigail dreaded going to meeting, since she just knew they would all be looking at her as if she would have 'fits' or fall jerking to the floor. "Mommy, I'd rather not go to meeting. Would you be really upset if I don't go?"

"I know what you're thinking and you're wrong. The brothers and sisters at Bee Branch have all been asking about you and you know what was in the paper so they know all about it. They'll welcome you with open arms and never say a word about your nerves. People that love you don't ask things just to be nosy, they're really concerned," said Sally seriously.

So Abigail went to meeting on Sunday and was hugged by every woman there. All the men smiled at her and said how pleased they were to see her. Abigail felt like she was part of a large, loving family and was encircled with love. She thought the singing was more beautiful than ever before and the prayer seemed to be just for her, even though no names were spoken. When the door was opened to accept members Abigail found herself starting to go up, but gripped the back of the seat and stayed where she was. Something had moved her, however, and tears of pure joy coursed down her cheeks. *Oh God, what is it you want me to do?*

Abigail and Sally walked back home, laughing and talking

with other members, who also walked, until they reached the cut-off to Stateline Ridge where they were alone. "I always enjoy that walk so much, don't you, Abby?"

Abigail smiled. "Yes, I do. Did you know that Mary Wyatt is getting married?"

"Yes I did. Her mother told me last week. He's a man who works at Number Six mine at Beartown. She'll probably live good. Miners get a good wage."

"She seems happy and that's more important than anything else, I guess," said Abigail.

Sally walked along without replying for a few feet and then stopped. "Abby, how do you feel about Lucas Sutherland?"

"I really like Lucas, Mommy, but I still don't want him or any other man to touch me . . . well, you know what I mean. Sometimes, I'd like to try, but I can't bring myself to do it."

"I think that man loves you . . . I don't mean he just wants to . . . well, you know. I think he wants to take care of you, make you feel safe, and cherish you. He certainly has been like that so far, and it seems like you and him can talk easy with each other."

Abigail walked along thinking that was true and that she really did like Lucas very much. "Mommy, I like Lucas better than any other man I've ever met except Grandpa and sometimes, the way Lucas acts toward me makes me think of Grandpa. I think if I wanted a boyfriend I'd want it to be Lucas. I'm just not ready yet. I don't want to feel like I'm doing something wrong all the time."

Sally jerked her head around and gave Abigail a wide-eyed stare. "You've felt like that a long time, haven't you?"

She's going to tell me, thought Abigail, but when she didn't, Abigail said, "Yes, I have, Mommy, a long, long time."

Sally picked up the pace and said, "We'd better hurry on home or that cow will be bawling her head off."

They walked on home in silent companionship, but each thinking their own thoughts. Abigail helped with supper and the other chores without Sally telling her to stop. In fact they worked side by side doing the dishes never speaking one word. Finally, Abigail asked, "Mommy have I said something wrong?"

"There you go again. You shouldn't always be thinking you're doing something wrong. As far as I know you've never done nothing wrong in your whole life. Other people have done wrong, but you've always just been a pretty little girl who tried to please everybody," said Sally, wiping the oil-clothed table vigorously.

"You're wrong there, Mommy. I've done lots of things wrong, but I've not stolen, or run around with boys or anything like that. Still, I know that the Lord is not pleased when I wish I had clothes like other girls and could go places like other people. That's being covetous isn't it? The Bible says that's wrong, doesn't it?" asked Abigail.

"Yes it does say that, but my thinking is if you never do no more wrong than that, you're in pretty good shape. I think doing devious things to get the things others have is worse. It's kind of like your Grandpa always told me, 'We can't keep birds from flying over our heads, but we don't have to let them nest in our hair.'" Sally said this with almost a smile as if mentioning her father made her happy.

"Grandpa was a wise man. I learned a lot from him. Was he always like that, Mommy?" asked Abigail as she hung the dishtowels on the rack above the stove.

"Your Grandpa was the best man I ever met in my life. He was the best friend I ever had," said Sally with a grim expression.

"What about your mother? Wasn't she good to you?"

"Mam wasn't good to nobody, especially her husband and children. Well, she was good to Dan'l. She acted like he was the only child she had," said Sally as she walked out of the room. She turned at the door. "You'd better get to bed. You've had a long day."

Abigail was soon fast asleep and dreaming of skating with Lucas. She felt so good gliding around the rink in his arms. The sound of power saws woke her at six o'clock. She frowned and turned over, then sat straight up in the bed listening. Sure enough there were power saws running down in the woods. She jumped out of bed, ran to the window, and pulled back the curtain. She saw two men with white hard hats using power saws. *One of those men is Lucas, but who is the other one? Surely Dad isn't using the other one. He's not used a power saw in years, according to Mommy,"* she thought.

She hurried to wash and dress, then almost ran into the kitchen. Of course her mother was already up and cooking. Nobody could sleep with that noise anyway. "Did they wake you, too?" Abigail asked, going to get the plates to set the table.

"No, I was awake when I heard a car pull into the drive. Garson grumbled, but got on up and went outside. He ain't come back yet, so I figure it must be Lucas. Garson would have been back for his shotgun if anybody else dared bring a power saw into his woods." Sally expertly flipped the bacon in the pan and turned back to the dough for her biscuits.

"You want me to make the gravy this morning? Daddy said it was good the last time I made it," offered Abigail.

"Since you're up you may as well make yourself useful so go ahead. Just be sure you get the flour good and brown before you start pouring in the milk."

Soon the smell of bacon, eggs, sausage, and fried green apples wafted through the open window. One of Sally's rare smiles appeared when the noise of the power saws stopped. "If the smell of food can't stop a man nothing else will, I don't reckon."

Abigail stepped out on the kitchen porch and sure enough, Lucas came walking toward her. "I thought I'd get over here as quick as I could and cut those trees before your dad changed his mind."

Abigail smiled. "Come on in and eat breakfast. Since you've already started, he probably won't stop you now." Abigail shyly put out her hand and Lucas clasped it warmly. They turned together and went back into the kitchen.

"Um, um, something sure smells good, Mrs. Dawson. I'm

surprised you cooked after I woke everybody up with my power saw," said Lucas.

"Your car or truck woke me and I woke Garson. I don't think he liked it much, but he wasn't going to allow you in his woods without him being there," replied Sally.

Soon Garson and a tall white-haired man came through the door. "Look who Lucas brung with him. This is Lucas's pa, John Sutherland. He's using that power saw just like he was still a young man. Mr. Sutherland, this tall woman is my wife, Sally, and that little red-headed runt is our daughter Abigail."

John Sutherland looked at Sally and smiled. "It's good to meet you, Mrs. Dawson. Your food smells good."

Sally nodded and said, "Thank you, sir. It's nice meeting you. You have a fine son."

Abigail had stood quietly beside Lucas, who now took her hand and walked over to his dad. "Dad, this is the girl who has worked herself to death trying to get enough money to go to college this fall."

John Sutherland looked at this petite young girl with big, sparkling, green eyes and a wealth of long, wavy, red hair and thought to himself that he could understand Lucas's attraction. He smiled broadly. "Hello, Abigail. We've heard a lot about you."

Abigail smiled back at him, but Lucas felt her hand trembling and pulled it up against his chest. "You should see this woman skate, Dad. She's so good that the rink manager took our picture to use in his advertising."

Suddenly Lucas looked down at Abigail who had taken a few steps back. "Hey, you know something? That man owes us twenty-five dollars each, doesn't he? Let's go collect it this Friday night."

Glad to move away from the white-haired man, Abigail grinned excitedly. "I guess we'd better, before he forgets it."

Chapter 27

Soon they were all seated around the kitchen table, but Sally made sure that Abigail was seated between herself and Lucas. She didn't know how Abigail would react to being too close to a man with white hair.

Breakfast was a pleasant meal and both Lucas and his father bragged on the cooking. Mr. Sutherland looked across at Abigail. "Did you do any of this, Abigail?"

Abigail turned red, but Sally broke in with, "Abigail made the gravy this morning, but she's as good a cook as I am. I taught all my girls how to be handy around the house."

Mr. Sutherland beamed a wide smile across the table at Abigail. "I suspected you could do more than skate, but that's what Lucas raves about."

Lucas looked at Abigail and shook his head. "Don't listen to him. Besides, he's out and gone so much that I don't get to talk to him that much. I've told Mom more about you than I have Dad."

Mr. Sutherland opened his eyes wide. "Don't you know that telling your mother is the same as telling me? We don't have any secrets from each other."

Lucas looked around the table, nodding his head and grinning. "That's the truth. If one of us got into trouble and asked Mom not to tell Dad, she always said she didn't keep anything from Dad. We didn't have a chance; Mom spanked us and Dad did too."

"Between the two of us I'm surprised any of you lived to be grown," said John Sutherland, rising from the table and thanking Sally for his breakfast.

Garson stood up too, and turned to Lucas. "Let's go, young feller. You don't want your pap to cut all the trees, do you?"

Lucas grasped Abigail's hand and squeezed it. "I'll talk to you before we leave. You are going to be here, aren't you?"

"I don't need to go anywhere since Dad already told Harve and Matty that I can't come back to work. I'll just be here helping Mommy." Abigail squeezed Lucas's hand as well and he leaned toward her, but she backed away her eyes widening in fright.

Lucas stepped back. "I was only going to whisper that you'd soon have your college money. What did you think I was going to do?"

Abigail looked down and mumbled. "I don't know. I'm sorry."

"It's all right, Abigail. You don't need to be sorry. All this takes time, but we'll work it out together. Remember, I'm your friend," said Lucas.

Abigail looked up with a smile. "I know and I really do appreciate it."

When the men were out of the house, Sally gave Abigail a long look. "You don't know how lucky you are, Abby. I wish to God I'd met somebody like your Lucas when I was young."

Abigail turned a startled gaze on her mother. "Mommy, didn't you love Daddy? How did you two meet anyway?"

Sally turned red. "I don't know if I loved him or not. I appreciate your Daddy, but I don't think he knows that."

"How did you meet him? You never do talk about yourself, but you don't act really happy," said Abigail.

Sally walked to the window at the end of the kitchen and stood looking out over the hills. "I met him at a church meeting. He drove Preacher Horn to church and he introduced us. I wouldn't ready to meet a man," said Sally sadly and turned toward the door. "I think I'm going to check on those white half-runner beans I planted," she said and hurried on out the door.

Abigail stood pondering what she had said as well as her actions. *I just know something happened to Mommy that she has never talked about. I'm going to ask Virginia the next time she comes home,* she thought and went back to her room to make her bed and leave the room clean. She also wanted to clean her shoes, handbag, and her suitcase in preparation for starting to college.

Abigail knew she was nervous about going to college. She wasn't nervous about learning, but didn't know if she was ready to handle meeting so many strange men. *Lord, please help me. You've helped me to learn what caused my fear and taught me that I wasn't filthy or nasty, but I still feel guilty, or something, if any man except Lucas touches me. Please just keep on helping me until I can be like I'm supposed to be. I need your help so very much,* she silently prayed.

The power saws were still going at ten forty-five that morning and Abigail had not only cleaned her own things and her room, she had also gone through the other bedrooms, making beds and leaving each room neat. She came from Damon's room and went out onto the porch to sit in the swing. When she heard the kitchen door slam shut she got up and went to the kitchen. Sally was there rattling pots and pans to prepare lunch.

"I'll help, Mommy, but you have to tell me what you plan to make," said Abigail, sitting down on the bench behind the table.

"You can peel and slice the potatoes, but since you make a good meatloaf why don't you work on that and I'll peel the potatoes. How long does the meatloaf have to bake?" asked Sally?

Abigail looked at the clock. "It takes an hour, but I should have it ready for the oven in ten minutes if I hurry."

"You do that and I'll do the bread and the other stuff. You'd better make a big one if this morning was any indication. Working men are big eaters," said Sally and chuckled.

The table was loaded with homemade biscuits, meatloaf, green beans, creamed potatoes, Sally's special coleslaw, and a variety of jams and jellies when the men walked through the door.

"Oh my! This is a feast! Do you feed like this at every meal, Mrs. Dawson?" asked John Sutherland, wiping his face with a large bandana handkerchief. All the hard hats had been left on the kitchen porch where they had washed their hands before entering the kitchen.

Sally smiled. "Men like to eat and I've raised a number of boys. Garson likes to eat too and I don't mind cooking."

Garson came through the door. "That's one thing I can say about my wife. There ain't a lazy bone in her body. Nobody has to tell her it's time to cook. She's always got it ready," he bragged.

Sally dropped her head, but looking at her, Abigail knew she was pleased. *I wish I could find out what is wrong between Dad and Mom,* she thought and smiled at Lucas as he came through the door.

"Abigail, the trees are cut and Mr. Dawson will get paid when the man comes to collect them. He'll be here tomorrow or Wednesday. He has to wait for one of the company trucks to be free," explained Lucas, not only for Abigail's benefit, but for Garson's as well.

Abigail smiled. "I've been cleaning all my shoes and things I'll take to college. I want to make sure everything is ready."

"What are you in such a hurry about? That college don't start 'til September does it?" asked Garson, motioning Mr. Sutherland and Lucas to the bench behind the table.

"It starts the first Monday in September, but I need to go over there on Saturday morning. That way I can look for all the places I need to be on Monday morning. I've never been farther away from home than Kyle's and there's so much I don't know," said Abigail, sounding nervous.

Lucas looked across the table and smiled at her. "You don't need to be nervous. The college will have people there on the first morning to help you get registered and pay your fees. You have already applied for this fall haven't you?"

"Yes, I applied back in the spring because I wanted to make sure my scholarship was still there," said Abigail.

"She'd better do good at that college. I've give up some

170

awfully valuable trees to help her," said Garson between mouthfuls.

"When I get a teaching position I'll pay you back, Daddy," said Abigail.

"If you don't quit and get married before you get me paid," said Garson, looking at Lucas.

"You'll get your money, Mr. Dawson. You don't have to worry about that," said Lucas adamantly.

"Ah ha! Did I hear a marriage declaration just now?" asked Mr. Sutherland.

Abigail gasped and turned red. Lucas saw her face and turned an angry glare toward his father. "What you heard was one friend stating that he had confidence in another friend. I just meant that Abigail would pay her debts. She's that kind of person."

Mr. Sutherland seemed to cringe in fright as he laughed. "Gosh! It don't take much to get you riled, does it, Son?"

Sally jumped up. "Here let me go take up some more green beans. There's plenty more in the pot." She arose with the bowl in her hand and went to the stove.

Talk became general after that and soon they were all finished with their meal except for the dessert, which was a large strawberry cobbler that Sally served piping hot along with two scoops of ice cream in each serving.

When everyone had eaten their portion of cobbler, Mr. Sutherland and Garson rose at the same time. "I don't know how the this family stays so slim, well, Mr. Dawson may be a little hefty, but the rest are almost skinny, and still eat meals like this," said Mr. Sutherland.

"We work it off, I reckon. That must mean that I work less than the others," Garson said, laughing and rubbing his stomach.

Lucas lingered until Abigail got up and, taking her hand, walked with her toward the kitchen porch. "I don't know if I'll come back in before we leave, but I'll be here at one-thirty on Friday to take you to Welch," he said, putting both hands over hers. He looked at her tenderly. "You are very important to me, Abigail."

Abigail smiled up at him. "You are important to me too, Lucas. I don't know what I would have done without you."

Lucas's face broke into a wide grin. "That sounds really good. I like knowing that I've helped you."

Lucas left then and Abigail stood thinking, *That's really true. I think the Lord wanted me and Lucas to meet. Maybe he was sent to help me.*

Chapter 28

The rest of the week seemed endless for Abigail. She did whatever her mother or father told her to do, but still her thoughts were constantly on Lucas. She went over and over all the ways he had been good to her and how many things he had done for her.

She and Sally were doing laundry and Abigail was catching the clothes coming through the washing machine wringer. She would shake them out and drop them into a wash tub that had bluing in it and was anchored on a wide bench. Then the wringer would be switched around and the clothes run through the wringer again and put in a basket to be hung on the lines.

"Mommy, how does a girl know if she's in love with somebody?" asked Abigail.

Sally looked across the wringer in shock. "In love! Are you in love with Lucas?"

"I don't know. I really like Lucas and I trust him, but I don't know if that is love or not."

Sally pursed her lips together. "I reckon there must be a difference in loving and being in love. For me, loving is the only one I know. I love your daddy and you children, but I don't know a thing about being in love. So, I can't answer your question."

"Didn't you and Daddy date for a while before you got married? That's when you find out if you're in love, I think," said Abigail, still in doubt.

"No. We didn't date as you call it. We just got married," blurted Sally and grabbed up the basket of clothes ready to be hung and made for the kitchen door.

Abigail was left still running the remaining clothes through the wringer. *They never dated. I wonder why?* Abigail thought, more and more puzzled about her parent's marriage. She knew that her mother had never talked to her sisters about her marriage, or at least not in her presence, and now she wondered if they had ever asked her about it. *Mommy seems different since I've been sick, but I don't know exactly how she is different. She seems more . . . approachable, I guess,* thought Abigail and wondered why.

On Friday morning, Virginia arrived with Beatrice and Cindy. Seeing her two nieces, who were nearer her own age, pleased Abigail. She hadn't seen them while she was in the hospital.

Virginia went out in the orchard where Sally was grafting a limb into a young apple tree. This left Abigail and the girls to chatter away. "Can you spend the night?" asked Abigail eagerly.

"We're going to stay the whole weekend. Daddy's run was out west this week and he won't be home. All of us have been dying to see you, but you know how it is when Daddy is at home," said Beatrice grimly.

"He don't want us to go anywhere and we have to almost tiptoe around the house when he's home. I wish he'd stay gone," blurted Cindy angrily.

Abigail put her arm around Cindy's shoulders. "Well, now how would you get over here if your Dad hadn't bought Virginia that big jeep she drives?"

Cindy giggled. "Maybe he could come home long enough to bring his payday."

They went through the house giggling and laughing as Garson came through the door. "Ha, I caught you! Now, I have two more workers to help me dig up that new ground." He looked so serious that Cindy believed him.

"Aw, Grandpa, don't make us work today. Besides I don't want to ruin my good clothes," whined Cindy.

"We'll get you some old overalls to put on, and I'll let you come in for dinner," he continued, looking at Abigail with a wink.

174

Joining in, Abigail said, "Let's go get our rig on. I can't work in these clothes either."

"Shucks! I wish we hadn't come. If one old man ain't bossing us around another one is," said Cindy rebelliously.

Virginia and Sally came through the door and Cindy ran to her. "Mommy, Grandpa is going to make us go out and grub in his old new ground. Don't make me go, Mommy. He's as bad as Daddy," Cindy pleaded.

Garson erupted in a loud belly laugh and everybody joined in except Sally. "Garson you'll have every one of your grandchildren hating you." She turned to Cindy. "Your grandpa is just fooling with you, honey. He doesn't have a new ground to grub."

Cindy gave Garson a malicious look and left for the swing on the front porch, with Beatrice and Abigail following her. After a little while, Virginia came out on the porch and said, "Beatrice and Cindy, your grandma wants you two to help her with dinner, so scoot. I'm going to swing with Abigail a while."

The girls loved Sally's kitchen and loved helping her cook and now eagerly scrambled to be the first to get there. Virginia sat down on the swing beside Abigail and put her arm around her shoulders. "How are you, little Sis? I'm sorry I couldn't get over, but Stanley was home and I couldn't get away. I called the hospital every other day and checked on you, though. Did they tell you?"

Abigail smiled. "I guess they did, Virginia. I was so doped up for the first few days I wouldn't have remembered if they had."

"You seem fine now. Actually you seem better than I've ever seen you. You look happy, Abby, and you haven't for years."

Abigail got up and looked in the living room then turned back to Virginia. "Did Daddy go out of the house?"

Virginia nodded. "He went out the kitchen door, saying he wanted to check on his sow that's trying to have a litter of pigs."

Abigail sat down again and turned to Virginia. "I want to ask you something and I don't want anyone to hear. If I promise never to mention it will you tell me something?"

Virginia looked puzzled. "If I know it and can, I'll tell you. What is it?"

Abigail hesitated. "I don't exactly know how to begin. I . . . do you remember when I was very young; maybe three years old?"

"Of course I do. I tended to you more than Alice. You were the prettiest little, bouncing, laughing girl I'd ever seen in my life. Everybody said you acted like a little butterfly darting here and there. I loved tending to you," said Virginia, giving her a hug, but then pulling back and looking at Abigail warily.

"Something happened to me when I was about three. I'd forgotten about it, but Dr. Fischer hypnotized me and I told him all about it. I just couldn't remember what happened after Grandpa slapped Mommy. Tell me what happened after that, Virginia. I really need to know," pleaded Abigail.

When Abigail said 'when grandpa slapped Mommy' Virginia gasped and locked her arms across her chest. Now she was sitting wide-eyed and looking grim. When she didn't say anything, Abigail put her hand on her arm.

"Virginia, please tell me. Dr. Fischer says to be really well I need to get that all out in the open and accept it. I can't unless I know what it is. I've thought and thought, but I can't remember anything after that," said Abigail.

"Daddy made me and Grandpa promise that we'd never mention any of this to a soul. Grandpa never did and neither have I. I don't like to break a promise, but I do want to see you well again. Did you ask Mommy?" Virginia asked.

"No, but a time or two it seems Mommy says one thing and it has another meaning. I may just be wishfully thinking, though," said Abigail.

Virginia wrung her hands together several times. "Tell me what you remember, Abby?"

Abigail told about taking her clothes off and Grandpa chasing the boy. She shivered but went on to tell of Sally's switching and name-calling until Grandpa had come in and slapped Sally. "I remember Mommy falling and me going to her, but after that I can't remember anything. That's what's keeping me all locked up inside, according to Dr. Fischer," explained Abigail.

Virginia began to push the swing rapidly with her foot, but seeing Abigail's face she stopped. "You won't tell that I told, will you?"

Abigail shook her head. "No, Virginia, I'll never tell anybody."

Virginia was as white as a piece of paper. "Mom went into a coma I reckon and you thought she was dead. You grabbed her around the neck and wouldn't let go. Grandpa had to pry your fingers loose. You kept saying, 'I sorry, Mommy. I sorry. I be nice. I not be nasty and filfy. I promise' and Dad told Grandpa to hold you in his arms and he went to see to Mom."

Virginia was crying and had such a sad expression on her face. "You kept crying and saying the same words over and over until you passed out. Dad brought the doctor to the house to see you and Mom. He said something about it being traumatic comas and asked what had happened. I don't know what Dad told the doctor, but he and Grandpa had words about it. Three days later Mommy came out of the coma and Grandpa told her that she had to tell you that she loved you and that you were not nasty and filthy. He put you in Mom's arms and she began crying. I'd never seen Mom cry before. She rocked and held you, whispering something over and over and finally you moved your hand."

Virginia got up and walked to the edge of the porch and stood looking off into the distance. In a wobbly voice she continued. "When we saw your little hand move, we all started crying. Grandpa kept saying 'Praise the Lord' and 'Thank you Jesus.'" Dad turned away, but I saw his big red bandana handkerchief come out to wipe his eyes."

Virginia turned back to Abigail. "That's all I know and that's the first time I've ever mentioned it to anybody. If you hadn't already remembered most of it, I wouldn't have told you the rest."

"Virginia, do you know why Mom acted the way she did? Why would she call me nasty and filthy? I was only three and really didn't know I was doing anything wrong."

"I don't know, but Dad knows and Mom thinks he doesn't love her because of it. I believe he does love her, but she never acts like she cares about him. Before that happened they used to laugh and kid, but they never did touch each other. Whatever it was, has made Dad very suspicious of girls. Alice and I never did those things Dad accused us of, but we did work in beer joints. That's the only jobs we could find. We both wanted to get away from home." Virginia had sat back down with her arms crossed over her chest.

"It's kind of like Grandpa said, 'you girls jumped out of the frying pan into the fire,' and he certainly told the truth," said Virginia, trying to laugh.

They were interrupted as Garson came through the door. "Are you women going to set out here and leave the cookin' to your mother and them two little girls?"

Virginia and Abigail both got up at once. "No, Dad. We just got to talking and forgot the time, I reckon," said Virginia and they both went in the door.

Chapter 29

They had just gotten in the door when Lucas's car drew to a halt in front of the house. "Here's your boyfriend, but he's early," said Virginia, looking at her watch and laughing. "If he says one-thirty is he always an hour early?"

Abigail turned red. "I think he likes Mommy's cooking." She turned back to the door and walked onto the porch. She stood waiting until Lucas came up onto the porch and shyly said, "Hello, Lucas. You're early."

"I know, but I had to see the man who bought those trees. He did come and get them, didn't he?" he asked, looking at Garson.

Garson stood up. "Yeah, he come yesterday and told me he'd send the check by you. Did he?"

Lucas pulled a long white envelope out of his shirt pocket and handed it to Garson. Garson opened it and nodded his head satisfactorily. "This means I'll have to go to Iaeger tomorrow to put this in the bank."

Abigail's eyes grew suspicious. "Aren't you going to give me what you said you would?"

"I think the word was loan, Abby. I'll bring your money back, but I aim to keep the rest in the bank for a rainy day, as Wilson says," Garson said, grinning.

Lucas put out is hand and Abigail placed hers in it. "How are you, Abigail?"

Abigail smiled happily. "I'm great! Can we stop at the skating rink and see if Mr. Gregory has our twenty-five dollars?"

"That girl is money crazy. All she talks about is money. I'd be careful around a girl like that, if I was you, Lucas. She's probably just after your money," said Garson with a chuckle.

"I don't think so, Mr. Dawson. I guess I'll have to wait and see," said Lucas, squeezing Abigail's hand.

Abigail dropped his hand and said, "I have to go help with the cooking. You sit here with Daddy. It's almost ready, I think."

Around the table Sally made sure that everyone knew that Beatrice and Cindy had done most of the cooking. Both girls smiled from red faces as everyone bragged on their cooking.

"Ginnie has to bring them back to their Grandma to learn how to be good cooks, don't you Ginnie?" joked Garson.

"Yeah, you're right. Mommy didn't teach her girls to cook. I couldn't boil water when I got married. All I could do was work in beer joints," said Virginia sarcastically.

Sally quickly jumped in when she saw how red Garson had turned. "Well, you had to cook things like hamburgers, and hot dogs in those places too. I'll bet you wouldn't have been hired if you couldn't cook."

Virginia smiled at Sally thankfully. "I sure did. I stayed in the kitchen the whole time I worked at Alvie Horn's. I was never out front and never sold one bottle of beer."

Never having heard this before, Garson opened his eyes in surprise. "Is that what you done out there? I was so mad that I quit going there at all. Seems like I judged you wrong, Ginnie. I wish you'd told me."

"That was a long time ago, Dad. I guess I've judged you wrong too." Virginia looked like she was about to cry and Garson cleared his throat.

Soon the meal was over and Lucas said, "Abigail, we'd better get on the road if you want to be on time for your appointment."

Abigail went to her room and came back with her purse and a thin jacket. She hugged Virginia and the girls and told her parents bye before walking through the door Lucas held open.

The family stood in the living room watching as Lucas went to the passenger side and opened the door for Abigail. Once she was seated, he closed the door and went to his side and got in.

"He's going to spoil Abby to death. He acts like she can't even open a car door and get in by herself. I'm going to have a talk with him. He'd best start like he's going to go on, else he'll make her lazy," said Garson.

"He's just using good manners, Garson, which you never learned, I don't reckon," said Sally and abruptly turned back toward the kitchen.

Garson looked at Virginia and grinned. "We've been together forty-five years and she still don't know when I'm joshing."

"She ain't the only one, Dad. I never did know, either. I think Mom is more . . . I don't know the word . . . approachable, I guess, than she was before Abby's stay in the hospital."

Garson sat silent for a few moments. "That's sort of shook us both up, I reckon. I know I've been rethinking some things. She may be too. I hope she is."

Virginia looked at her father in astonishment. It was the first time he'd acted like he wanted a conversation with her. She really didn't know what he was referring to, but stood looking at him expectantly. When he made no further comment, she followed Sally into the kitchen.

"Mom, that Dr. Fischer sure has helped Abby, hasn't he?" she said as she started raking plates and stacking them.

"Him and the Lord together, I think. I always believed that the Lord gave the doctors gifts to heal people and we should use their gifts, but the praise belongs to the Lord."

"Sometimes, I'd like to talk to a doctor like that. He might help me to figure out some things that have puzzled me all of my life," said Virginia, putting the plates in the hot soapy water on the side table by the stove.

Sally's head jerked around. "Don't tell me some man's been at you too," she said with a shiver.

Virginia felt so sorry for her mother. She could just feel what Sally had gone through while Abby was sick. Trying to ease her pain, Virginia said, "No, Mommy, I can honestly say that no man has tried anything with me, except Stanley of course. We got married though. I guess I just wasn't pretty enough to attract a man."

"You don't have to be pretty, Ginnie. You just have to be available and too cowardly to tell," blurted Sally sadly and then clamped her lips together, grabbed the scrap plate, and went outside to the slop bucket.

Meanwhile, Lucas and Abigail had laughed and talked down Bradshaw Mountain and were now in Caretta. "I'll bet this was once a nice thriving little community before the major coal seams, those that were easily accessible, worked out or, before these environmentalist groups began raising a ruckus about air pollution," said Lucas.

"I never was up through here so I don't know, but the houses are still nice. There must be other houses up one of these roads, since they have a large church, school, and post office," said Abigail.

"Probably, but even if they are, this place will keep getting shabbier and shabbier. Coal built this part of the country, but people in charge haven't been collecting enough B&O taxes and when they do it isn't put to good use. With its huge deposits of coal, this county should have water and sewage systems, good roads, and all kinds of businesses. They don't because the coal companies elect the representatives and, therefore, can do whatever they want to do as payback."

Abigail had studied enough civics and local government to know what he was saying, but hadn't yet formed any opinions, so she didn't say anything. They rode along in companionable silence until they came into Coalwood.

"This is a much nicer community, isn't it? I like the houses and how neat they're kept," said Abigail.

"It should be nicer. Old man Carter, who sold out to Olga Coal Company, built this town and fixed it nice for his wife." Lucas pointed left at the intersection. "It's really nice down in the real town. They have a clubhouse, a swimming pool, and tennis courts."

"I think Gary does too and they have a golf course as well,

did you know that?" asked Abigail, eager to tell him something that he didn't know.

Lucas smirked and then smiled. "I've played golf there, so I did know it. In my job I go all over the place and I know most places in southern West Virginia and a lot of the north and east as well."

Abigail sat feeling so ignorant and Lucas saw her crestfallen look. "Why are you looking like that? Am I being a smart aleck?"

"No, but I feel so dumb. I've not been anywhere and I don't know much. I'm sure you get bored trying to talk to me."

Lucas picked up her hand that lay in the seat between them. "No, Abigail, you do not bore me. I'm ten years older than you and I have been out in the world a lot longer, that's all. Once you go to college you will know much more than I could ever know. You are very intelligent and have great insights into many things, especially religion."

"You're twenty-eight! I've wondered how old you were, but didn't want to ask," said Abigail.

Lucas grinned. "You didn't want to bother an old man, I guess."

That's not old, Lucas. Sometimes I've felt like I was a hundred and it didn't really matter. I've not been very happy, Lucas."

His hand squeezed hers gently. "I know, Abigail. I thought I had caused it and I felt bad, but I didn't cause it, did I?"

"No, Lucas, I think my mother caused it, but I don't think she could help it. Dr. Fischer hypnotized me and I remembered something that happened when I was three years old. In that episode, my mother truly caused me to be traumatized all my life. Even though that old man scared me to death, his attack was the cause of me getting at the root of my problem. Like the Bible frequently tells, sometimes the Lord uses evil to bring about a lot of good."

"That's true and I'm so glad you can talk to me about it. I'll always be here for you, Abigail, because I want to be . . . your friend," he finished hesitantly.

By this time they were pulling into the hospital parking lot. Lucas opened her door and helped her out. They walked together, holding hands, into the hospital and on into Dr. Fischer's office.

When Dr. Fischer saw them coming, holding hands, he met them with a wide smile. "Do I smell romance in the air?"

Lucas shrugged his shoulders. "I'm still just her friend, Dr. Fischer."

Dr. Fischer looked at Abigail. She slowly smiled. "He is a very special friend, though."

Dr. Fischer turned back into his office. "You can say that, again. He's the best friend a girl could ever have, in my opinion. Right now, though, he'll have to wait out here and you and I will get started."

Lucas nodded, picked up a magazine, and sat down to read. Abigail followed Dr. Fischer on into the office and took a seat in a comfortable chair. Dr. Fischer pulled up another chair facing her.

"How have you been this week? You look really well, almost happy. Are you happy, Abigail?"

"You're right. I'm almost happy. Dad sold his trees and has the money for them, but Lucas had to come over and cut them. I met Lucas's father. He has white hair and it didn't bother me as much as I thought it would. I didn't get close to him, however. I felt silly, but I just didn't feel comfortable."

"A person's hair color will eventually go unnoticed, but it may take a little more time. You are smart enough to know that hair color does not make one good or evil, so that will pass. Believe it or not, you will someday like the touch of a man; I mean a man that you love," said Dr. Fischer.

"I asked Mommy how one knows if they are in love and she said she didn't know anything about being in love, but that she loved Daddy and her children. I asked her if she and Daddy dated and she said no, they didn't. Isn't that strange, Dr. Fischer?" asked Abigail.

Dr. Fischer sat thinking. "I think she's right about loving and being in love being different. A person is very fortunate if they are in love and love their mate as well. Being in love is that fairy tale wonder that one dreams about, but loving is sometimes hard, but worthwhile in the long run."

Abigail beamed a smile at Dr. Fischer. "I think I may be in love with Lucas, but I can't let him touch me other than hold my hand. I'm afraid . . . I don't want to feel guilty."

"Did you ask your sister about the incident where your mother called you names and whipped you?"

Abigail told Dr. Fischer all that Virginia had revealed to her. "I think something has happened to Mommy similar to what happened to me, or at least some encounter that was unpleasant with a man, but I don't know that. Virginia said that Daddy made her and Grandpa both promise to never tell about the incident with me. I don't know if he was protecting me or her."

Dr. Fischer had a furious frown on his face. "He was probably afraid he would look bad in the eyes of the neighbors. Instead they both ruined your childhood. That's really child abuse, Abigail, even though they say they love you."

"They do love me. You don't understand that people back in the mountains don't show their feelings very easily," defended Abigail.

Dr. Fischer looked embarrassed for a moment. "I'm sorry I reacted as I did. There may be more to the story than you were told. I did feel compassion for your mother as she rocked and cried when you held her hand," said Dr. Fischer.

"Until you hypnotized me, I could never remember my mother calling me any names, slapping or spanking me, or anything like that, but she is just not a hugging, petting kind of person. I now know she did those things that one time, but I think she's regretted that all her life," said Abigail.

Dr. Fischer looked at Abigail for a second. "Abigail, when are you ever going to allow Lucas to hug you or hold you? You'll never know whether it will bother you unless you try. I feel that most of it is in your mind and you think about every move you make when you are around him. Why not relax and just be spontaneous?"

Abigail dropped her head. "I've been thinking about it, Dr. Fischer. Maybe I'll get up the nerve to take a chance sometime."

Dr. Fischer stood up. "Poor Lucas! How would you like to be in his shoes?" Abigail raised a startled gaze to him and started to speak, but instead went to the door. She turned and said, "Am I to come the same time next week?"

The doctor smiled and said, "Yes, the same time. Bye."

Chapter 30

On the way home, Abigail and Lucas talked and laughed. They stopped in Bradshaw and ate, then stopped at the skating rink. Mr. Gregory jumped up from his seat in surprise when he saw Abigail. "It is good to see you, young lady. How are you?"

Abigail smiled. "I'm fine and I want to apologize for the ruckus I caused. I'd just gone through a bad experience and hadn't really gotten over it. That's the only explanation I have, but I am sorry."

Mr. Gregory smiled. "You're better and that's good enough for me. I've held the pictures, but if you two will promise to be back next Friday night I'll start circulating them."

Abigail looked at Lucas and eased her hand into his. "What do you think? Can we go to Welch next Friday and go skating also?" she asked.

Lucas held her hand tenderly and smiled. "We can if you want to. I sometimes take a half day off on Fridays anyway."

"All right, Mr. Gregory, start circulating," said Abigail, smiling widely.

"You look different, but I don't know how," Mr. Gregory said as he studied Abigail. "She's prettier than she was, isn't she, Mr. Sutherland?"

Lucas grinned. "I didn't think she could get any prettier, but now she has a . . . a brightness about her. She's like a bright ray of sunshine."

"That's it! It's that happy look in her eyes, or something," said Mr. Gregory.

Abigail turned red. "Stop it you two. You are embarrassing me to death. I'm just like I've always been except I'm happier than I ever remember being in my life."

"I guess this young feller had a lot to do with that, didn't he?" asked Mr. Gregory, raising his dark bushy eyebrows.

Abigail looked at Lucas and smiled. "Yes, he did, Mr. Gregory. Lucas has had a lot to do with it."

Lucas smiled and squeezed her hand and Abigail turned to go, but stopped. "What about our money? You promised us twenty-five dollars each."

Mr. Gregory took out a blue bordered handkerchief and wiped his large, bulbous nose before pulling out his billfold. He turned his back and fumbled for a while, then turned around. He placed a twenty and a five in front of Abigail and then another twenty and a five beside it. "I was hoping you two would forget about the money when you got a look at these pictures." He opened the desk drawer and pulled out a long yellow envelope. From this he pulled out a bright glossy picture. He was as good as his word. Both Abigail and Lucas could be seen but only the sides of their faces. They both stood looking and Mr. Gregory said, "I've got another one I wish you would let me use. Just look here."

The next picture he pulled out showed them waltzing close together, but their faces were turned away from the camera. Abigail's hair would be a dead give-away to anyone who knew them, however. Abigail gasped in pleasure. The picture was wonderful. "Gosh! It is a good picture, isn't it, Lucas?" said Abigail, looking up at Lucas.

"It sure is. How much will you take for that picture, Mr. Gregory?"

"It's free if you'll let me use it one time."

Abigail and Lucas stood looking at the picture. "What if we got matching outfits . . . say blue pants and vest for me and blue skirt and vest for Abigail and allowed you to make a similar picture?"

Mr. Gregory jutted his lower lip out and wiped his nose again. "How soon could you do that?"

"If Abigail will agree we can be ready two weeks from today," said Lucas.

"You come back fixed up like that and let me take the

pictures and I'll give you both pictures after I use them one time."

Lucas looked at Abigail and she nodded. Lucas put out his hand to seal the deal. Hand in hand Lucas and Abigail left, each with twenty-five dollars they didn't have before.

When Abigail got in the car, she waved her money. "When Dad gives me the money he promised, I'll have enough money to go to college. The Lord has certainly been good to me."

Lucas pulled his twenty-five dollars out of his shirt pocket and placed it in her lap. "There's another twenty-five to help on expenses."

"Now, Lucas, I can't take your money. Mommy always told her girls not to take gifts from men." Then she gulped. "I already have taken gifts from you, though, and Mommy never said a word."

"I'm very persuasive. On the trips to the hospital I talked them into giving me a few extra privileges," said Lucas and laughed at Abigail's surprised expression.

"I guess they thought I'd lost my mind and it wouldn't matter if you gave me gifts."

Lucas reached over and clasped her hand. "You know better than that, Abigail. It was just that they knew that I really wanted you to get better and that I cared for you. They didn't, nor did anyone else; think you'd lost your mind."

Abigail grinned. "Well, if it took that to make me feel good inside the way I do now, it was worth it."

Lucas smiled and drove slowly out of Stringtown through Jolo, thinking about how things had worked out since he first met Abigail. "You know what I think?"

"About what!" Abigail looked at him curiously.

"Us. I think that the Lord has used all this for us to meet and lo . . . become such good friends. I had never tried to pray in my life until I couldn't find you after I saw you walking out of Collins Ridge that day."

Abigail looked at Lucas with bright shining eyes. "I know you've been praying for me, or did while I was in the hospital. I dreamed of you praying for me several times."

Lucas looked sober. "You know it is strange, but I'd never even tried to pray until that Collins Ridge incident. Then when I didn't find you I began to think that there was nothing in prayer after all. When Kyle invited me to visit your home with his family, I didn't really want to go. The only reason I did was in hopes that I could ask someone about you. I was so shocked when you walked through that door when we were eating. I'm surprised that I didn't choke. The first thought I had was that God had heard my prayer after all." Lucas stopped as if he was trying to gain control of his emotions or something.

Abigail squeezed his hand. "Are you all right?" she asked, leaning toward him.

By this time they had turned down Stateline Ridge and Lucas pulled to the side of the road to allow another car to pass. He didn't pull back out immediately, but turned toward her. He picked up both her hands. "Abigail, the day I went to church with you something happened to me. I was going just to be with you, but once inside, the singing was so beautiful that I completely forgot my surroundings. I can't really describe what I felt. There's just no words that could come close to describing the peace and love I felt. I thought that little wrinkled old woman looked like an angel. You know the one who sat on the second row back. She's very thin."

Abigail nodded. "Yes, that's Angeline Hagerman. I don't think she's as old as she looks, but she is one of the best people I know of anywhere. She has the purest, clearest soprano voice I've ever heard."

"Do you know what I am talking about? I mean do you understand whatever it was that came over me during the singing?" asked Lucas.

Abigail smiled. "I think you received the blessing of His spirit for the first time. I don't know that for sure, but I have felt something similar. Then I would become afraid that someone would see me crying and try to get me to unite with the church, so I always got up and went outside."

They sat looking at each other until Abigail became uneasy and said, "We'd better get on home before Daddy follows us."

Lucas dropped her hands and pulled back into the road. They drove on down the ridge without talking, but when they were on the last curve before reaching the house, he said, "Well, we have a lot to tell your folks, don't we?"

"Yes we do, but Lucas, where are we going to get costumes? I intended asking you as soon as we left the skating rink, but I forgot it when we started talking about praying."

Lucas smiled. "My mom is a wizard at finding costumes. You write down your sizes and I'll get her on to it next week. I don't know how she does it, but my mom can work out solutions to almost any problem."

"How old is she, Lucas? Your dad looks to be in his sixties, but that may be because of his white hair."

"Dad is sixty-four, but Mom is only fifty-six and she looks young. She's not a very big woman, but she's bigger than you. She's like you in many ways, though."

"Good or bad ways?" asked Abigail.

"You don't have any bad ways except not letting me touch you. I'd like it if I could hug you once in a while."

Abigail sighed. "I'm just not there yet. I honestly wish I was, for then I'd know I was normal, but Dr. Fischer told me not to force it."

"That's all right. You just do what the doctor tells you, but I'm going to keep on praying that the Lord will work a miracle," said Lucas as he pulled to a stop before the house.

Garson came out on the porch just as they got out of the car. "I was beginning to get worried. Did you'uns have any trouble?"

"We stopped in Bradshaw and ate supper and then stopped at the Skating Rink to get our money that Mr. Gregory promised us," said Abigail.

Garson grinned. "There she goes talking about money again. A man will have to be rich to keep her if she ever decides to marry."

"No they won't, Daddy. I'll be teaching and making my own money."

Chapter 31

All the following week, Dr. Fischer's saying, "Poor Lucas. How do you think he feels," kept going through Abigail's mind. She wondered if Lucas was in love with her. She knew he wanted to be more than a friend, but then she would remember what her girlfriends had told her about what sometimes happened on dates and shivered.

She had started reading her Bible again and often would read several chapters at night before she put it down. After closing the Bible, she lay thinking, *Lord, I don't know why I want to read. I don't really understand any of it. Oh, I can read the literal word, but I know there is a spiritual meaning and that's what eludes me.*

On Thursday night, she picked up the Bible and it fell open to the fourth Chapter of John and the eighteenth verse, which read, "There is no fear in love; but perfect love casteth out fear: because fear hath torment. He that feareth is not made perfect in love." Abigail closed the Bible and got out of bed and knelt beside the bed where she whispered her petition: "Lord, fill me with love so that I won't fear. I have been so tormented and I don't know how to get free of this torment unless you help me. Please God, fill me with your love," she begged with tears running down her cheeks.

When she finally went to sleep, she dreamed that she and Lucas were walking hand in hand down a dirt road. In the background she heard the church members singing. She didn't see any faces that she could recall except Angeline Hagerman. Then Lucas took her hand and they walked to the edge of the water together. Abigail woke up with a start. *Why would I dream something like that? I wouldn't go out in the river. I can't swim.*

She puzzled over the dream until she eventually went back to sleep, but the next morning she still remembered holding Lucas's hand and walking toward the river. She didn't mention it, however, since she feared her mother would think she was having a relapse.

She thought about her dream off and on all day and still had it on her mind when Lucas arrived at one o'clock to take her for her counseling session. She'd heard his car as she finished getting dressed and hurriedly brushed her hair before leaving the room. Lucas was sitting in the living room talking to Garson, who had finished up in the barn where he had been shoeing the horse.

"Hello, Lucas," she said, coming into the room. Lucas jumped to his feet, smiling widely.

"I see you're ready. Do you want to go early and look around town before your session and then go out to Sterling Drive-In and get supper this evening?" Lucas asked.

Garson spoke up. "He's trying to get away as fast as he can. He's afraid I'll ask him to help me put the other shoe on that cantankerous horse."

Lucas laughed. "He'd be more than cantankerous if I tried to shoe him. I wouldn't know how to begin."

Abigail looked at her mother who had come in from the kitchen. "Mom, do you and Daddy mind if Lucas and I go now since he wants to take me out to look around town before the session?"

"If your Daddy thinks it's all right, I don't mind," said Sally, looking at Garson.

"Since I can't get him to help me shoe the horse and you can't help me either, you may as well go on. It'll save us some money 'cause Sally won't have to cook much if it's just us and Damon," Garson said and then let out a loud guffaw when Sally gasped in embarrassment.

"Your mother ain't got me figured out yet and we've been married forever," said Garson, still chuckling.

Abigail and Lucas laughed as he took Abigail's hand and they started for the door, but stopped as Lucas said, "I wanted to remind you that Abigail and I plan to stop at the skating rink for a while as we come back. That means that we probably won't be back until about eight-thirty. Is that all right? I promise that I'll keep her safe and take good care of her."

Garson looked at Sally and she looked back at him. "Seems like that's an awful long time for you'uns to be out by yourselves," said Garson.

"Mr. Dawson, if somebody wants to do something wrong it doesn't take long. I promise you that Abigail will be treated as carefully as if she was in a church crowd," said Lucas.

Garson rose from his chair. "I trust you, Lucas, but Abby has been in so much trouble and we stay afraid for her all the time."

"I understand, Mr. Dawson, but I promise you that you don't have to worry when Abigail is with me."

"Well, go on then, but be careful driving. The air feels like its heavy with rain and that makes the roads slick," said Garson, walking toward the kitchen.

To the surprise of Lucas and Abigail, Sally came over and hesitantly patted Abigail's shoulder. "Go on, honey, and enjoy yourself. It pleases me to see you so happy," she said as she awkwardly stepped back from Abigail.

They went on out to the car, but when they were driving away, Abigail turned and looked back to where her mother was standing on the porch, watching them leave.

"How strange! Mommy has never before acted like she just did when I went somewhere, or told me to enjoy myself. Do you think there's something wrong?"

Lucas smiled and shook his head. "No, Abigail, I don't think there's anything wrong. I think the Lord heard my prayers."

"You mean you've been praying for Mommy?" asked Abigail.

"I've been praying for your mother and your father, Abigail. There's something we don't know about that is keeping them from sharing their lives, I think," said Lucas quietly.

Abigail really enjoyed her evening with Lucas. They ate at the Sterling Drive-In on Browns Creek Road above Welch after she had been to see Dr. Fischer. That session went really well. Abigail was told that she could start coming every other week.

Before the session with Dr. Fischer, they had walked down Main Street and Lucas bought her a music box that she had admired in a music store window. However, their visit in Welch wasn't finished. After seeing Dr. Fischer they went to the Sterling Drive-In first and then came back through town and stopped at Franklin's Dairy Bar and ate strawberry sundaes, laughing and talking happily before leaving Welch for the skating rink. Abigail rode along smiling happily, in remembered enjoyment of the entire evening.

Lucas drove slowly back over the mountains. He turned on the radio and they listened to Dean Martin singing "That's Amore" and other songs. Abigail sat entranced. She had no idea that being alone with a man could be so nice and comfortable.

From listening to other girls and women talk, she had gotten the impression that there was always tension around men. Tonight she didn't feel any tension at all and now she looked forward to skating in Lucas's arms. "I wonder what it would be like to slide over and sit close to Lucas in the car," she thought and then remembered what Helen Crouse in high school had said happened to her and Abigail shivered.

Lucas noticed her shiver and asked, "Are you cold? I can stop and get your jacket if you want me to."

"No, I'm all right. I just do that sometimes. I guess it's my nerves."

"I'm anxious to get on skates again, aren't you?" asked Lucas.

Abigail smiled. "Yes, I love to skate. Charles and Sylvia taught me. They said I was a natural because they only held onto me for one round and then turned me loose."

"They told you the truth. You are so relaxed on skates and skating with you is like a rhapsody in motion, if that makes any sense," said Lucas.

"When I'm on skates it is almost like I become somebody

else. I feel like I've been given wings. It's a glorious sensation for me. Is that the way you feel?" asked Abigail.

Lucas grinned. "When I'm skating with you I feel something like that. I feel ten feet tall, especially when we're waltzing. To me that's the best part of skating. I don't think I ever enjoyed skating as much as I do now."

"Did your mom think she could find those costumes? I thought about them this week and Mommy can sew almost anything if she can see a picture of what is wanted," said Abigail.

"She found the pants and two vests, but she hasn't found a skirt yet. Do you think your mother could make one?"

"Can you get her a picture of the type of skirt you have in mind? She'll make one, but if you were thinking of a short skirt, Mommy won't make it. She doesn't believe in girls wearing their dresses too short."

"I saw one that was a little above the knees, but not any shorter than that. Would she have a problem with that length?" asked Lucas.

"I don't know. I'll have to ask her. Maybe if I wore tights underneath she wouldn't object," said Abigail.

"You'd burn up in tights in this weather. It's not like you would be turning somersaults," said Lucas in what Abigail thought was an angry tone.

"Well, don't get mad at me. You asked me and I told you what I thought."

Lucas grasped her hand. "I'm not mad at you. I'm sorry if I sounded like I was. I'm just not used to such strictures as to dress. I don't believe in girls or boys putting their bodies out for display, but a skirt down to the knees is certainly not showing much. What do you think, Abigail? Don't tell me what your mother feels. I want to know how you feel about it."

"I don't want Mommy to think I'm fil . . . not a nice girl, but lots of girls in school wore their dresses shorter than mine. I thought they were very good girls, said Abigail.

They had arrived at the skating rink and Lucas said, "Well, I guess we'll have to take the chance if Mom can't find a skirt for you within the next two days."

Chapter 32

The pattern Lucas brought to the house on Tuesday showed a girl with a skirt about an inch above the knee. Sally looked at it a long time. Then she felt of the soft dark blue material. She looked up at Lucas and said, "I can make the skirt, but if Garson sees Abby in it he's apt to throw a fit."

"I wasn't planning to wear it around the house, Mommy. It's just for when we are skating for the picture," said Abigail.

Lucas had stood by not saying anything, but now he said, "Mom found the pants for me and the two vests, but she couldn't find a skirt that size anywhere. She found this pattern in a craft shop in Lewisburg and the cloth also."

Sally smoothed her hand over the material. "It's got a nice feel to it and I believe it'll make a pretty skirt. You even brought the thread and zipper." She unfolded the material and something fell out. She stooped to pick it up. "It's a button for the waist band. Your mother thought of everything, didn't she?"

Lucas smiled. "That's the way she is. If she's making a new recipe she gets everything it calls for and has it out on the counter before she starts."

Sally smiled. "That's a good way I guess, but I usually make things that I've stored the recipe for in my head. Sometimes I've thought of a recipe or made up one that I'd like to try, but had no way of getting the stuff I needed for it."

"Your head is full of good recipes, Mrs. Dawson, so I guess your way is as good as Mom's," said Lucas tactfully.

Sally got up and put all the material back in the bag. "I'll have this done by Friday, but Abby may have to wear her pants under it until she gets to the skating rink." At Abigail's astonished look, she said, "I know that sounds like I'm encouraging you to sneak and do something you shouldn't, don't it? I just don't feel that an inch above a person's knee is more shameful than an inch below the knee. I don't even know that your daddy would object, but just to be on the safe side I think we'd best not say too much about it."

Lucas was as astonished as Abigail. He'd never seen Sally wear anything except the mid-calf dresses, hose, and a hat. Of course, he had only seen her at church and when they made the trips to Welch to see Abigail, but she wore that dress length at home also. When he'd met Virginia and Alice they both had dresses that reached below the knees, but at home they wore jeans, as did Abigail. *That's sure a different picture than I had painted of Mrs. Dawson,* he thought, but kept it to himself.

Abigail had similar thoughts and wondered why she had always thought that her mother was the strict one about dress codes and morals. *Could it be that Sally acted that way for fear of upsetting Garson?*

Abigail went into the kitchen to help with preparing supper, since it was now a quarter to five and they never ate later than five-thirty. Damon always came home at that time from his mail delivery job and Garson always came in from whatever project he had been doing on the farm at the same time. *Our family certainly lives on a strict schedule,* she thought, remembering that nine o'clock had always been bedtime for everybody unless they had to be gone for some reason. On such occasions, Garson still expected them to be home by eleven o'clock and not a minute later.

Sally came in and Abigail had the table set and hot pads down for the bowls of hot food at five-thirty. Sally went to the kitchen door and yelled. "Supper's ready!"

Garson came in grumbling because he didn't have his project finished and Sally said, "You can't have it both ways. You told me when we were first married that you wanted supper on the table no later than five-thirty. Unless we've been gone, I've always had it ready at that time."

Garson, who was already seated, glanced up in surprise. "Do you mean to tell me that this rigid pattern of yours over the years is because I was kidding you when we first married?" When Sally nodded, he said, "Well, if that don't beat all."

Both Damon and Abigail looked surprised. Something was happening in her family and it all started when she got sick and was in the hospital. She ate her supper, pondering this, until Sally said, "Abby, is something wrong? You're awfully quiet."

"Yes, I'm all right. I guess I was just thinking about skating on Friday night," she lied and then felt bad for doing it, but she didn't want to say anything about what her dad had said.

Lucas looked at her as if he knew what she had done and smiled. Abigail wondered if he could read her mind and then gasped when he said, "If she's going to think about skating all week she'll be worn out by Friday, won't she, Mrs. Dawson?"

Garson took his last bite and pushed his plate back. "Abby can't fool me. I surprised her by lettin' her see that I ain't the ornery cuss she always thought I was. It just slipped out, I reckon."

"You're right, Dad, and I'm ashamed that I lied, but I was afraid of getting you upset."

Garson gave her a speculative look. "I ain't near as bad to get upset as you young'uns always acted like I was. I don't know where that idea came from. I carry on a whole lot, but it takes a heap more than that to make me mad."

Knowing that her mother had always cautioned them to be quiet, use good manners, and to respect the wishes of their father, Abigail was more puzzled than ever. Sally had certainly believed that Garson would rage and rant if everything didn't go his way, but now Abigail wondered about that belief.

"Is everybody ready for apple pie?" asked Sally, rising to her feet.

Lucas shook his head. "Not me, Mrs. Dawson. I couldn't eat another bite, but thank you." He too arose from the table as did Abigail. They stood looking at each other and Lucas asked, "Do you want to go for a walk to settle this food?"

Abigail looked at her mother. "Can we leave the dishes until I come back? We won't go far."

"I don't reckon the dishes will know you left them for an hour," said Sally.

Lucas and Abigail walked down through the orchard, stopping to look at a bird's nest and each picked a particular apple off the golden delicious tree. "I picked out the best one. Your apple has a worm hole in it," said Abigail, laughing at Lucas.

"I'll bet mine tastes better. The worm has already tasted of it and liked it well enough to stay for another bite," said Lucas as he bit the place out with the worm hole and spit it on the ground.

"Phew! Weren't you afraid you'd bite the worm? That almost makes me sick."

Lucas held the apple up and pointed. "See, the worm is still there. He's gone for the core. They always do."

Abigail picked one up from the ground that had several places in it. "Here, bite this one since all the worms go to the core."

Lucas laughed. "No, too much protein."

Abigail ran down below the tree and yelled catch as she threw an apple at Lucas. He caught it, but it broke apart in his hand. He threw it down, shaking the mess off his hand and then looked up with a gleam in his eyes. "You did that on purpose, my friend, so I think I'll return the favor." He grabbed up an apple to throw, but Abigail jumped behind the tree and he missed.

That began a chase that soon had them both panting for breath before Lucas caught Abigail at the bottom of the orchard near the fence. "Okay, I caught you. What kind of reward do I get for winning the game?"

Abigail turned a happy smiling face up to him and he pulled her into his arms. Abigail stood still and didn't shiver until she looked over Lucas's shoulder and saw her mother standing on the back porch, and suddenly she felt guilty. She shoved Lucas away from her. "I don't want . . ." Then suddenly she started crying and shivering. Lucas stepped back with such a hurt look on his face that Abigail couldn't stand it. She turned and starting running back toward the house.

"Abigail, please, please wait," called Lucas with such a sad voice that Abigail stopped.

He came up to her and asked. "What happened, Abigail? I didn't do anything but put my arms around you. You were fine at first and then you froze. I want to know why. Do you know what happened that made you change?"

"I saw Mommy looking at us and I felt guilty or afraid of what Mommy would think." They were standing in front of a tree and Abigail leaned against the tree. She still had tears in her eyes, but now they were tears of sorrow for Lucas. She knew she had hurt him and she didn't want to hurt Lucas. She put her hand on his arm. "Please forgive me, Lucas. I don't want to be like this and I don't want to hurt you, but I can't stand for Mommy to think I'm bad."

"Think you're bad! Why in the world would she think that? You need to talk to your mother about how she makes you feel. She may tell you something that will change your whole attitude," said Lucas, putting his hand over hers.

Abigail stood thinking that Lucas was right, but she didn't think she had the nerve to tell her mother what her hypnosis had revealed. "I can't do that, Lucas. Mommy has kept her secret all these years. What if I tell her and she has a heart attack?"

Tired and exasperated, Lucas grasped her shoulders. "Abigail, I think I've been patient and tried to help you in every way that I know how, but don't you think you should meet me halfway? Do you want to live like this the rest of your life? All you need to do is talk to your mother. Even without that you could just t relax and let me hold you? That's all I want to do, at least at first."

"Lucas, I'm sorry, but I just haven't been able to probe any more. I can understand if you want to stop seeing me. I really don't know why you've kept coming back anyway."

Lucas looked at her angrily. "I keep coming back because

I love you, but you've been so wrapped up in how you feel that you've never thought how I might feel. I have feelings too, Abigail, and I'm about at the end of my rope."

Abigail looked up at Lucas, her eyes brimming with tears. "I'm so sorry Lucas. I truly want to be different. If Mommy hadn't come out I might have . . . I just don't know anymore. Just don't come back anymore. I don't like to see you hurt."

Lucas grabbed her by the shoulders. "I'd like to shake some sense into your head. There is nothing wrong with men and women hugging each other. You tell me what you think is wrong with that."

Abigail trembled. "Lucas, I know there is nothing wrong with you hugging me. I tell myself that all the time. I'll make up my mind that the next time you come I'll be different, and then I can't. Will you please pray for me?"

Her large green eyes were filled with such a forlorn expression as she looked up at him that he dropped his head in his hands and moaned. Finally he looked at her and said, "Let's both pray because I'm coming back Friday and we're going to skate. I'm also going to put my arms around you while we're skating."

Suddenly Abigail remembered her dream. "Lucas, night before last, I dreamed that there was a church crowd, but I don't remember anybody I knew except Angeline Hagerman. In the dream you and I were holding hands and walking down a road, but we could hear the singing. We walked to the edge of a river. Then I woke up. I couldn't understand what I was doing going toward a river. I've always been afraid of water and never learned to swim. Don't you think that is an unusual dream?" she asked.

Lucas grasped her hands. "It's a good dream, Abigail. I don't know the meaning of it, but at least you and I were together and that is good. If it means anything, the Lord will reveal it to us. We just need to pray."

Abigail was happy again and her eyes were shining like emeralds. "I think you're right. We both need to pray and since your mother told you to pray, please ask her to pray also."

Chapter 33

When Lucas left, Abigail stayed close to Sally all evening. She thought that somehow the conversation would be brought around until she could bring up the subject of her trauma. It was almost as if Sally sensed her intentions for she stayed in the same room with Garson and then followed Damon out to the rabbit hutches where one of the does had just delivered. Abigail laughed at Damon's stricken look when Sally said, "Damon, you're either going to have to start eating rabbit or buy some land and start a rabbit farm. You started out with a male and a female and now you have twelve rabbits."

That started a conversation that followed them back in the house and got Garson involved. "It's a good thing people don't multiply like that else we'd have to find another planet to populate."

Abigail didn't get to talk to Sally that evening or the next day because Sally said she had to go to the grocery store. "I'm out of salt, soda, coffee, and things I can't grow." Even though Sally and Garson only went to Jones and Spry Store in Bradshaw they were gone almost all day.

There was no talking Friday morning either, since the measuring and sewing was started. All of the attention was centered on making sure the pattern was placed correctly and then the material was pinned so it wouldn't slip. Once that was done, Sally said, "Now, go off and do something else and don't come near me or speak to me until I get this done. If I get distracted I'll ruin this pretty material."

Since Abigail did not have a session that week, Lucas didn't show up until five-thirty. Until he came Abigail was on 'pins and needles' as Grandpa had always said when she couldn't be still. *Lord, please don't let Lucas stop coming to see me. I need him,* she pled silently as she went about her usual chores.

True to her promise she had knelt each night and poured out her heart to the Lord, but she didn't feel like the Lord had even heard her. *Maybe Lucas and I aren't supposed to be together. I begged the Lord to change me and, like it says in the Bible that love casteth out fear, I begged the Lord to give me that kind of love. I'm still afraid, though, so I guess He doesn't think it's time,"* she thought morosely. However, when she saw Lucas's car pulling up before the house, she was all smiles.

Abigail had taken her bath and put on a white blouse with a turned back collar and a button down front, but she was wearing her jeans. She had tried on her skirt and it fit perfectly. "Oh! Mommy, it's beautiful. It doesn't look too short, see!" She twirled around.

Sally smiled. "It is pretty even if I did make it. Turn around again." Abigail twirled around and Sally shook her head. "The material is heavy enough to keep it from flaring up and showing your drawers. I think it's fine."

Abigail stood with the skirt on and Sally said, "Why don't you wear your jeans until Lucas comes with the vest. Maybe you'll look so pretty your daddy won't notice if the skirt's a little short."

Abigail was standing in the middle of the living room when Lucas knocked on the door. "Come on in," yelled Garson, never taking his eyes from *The Virginian*, his favorite western.

When Lucas walked in he looked so handsome. He already had his outfit on. The crisp white shirt, blue vest, and blue pants made him look like a teen idol. He had Abigail's vest on a hanger with plastic over it. "Here's your vest. Did your mother make the skirt?"

Abigail nodded yes, but stood looking at him admiringly. "You really look sharp, Lucas. Some girl will try to snatch you up tonight," she said and laughed.

Lucas looked at her and said, "I hope she does, if she's the right girl." Then he pointed to his vest and pants and raised his eyebrows in question. She nodded yes, but slanted her eyes toward her dad.

Lucas grinned in understanding and followed her to the kitchen. "Mrs. Dawson, did you get your sewing done?"

Sally looked around and grinned widely. "Yes, I did. Just wait until you see it. That material was so easy to work with."

Abigail had gone on to her room with the vest in her hand and soon she came out and stopped in the kitchen doorway. Everybody turned to look and she twirled around. She looked like a small elf as she almost danced over to Lucas and stopped. "Well, what do you think?"

Nobody had noticed that Garson had come into the kitchen, but they took notice when he said, "Pon my honor if a fairy ain't flew right into our house. Turn around here Abby and let your daddy look at you."

Abigail turned around slowly as her joy all left her. Now she looked like a drooping bluebell. Garson looked at her and said, "What happened? I walked to the door and saw a little fairy almost dancing and now you look like the world has come to an end. Am I that ugly?"

"No, Daddy you're not ugly. I was afraid you'd be mad about my outfit. Lucas and I were supposed to dress alike tonight and Mommy made . . ."

"Stop, stop right there," ordered Garson. "Why wouldn't I like your outfit? Its plum pretty and you are pretty as a store bought doll. In fact you both look sharp. Course I wouldn't be caught dead in Lucas's outfit, but I ain't young like he is."

Impulsively Abigail ran and hugged her father. "Thank you, Daddy. Thank you so much. You've made me so happy." Abigail had tears in her eyes as she turned back to Lucas, smiling.

Garson and Sally both stood still in amazement when Abigail had voluntarily hugged her father. They looked at each other and smiled. Garson walked over closer to where Abigail and Lucas stood and said, "I do have one stipulation."

Abigail quaked and grasped Lucas's hand. Lucas said, "What's that, Mr. Dawson?"

"When that man takes them pictures you've got to promise to bring one home for me and Sally."

A wide grin broke out on both their faces and Lucas put out his hand. Garson shook it as Lucas said, "You've got my promise on that."

Soon Lucas and Abigail were driving out of Stateline Ridge. "Wasn't your dad a surprise? Your mom had us both scared that you'd have to sneak out of the house and neither of us wanted to sneak."

Abigail sat thinking and then aloud she said, "Lucas, it is almost like Mom expects Dad to act or be a certain way and yet he isn't like that at all."

Lucas agreed that it did appear that way. "Abigail, for some reason I believe that the part your Mom played in traumatizing you for so many years, and it still isn't over, is also something that has affected her as well. You didn't talk to her, did you?"

"No I didn't. I'd made up my mind to talk to her, but I could never get her alone. I've stayed right with her since you left that evening. I mean literally right with her except when we were asleep or when she and dad went to Bradshaw on Thursday. I just never could get her alone. She was either in the living room with Dad or, believe it or not, she even went with Damon out to the rabbit hutches. Then this morning she wouldn't let me say a word while she was making the skirt. In fact she told me to get out of her way and not even talk to her until she got it done."

"Sounds like she suspected something," said Lucas thoughtfully. They rode on into Stringtown without talking. Just before they pulled in Lucas turned to Abigail. "You look especially pretty, so don't get all panicky if some guy whistles or wants to skate with you. I'll be right there to ward them off."

"Thanks Lucas. I know you'll watch out for me. Besides, once we start skating I forget about everything and everybody," said Abigail.

When they walked into the rink people stopped skating and Mr. Gregory came hurrying over. "Wait till I get my camera ready. This is going to be good. Where did you get your outfits?"

"We have family that knows how to find things or make things. We did a little of both," said Lucas, laughing.

People were gathered around oohing and ahhing at the outfits and in Abigail's opinion, the girls were eyeing Lucas as well. Lucas held Abigail's hand possessively and Abigail didn't mind at all.

Soon they were on the floor and, as usual, they skated one round just holding hands. Then the music changed to the "Tennessee Waltz" and Lucas swung Abigail into his arms. From then on Abigail was in another world and didn't want to leave it, but finally the music stopped and they glided off the floor. Lucas's arm was around Abigail's waist and she didn't mind at all. She also didn't mind the roar of applause as they went off the floor.

Mr. Gregory came over. "I got some really good shots. If they're as good as I think they are you're going to have some mighty fine memories to look at."

Lucas was on his knees taking off Abigail's skates. "Since we put on a good show for you, couldn't you get us something to drink?"

"I certainly could, son. What do you want?"

"I want a coke and Abigail wants a bottle of water," said Lucas as he finished and rose to his feet. He turned to sit down when a girl with long blond hair came over.

"I think I could skate like that with you. Do you want to give it a try?" she asked, smiling flirtatiously.

"No, he doesn't want to give it a try. He is taking me home," said Abigail, glaring at the girl, who glared back and looked at Lucas, expecting a different answer.

"She's right. Her wish is my command. She's got me under her spell," said Lucas, smiling at Abigail and not even looking at the girl, who bent a malevolent stare at Abigail.

Mr. Gregory came back with their drinks. He looked at Abigail for a moment. "The man that scared you that night died. I saw it in the paper. He'd have gone to prison if he hadn't died. I've learned a good lesson though and everybody has to show what's in their pockets before they come in here from now on."

As they rested, a man with a shock of white hair walked over and Abigail didn't flinch. She knew this man. Abigail put out her hand. "Adam Hagerman! Mr. Hagerman, how are you? I haven't seen you in five or six years."

"I'm plum sorry about what happened to you. Are you all right now? I was here that night, but there was such a crowd I couldn't get to you. I got to that man though and helped to hold him. You was so tore up that night you wouldn't have recognized me anyway."

"Mr. Hagerman, that man attacked me three years ago and I got away by jabbing my finger in his eye. He came back to kill me, according to the paper, but anyway after that attack a man with white hair always threw me into a panic. I didn't know what I was doing, but thank God I had Lucas to take care of me," explained Abigail.

Adam Hagerman patted her hand. "Well, that explains it. I'm real sorry that I couldn't have been more help to you."

Abigail smiled. "Don't worry about it, Mr. Hagerman. We're still friends." Before he turned away, Abigail said, "Oh, Mr. Hagerman, this is my friend, Lucas Sutherland. He's the best friend I've ever had. Lucas, this is Daddy's friend Adam Hagerman."

The two men shook hands and Mr. Hagerman left. Then Lucas and Abigail got up to go. Mr. Gregory came over. "Are you two coming back next Friday night? I'd really like for you to come on Saturday night. I could advertise and I'll bet I wouldn't have no place to park all the people."

Lucas looked at Abigail. "Do you want to come on Saturday night instead of Friday, next week?"

"I don't know if Daddy will want me to, but I will if he'll let me."

"I'll find out when I take her home, Mr. Gregory," said Lucas and then added, "I'll either stop back by or I'll call you before Monday. I just thought of something though. We can't stay for hours, so how can we sneak in here and out again in about an hour?"

Mr. Gregory turned toward his office and said, "Follow me."

Lucas and Abigail walked along behind Mr. Gregory as he went through his office and down a narrow hallway to a door at the end. He opened this door and stepped out into a seemingly vacant lot. There was one car parked there and Mr. Gregory said, "That's my car. Come on and I'll show you how to get here from the highway."

An alley only wide enough for one car circled around behind two buildings and came out between two houses about fifty feet up the road from the skating rink. Once they saw where to enter the alley they retraced their steps and followed Mr. Gregory back into his office.

"All right, we'll be here from eight until nine next Saturday night with her parents' permission," said Lucas.

"Good! That's probably the best time to draw the biggest crowd anyway," said Mr. Gregory, following them out of his office as they turned to leave.

Chapter 34

When they were in the car and driving up the road Lucas looked across at Abigail. "You were wonderful tonight. Were you as relaxed as you seemed to be?"

"I was when we were skating, but I got upset when that girl got flirty with you."

"Were you jealous?" asked Lucas, trying to keep from smiling.

"I don't know. It just made me mad. She was acting as if she would be better to skate with than I am. Also she was looking at you in a way that I didn't like. Is that being jealous?"

"I was hoping you were jealous because that would mean you care about me. I would like that."

"Are you serious? You know that I like you. I've told you I do and, believe me, I wouldn't be in this car with you if I didn't like you. I don't understand you, Lucas."

Lucas heaved a long sigh. "Abigail, I know you're eighteen, but as far as knowing anything about life you're more like thirteen."

Abigail didn't answer because she was afraid he'd begin talking about hugging and things like that. She decided to change the subject since she didn't know what to say anyway. "Lucas, are you going in to ask Daddy about my going skating on Saturday night?"

"That's the only way I know to find out so I guess I'll have to. That shouldn't be a problem since he stays up until we get back anyway," said Lucas, knowing that she had deliberately changed the subject.

He drove along thinking that Abigail blew hot and cold.

Inside the rink he had skated with her in his arms and encircled her waist as they went back to their seats and also when the Hagerman man came over, but as soon as they were outside she kept her distance. *I'm getting awfully tired of being treated as if I'm a rapist or some kind of psycho,* he thought bitterly.

Suddenly Abigail reached over and touched his arm. "Lucas, if I slide over beside you, will you not touch me, but just let me sit beside you?"

Lucas drew in his breath. "Slide over here, woman. I'll promise anything you want."

Abigail slid across the seat as Lucas drove up the mountain and he suddenly started singing, "That's Amore."

"I didn't know you could sing. That's good! You have a nice voice. Do you sing a lot?"

"Just when I'm happy!"

Abigail hesitantly joined in and found that their voices blended well so she continued singing. They went from one song to another as they finished their drive home. When they pulled to a stop in front of the house, Lucas looked down at Abigail nestled at his side and said, "Now, what is wrong with sitting beside a man and singing songs?"

Abigail straightened up and slid back to her side, but she smiled back at Lucas. "Nothing! Absolutely nothing was wrong with it. I liked it. In fact I may try it again sometime," but seeing Lucas's look she quickly added, "On the same terms, of course."

Lucas' face fell. "What's the difference in my shoulder touching you and my arms touching you?"

"Nothing I guess, except that a shoulder doesn't have hands," said Abigail with a slight shiver.

"Good God! Abigail, who put such weird ideas into your head? Every time a man touches you it doesn't mean that he has some lecherous thought in his head."

Abigail dropped her head. "I so wanted this night to end with us as happy as we were coming up the mountain, but you ruined it. Why do you always have to bring up about hugging and touching?"

Lucas glared angrily at her. "I didn't bring it up. You put those strictures on sitting beside me in the car. You are treating me as if I was the dirtiest scum of the earth. I don't attack women and I don't put my hands where they are not wanted." He shoved the door open and got out and stomped toward the porch without offering to open Abigail's door.

Abigail didn't understand why Lucas was so upset, but then there was so much she didn't understand about men. *I have always been given a different idea about men than what Lucas says,* she thought and slowly got out of the car to follow Lucas up the steps.

Garson opened the door. "You're back early. Come on in and tell us about it. Did he get some good pictures?" When they were inside and Garson got a good look at Lucas's face he was surprised.

"Who put a burr under your blanket? You look mad enough to bite nails," blurted Garson.

"I am mad, Mr. Dawson, and I'm tired of fighting a losing battle."

Garson looked at him speculatively and intuitively sensed that this had to do with Abigail's problem. "Are you giving up?" he asked as Lucas moved to the side.

Abigail was standing behind him and now silent tears were running down her cheeks. "Lucas, I'm sorry. I am trying. I honestly am, but . . .," Abigail covered her face with her hands and ran past him and into her bedroom and slammed the door.

Neither Lucas nor Garson said anything for a moment, but Garson slowly turned to look at Sally, who had come in from the kitchen. The look they exchanged was filled with something, but Lucas couldn't understand it. Sally, however, dropped her head and remained silent.

"I don't have the answer, but I feel certain I know who does. I thought that doctor had helped Abigail, but I guess he didn't," said Garson.

"He has to a point, Mr. Dawson. She is more relaxed in a crowd and seems fine with me most of the time." Lucas dropped his head dejectedly. "I was so sure that the Lord wanted me to try to help Abigail, but maybe that was just me. That may not be the Lord's purpose at all."

Sally's head jerked up. "No, you're not wrong. You've done your part, but I've not done mine." She rose from the sofa and left the room.

Garson turned to Lucas. "Does this end your skating and you taking Abby to the counselor?"

"Right now I feel like leaving and never mentioning her name again, but I'm tired and upset tonight. Can you get Charles or somebody to take her for her session next Friday?"

"I'll get somebody, but I'm going to tell that doctor that he's running up a big bill and not helpin' any," said Garson.

Lucas turned to leave and then stopped. "Abigail and I were supposed to skate on Saturday night next week from eight until nine o'clock if you would permit it. I told Mr. Gregory I'd let him know, but right now I just don't care."

"She has my permission if you change your mind, Lucas. I know you love Abby and you've went along with her wishes longer than I would have. I wish it hadn't come to this, but I can't say as I blame you. The only thing I will say is she's been livin' with this for nigh onto fifteen years and I don't think she's going to get over it in a matter of weeks."

Lucas started on out the door. "It's been months. It's been nice meeting you, Mr. Dawson. I . . . I hope that Abigail gets better."

Sally came back in the room. "Lucas, please don't give up, yet. I know the Lord sent you to Abby. I think that you'll soon see a difference in her attitude. I've been praying, but the Lord wants more than that, I guess."

Lucas, who had now cooled down, gave her a level look. "Mrs. Dawson, I . . . well, I think you are the only one who can help."

Sally nodded solemnly and asked, "Does that mean that you won't give up?"

Lucas looked at this woman, who seldom smiled or showed any emotion, and realized she was willing to sacrifice anything for her child. "Mrs. Dawson, right now I feel drained. I don't know if I can keep trying."

Sally whispered, "I hope you can, Lucas. I didn't think God would let you give up."

Lucas went down the steps thinking, *Then God must be working on you, Mrs. Dawson, for I'm ready to call off the fight.* He drove away without looking back, but that didn't lessen his agitation.

His drive back to Ronceverte seemed the longest he'd ever driven. He drove through Bluefield, Peterstown, and Union without even realizing where he was. When he reached home around one o'clock in the morning he crept silently through the door and up the stairs to his room thinking he would get the whiskey he had buried in his closet. It had been there since he had visited Abigail's church and had that wonderful experience during the singing. Now, he thought it had all been his imagination. He undressed, but the urge to get the whiskey kept pestering him. Finally he gave in and delved into his closet, coming out with a bottle. He looked at it, unscrewed the lid, and turned it up. With the first swallow he shivered and turned it up again.

The next morning, Mrs. Sutherland saw Lucas's car in the driveway and kept listening for him to come clattering down the stairs. When it was eight o'clock and Lucas hadn't appeared she became worried. She went hurriedly up the stairs and knocked on his door. She waited and the only noise she heard was a muffled groan. She opened the door to be met with the smell of whiskey wafting through the air.

"Lucas, Lucas, are you all right?" she asked as she stepped inside the room.

Lucas opened blurry eyes and winced as the sunlight shining through his window blinded him. He sat up in bed, grabbed his head and groaned. "Get me some aspirin, will you?" he asked.

His mother went back out into the hall and into the bathroom at the end. Soon she was back with two aspirin tablets and a glass of water, which she handed to Lucas. He swallowed them down without opening his eyes. Mrs. Sutherland patted his shoulder. "Take a hot shower and come down to the kitchen. I'll have some hot coffee ready."

Chapter 35

Lucas not only had a headache, but he was filled with remorse. *Lord, I'm so ashamed. Taking a drink wouldn't have bothered me, but turning to the bottle instead of you is what I'm ashamed of. Please forgive me.* Lucas had been looking in the mirror, but now he suddenly dropped to his knees on the bathroom floor. *Please, please Lord; work a miracle in somebody to help Abigail. I do love her, Lord, you know I do, but I've done all I can do. I'm just turning it over to you, Lord. If you want me to give up on it, give me a sign. Lord, I'm begging in the humblest way I know how. In Jesus's name I ask these things. Amen*

Lucas got to his feet and wiped tears from his eyes that he hadn't even known he'd shed. He felt easier and thought that the Lord had forgiven his turning to drink. *Maybe he is giving me strength to accept his will. I know I'll carry Abigail in my heart all my life, but with God's help I can live without her.*

Later he told his mother what had transpired and that he had decided to not go back to the Dawsons. "I still love her, Mom, but I am so frustrated. I've had to watch every move I've made since I first met Abigail and I guess the strain just got to be too much."

Mrs. Sutherland sat circling the salt shaker with her finger. "Well, the Lord has his way in a whirlwind and he can take care of this as well."

"I know that all of this has something to do with her mother, but I don't know how or what. She told me that Dr. Fischer had hypnotized her and she remembered something that happened before she was three years old and that it had to do with her mother," said Lucas, whose head was still aching.

"I thought you were supposed to go over a boundary of timber somewhere in McDowell County this week," said Mrs. Sutherland.

"That's in the Burkes Mountain area above Northfork. That's miles from the top of Bradshaw Mountain."

"You're in no shape to go today, are you?" asked his mother.

"No, I'm not and I'm ashamed of myself. I knew better, so I guess I deserve more punishment than this splitting headache."

"You're not the first man to get drunk, Lucas," replied his mother.

"No, but that's not what I'm ashamed of. I turned to the bottle instead of to the Lord. I thought I was stronger than that. I think I must be like Cain, who offered all he had, but he didn't bring a sacrifice. He kept back his heart. You see Mom, I kept praying and trying to do things so the Lord would bless my efforts, but I think my heart didn't believe. I thought I could do something. I guess I was trying to bargain with the Lord," said Lucas.

Mrs. Sutherland smiled a loving, contented smile. "Lucas, did you ever think that perhaps the Lord is using Abigail and her sickness to bring you both to Him?"

Lucas suddenly remembered the dream that Abigail had told him about. "Mom, Abigail dreamed that she and I were in a church crowd, but she didn't remember any of the faces except Angeline Hagerman, the old woman I told you about that sang like an angel. Anyway, in the dream, she and I were holding hands and going down a road to a river. She said then she woke up and thought it was silly, since she is afraid of water. Do you suppose her dream meant that she and I would be called to the church?"

Mrs. Sutherland didn't understand what he meant by "calling," but she did understand that people had dreams foretelling things if the Lord wanted them to do something. "It may mean that the Lord wants you and Abigail to be baptized."

Lucas was at first startled, but then said, "Her dream

happened more than two weeks ago and yesterday I got so frustrated that I left her crying. She'll probably not speak to me again." Lucas rose from the table and, taking his cup of coffee, went out onto the front porch and stood pondering as to what he should do about Abigail.

Back in the Dawson household both Abigail and Sally spent a restless night; each wrestling with their own demons. Sally had sworn that she would never even think of that long ago episode again, but the Lord had impressed upon her mind that she had to talk about it in order to save Abigail. Abigail's demon was the knowledge that she had treated Lucas like a yo-yo and knowing that it was unfair. They both awoke feeling worse than they had when they'd gone to bed.

Sally almost dragged herself to the kitchen and started preparing breakfast and was soon joined by Abigail. "Good morning, Mommy," said Abigail, getting the plates from the cabinet.

"Good Morning, Abby. How did you sleep?"

"I guess I slept, but it didn't seem like I had ever been asleep when I heard you in here."

"I didn't sleep much either. I hope I didn't keep your daddy awake with my rolling and turning," said Sally.

Garson came in before the gravy and biscuits were on the table and sat down at his place anyway. Sally looked startled. "You're early and breakfast ain't quite ready yet."

"Well, I'll not beat you up for that. I know I'm early 'cause I've got something I want to say. After Damon leaves for work, I think the three of us need to have a long talk," stated Garson in a very positive voice.

Sally gasped. "Seems like the Lord pressed on me all night to talk about something but still I begged the Lord for some kind of sign and he just gave it to me. I guess he does want me to talk."

Abigail looked from one to the other, and thinking they wanted to talk about her and Lucas, she said, "I know that you both think I've done Lucas wrong and I guess I have, but I just can't get past feeling guilty if a man touches me. I mean it is all right if I touch them, but if they put their hands on me then I feel guilty."

Garson grimaced. "Abby, just wait until Damon goes to work and then we'll talk."

Damon came through the door dressed for work. "I heard someone say my name. Am I late for breakfast?"

"You late for breakfast! Your nose wouldn't let that happen," said Garson.

Damon laughed. "I just appreciate Mom's cooking and want to let her know it."

"Yeah, I'm certain that's the only reason you hurry to the table." Garson looked at Damon and smiled.

Soon breakfast was over and Damon left for work driving Garson's truck. "That boy needs a car, but I can't see no way of him getting one unless he works it out. I don't know if he saves a cent of what he makes, do you?" He asked, looking at Sally.

"Yes, he has a box in his room and he's been putting so much each payday in it, but I don't know how much. Now, though, he's interested in that Cantrell girl and if she'll date him, he'll probably spend it all just to show off."

Abigail sat deep in thought and not adding one word to the conversation. Both she and her mother had gotten to their feet to clear the table, but Garson said, "You two set down here at the table. It's as good a place as any to talk."

Sally went to the sink and washed her hands and stood drying them over and over. Garson looked at her and said, "Come on. Bring that towel with you if you can't let it go."

When they were all seated, Garson said, "I'll start first and I'm pretty blunt. Abby, you're going to hear some things that may shock you, but things have been left too long already."

Sally sat twisting the dish towel around and around, to then straighten it out and start over. Abigail put her hand out and touched her mother's arm. Sally jerked back and then seemed to become rigid. Garson got up and went to the sink, filled a glass with water, and brought it to Sally.

"Here, Sally, drink this and try to relax. You may learn something today that you didn't know as well."

Sally took the glass in both hands and drank it down and sat back in her chair. "Abby, when the doctor hypnotized you, exactly what did you remember?" she asked.

Abigail wet her lips. "I don't want to hurt you, Mommy."

"I know you don't, Abby, but you've been hurt enough. I need to know what you remembered so I can tell you the rest." Sally was plucking at her dress sleeves and biting her lips in an almost rhythmic pattern, but she said harshly, "Go on, tell us what you remembered."

"I remembered a boy asking me to play a game with him. When I wouldn't agree he offered me a whole pack of gum and then I said I would. The game was that we take all our clothes off. I didn't think it was bad since I had to take them off when you put me in the tub. I started taking them off, but the boy wanted to help me and I didn't want him to. You said to not let boys touch me under my clothes. Grandpa heard me crying, I guess, for I remember Grandpa coming and hitting the boy with his cane and chasing after him. Then you came and you started calling me dirty, filthy, nasty, and whipping me. I started crying and running toward the house, but you kept hitting me and telling me I was bad. I remember Grandpa coming in and he slapped you. You fell down and I thought you were dead and I had killed you." Abigail stopped and began sobbing brokenly.

"Stop crying and tell us what happened then?" said Garson, who was pale as a ghost.

Abigail pulled a tissue from her pocket and blew her nose. "I remember running to Mommy and putting my arms around her neck and saying I was sorry and I wouldn't ever be bad again. Mommy didn't answer. That's all I remembered."

Garson looked at Sally for a few seconds. "This is the part I can tell. Virginia knows most of it, but she don't know all of it. Since your Pap died, me and Virginia were the only people that did know. I should have told you, but old Doc cautioned all three of us that we must never mention any of it. Also, I was always afraid it would make you sick again. Now, I wish I had. We would have been a lot happier if I had, I think." Abigail was seeing an expression on her father's face that she'd never seen before. Sally sat as if waiting to be shot and had lost her ruddy complexion.

Garson cleared his throat. "I come in while Abby was holding on to you and crying. I told your Pap to pick Abby up and I got Virginia to help me carry you to our bed. I washed your face, but nothing seemed to work. I was scared to death about you and Abby too. She had passed out or something. I told Virginia to stay with you and I got back in my truck and went to Bradshaw to get old Doc Harrison. He come out and took a look at you and said it was some kind of paralysis. Anyway, he give you a shot and since Abby was still out, he give her some medicine too. Your Pap told Doc what had happened and at first I got plum mad because he had slapped you. Doc said that your Pap did the right thing and I guess he did." Garson got up and went to get himself a glass of water then sat back down. He dropped his hands onto his knees and sat looking at Sally and drew in a long breath.

"You're not going to like what I'm about to tell you, but I'm doing it to help Abby and hope it will help you, too."

Sally didn't say anything, but looked at Garson as if she was hypnotized. Garson cleared his throat and renewed his story. "Doc came every day for the next three days, but you didn't come out of it. Abby didn't either and we were all worried to death, especially me and your Pap. Anyway, the next day, old Doc came, and finding you both still in a coma, he said, 'Garson, I'd like to try something on Sally. I can promise you that it won't hurt her and it just might help her. I think it's the only way we're going to get at the truth.' I talked it over with your Pap and with Virginia and we decided to try it. We all sat down around your bed and the old Doc gave you a shot which he said was the new treatment and then he told us to wait about eight minutes. We waited and then Doc started asking you questions about when you was a girl."

Sally jumped up almost turning her chair over. "He had no

right. You shouldn't have agreed." Then she looked at Abigail and sat back down. Still looking at Abigail, she said from lips that moved in spasmodic jerks. "I promised the Lord, so just go ahead."

Garson looked at Sally with such compassion that Abigail wanted to cry. "You had a rough life, Sally, and I'm so sorry. Anyway, by his questions we learned that your Mammy's brother came back from the War and made his home with your folks. He was good to all the young'uns, but you were his favorite. He started touching you in private places and when you got upset he always petted you and gave you money. You wanted to go to school and needed money so you went along with him until he caught you in the woods one day. He hurt you and made you feel dirty and filthy, but he said if you told your Pap that he would kill him. So you didn't tell. This went on for a year, but during that time I started coming around with the idea of sparkin' with you."

Garson paused and took a deep breath. "That's what you told the Doc and then you went to sleep. You slept long enough for Virginia and Alice to get supper ready and then you suddenly woke up. Abby was still out. You started asking for her. Do you remember your Pap putting Abby in your arms? He told you to tell Abby that you loved her and that she wasn't nasty and dirty. You started cryin', Sally, and you rocked and held Abby, whispering to her, and finally she moved her hand. Your Pap started praising God and I was mighty glad, but I had that uncle on my mind and if he hadn't already been dead I would have killed him. A lot of people thought your Mam poisoned him, 'cause he seemed to be in good health 'til after you run away from home and then he just up and died. When your mam was sick, before she died, she said it was easy to put rat poison in a person's food."

Sally started crying. "I hope she did. He deserved to die. I was pregnant when I ran away and you found me, Garson. I didn't have no place to go and didn't know what to do. I begged you to marry me when you didn't love me. I'm sorry. I'm so sorry. I shouldn't have done you that way. You've always thought Kyle wasn't yours, but he is. I know that for sure." Sally swallowed, grimaced and continued.

"I lost that devil's child and I wanted to. I took turpentine, but I would have probably lost it anyway. Granny Betty, the midwife said that women under a lot of stress often lost their first babies. I certainly was under stress for I knew if I wasn't married and Pap found out where I was that he would make me come back. I would rather have died than have to come back to that. I've felt so dirty, nasty, and filthy all my life and so guilty for doing you wrong. I think I'd carried all that so long that when I saw my sweet baby and that boy helping her take her clothes off, my uncle flashed before my eyes and I went wild. I'm so sorry, Abby, so, so sorry. I've messed up your life and your daddy's life. I hope to God you can both forgive me, for I'll never be able to forgive myself."

Abigail started to go to her mother, but Garson got to her first. He knelt in front of her and put his arms around her and, laying his head in her lap, Garson Dawson cried like a baby.

Chapter 36

Sally sat stunned for a moment and then she bent her head over Garson's and started crying as well. Abigail stood looking at the only display of affection she had ever seen between her parents. She was amazed and so very touched. She didn't want to break in on this touching and private moment, so she tiptoed from the room.

She was so caught up in what she'd just learned that she didn't realize she had gone to the orchard until she stumbled on a fallen branch. She steadied herself and looked around her. Seeing the Rome Beauty apple tree that her Grandpa had loved, she made for it and sat down on the little bench he had placed beneath it. *Thank you, Lord. Now I know that Mommy wasn't seeing me so long ago, she was seeing herself and calling herself all those vile things. She has suffered all her life because she was afraid Grandpa would get hurt. Poor Mommy! Lord, please let this be a new beginning for Mommy and Daddy. Please Lord. I'm begging in the only way I know how. Please look down on them in mercy.* Abigail sat crying for her mother's sad story and also for the relief it gave her.

Abigail sat for a long time, thinking of how afraid she had been all her life. *I didn't know why, but I was always afraid of doing something that would make Mommy think I was bad. I don't have to be afraid anymore.* Abigail sighed happily and thought how good it would be to tell Lucas. Then she remembered how she had hurt Lucas and what he'd said to Sally when he'd left about being ready to call off the fight.

He'll not come back again and it's my fault. I wish he would come back so I could at least tell him that I'm free, thought

Abigail sadly. Now, everything she'd experienced paled in comparison with what her mother had been through.

Abigail slowly walked back to the house, wondering how to act when facing her mother again. *I'll just act as if nothing has ever happened. I'll go in and start peeling potatoes for supper and ask whether she wants to boil them or fry them.*

When she walked into the kitchen she was surprised to see Garson peeling the potatoes. Sally was rolling out dough for some kind of pie and when she saw Abigail, she turned red but kept on rolling the dough. "What are you making, Mommy?" asked Abigail.

"I told her I'd peel the taters if she'd make me a big strawberry cobbler," said Garson, laughing merrily before continuing. "She's been watching me though. She says I'm wasting half of each tater."

Abigail laughed. "You'll learn, and then I won't have a thing to do."

"You've suffered enough at my hands, Abby," said Sally sadly.

"Mommy, don't even think that. What I've been through is nothing compared to what you went through."

"I know, but you were just a sweet, happy, little baby and I ruined all your young years. I wish there was some way I could make it up to you, but I know it can't be undone."

Garson had finished the potatoes and rose to his feet. He put his arm around Sally and said, "Didn't I tell you to not cry over spilled milk. What's done is done and can't be changed, but what we do with the rest of our lives will make the difference. Ain't that right, Abby?"

"You're right, Daddy. Let's make a promise to each other. We've all helped each other today, so let's promise that we will put this behind us and leave it between us. Don't you think that's a good idea?" asked Abigail.

Both Garson and Sally looked at Abigail with tears in their eyes. Garson said, "Thank you, Abby. You said the very thing that your mother needed to hear. I needed it too, but not as much as your mother did."

When Damon came home and found Garson in the kitchen while Sally was cooking, he was amazed. "What are you doing in the kitchen? Don't you know you'll make Mommy nervous and she'll ruin our supper?" he asked.

Garson laughed merrily. "We've made some new rules in this house. If your mother can help me in the garden then I can help her in the house. In fact we've decided to teach you to cook as well."

"What if I don't want to learn to cook?"

"Who's going to cook for you when me and your mother take a vacation?"

Abigail and Damon both were goggle-eyed in amazement. "You're not taking no vacation, Dad. That's just one of your jokes," said Damon.

Garson laughed. "Well, I did just think of it, but now that I have, I think it might be a good idea. What do you think, Sally?"

"I think I might like to go visit some places, but not until after supper."

They all started laughing and Sally smiled happily. Abigail got busy and set the table with Garson's help, which amazed Damon further. Soon supper was on the table and they all sat down. Before Garson could reach for the first bowl, Sally said, "Garson, could we please bow our heads and return thanks."

Garson nodded and for the first time the Dawson family bowed their heads in a silent prayer of thankfulness. Three of those present were thankful for more than the supper they were about to eat.

When supper was over, Abigail offered to wash the dishes and her offer was accepted. Garson and Sally walked out into the orchard and Damon hung around in the kitchen. "Abby, what's brought on this change in Mom and Dad? I've never seen them act like this before, have you?"

Abigail looked at Damon and smiled. "No, but it's nice isn't it? I think it is because they know that I am better. They're just parents being thankful I guess."

"If you being better has brought about that much change I think I'll get sick," said Damon.

"I couldn't help getting sick," scolded Abigail.

"I know it. I was just kiddin'. Can't you take a joke?" asked Damon.

Abigail laughed. "Now, don't start being like Daddy. I couldn't tell half the time when he was joking. Most of the time I thought he was serious."

Later, going to hang out the dish towels, Abigail saw her parents sitting side by side on the very bench where she had sat earlier in the day. They looked so content. *Lord, please keep them like this with each other. I love them both so very much,* begged Abigail.

Friday came and Lucas didn't show up, but Charles came and drove Abigail to her counseling session with Dr. Fischer. Abigail told Dr. Fischer what she had learned and how relieved she felt. Dr. Fischer smiled. "I could tell that something had happened as soon as you walked in." Dr. Fischer sat looking at her with a pleased expression. "So, your life is about where it should be isn't it?"

"No, it isn't, Dr. Fischer. I've chased Lucas away. I miss him so much, but I caused it. I just couldn't relax and be like a normal girl. Lucas got tired of it and he won't be back. I think if I'd known what I know now I could have been different, but it's too late now. I'll just have to live with it. Anyway, I can go to college now and I have Lucas to thank for that too," said Abigail sadly.

Dr. Fischer picked up her hand and held it between his own two hands. "Abigail, why don't you write to Lucas? Just tell him what you've told me? I feel that he would understand and everything would be all right."

"I don't know that I will be different. I think I will be, but I've thought that before and I was wrong. I don't want to tell Lucas something and then not do it," said Abigail.

"Well, you think about it. You never know unless you try," said Dr. Fischer, rising to his feet. "I think I won't need to see you but once each month for a while. After that we may go to once every six months, then once a year and then not at all. How does that sound?"

Abigail smiled. "That's good, since it is expensive to make these trips and Daddy doesn't have a car. He only has a timber truck and he's not the best driver in the world; especially in towns."

Charles could see a difference in Abigail when she came back to the car. "He must have given you a gold watch. Your face looks happy."

"I don't have to come over here but once each month for a few months and then every six months, then a year, and then not at all. That's a big relief for me and for Daddy as well."

"I was wondering how you were going to be able to come here so often and still go to college," said Charles as he pulled into a line of traffic.

Charles never once asked why Lucas hadn't taken her this time and Abigail wondered about it, but didn't ask. They talked and laughed over the mountains and on into Bradshaw. As they went through Stringtown, Charles said, "Pictures of you and Lucas skating are splashed on posters all over the county. Did you know that?"

Abigail looked startled. "No, I didn't. Where did you see one? I'd like to have one as a keepsake."

"Aren't you and Lucas going to skate anymore? I've heard people talking about coming to see you two skate. So you must be really good," said Charles.

Abigail dropped her head. "I don't guess we will, Charles. I just can't . . . Well, I still don't like to be touched and Lucas has given up on me."

"He's got his arms around you in those pictures!"

"I know. When I'm skating, I forget everything but the music and the movement. It's when we're by ourselves that I get scared or something. Lucas never did anything but hold my hand. I wish to God I could be different. I think I love Lucas, but I guess I'll never find out for sure."

"You should write or call him and just tell him you love him.

He's a really nice young man. Kyle thinks the world of him," said Charles.

"Charles, I've never been in love. I don't know if it's real or not and I don't want to tell Lucas something and then find out it isn't so."

Charles looked solemn. "Like Sylvia says, I think you'd better do some praying."

Chapter 37

Lucas didn't show up that Friday night, nor did he come on Saturday night when they had planned to go skating. Abigail cried herself to sleep both nights, but on Saturday night, she again dreamed that she and Lucas were walking toward the river hand in hand. She woke up and knew that she would never again be afraid of Lucas's touch and she didn't know how the dream caused that feeling. She knew it had, but couldn't understand why. *Thank you, sweet Jesus. If you'll send Lucas back to me I will welcome him with open arms,* she promised.

Sally had asked Abigail on Saturday evening if she planned to attend meeting with her at Bee Branch on Sunday. "No, Mommy, I don't think I want to go. I'll just stay here and have dinner ready for you and Daddy."

Sally didn't pressure her as she normally would have. Abigail thought it was because her Daddy had half-way promised he would go to meeting on Sunday. Much to Sally's surprise, Abigail was up making coffee when she entered the kitchen. "Abby, what are you doing up so early? You said you didn't want to go to meeting, today and I planned to just let you sleep."

"I changed my mind. I believe I'll feel better going than I will just being here by myself," said Abigail.

"Good. I'm real glad you're going, Abby. The Lord knows what you need when you don't even know yourself," said Sally. She walked over and hesitantly put her arms around Abigail. "Honey, I've been trying to pray that I'll live to see you happy again like you always were before I ruined it for you."

Abigail pushed back and looked at her mother. "Mom, remember our promise. Just put all that behind you and forget it ever happened. I love you and I want you to be happy. You and Daddy act happy now and that is worth it all to me."

Sally said, "Abby, I want to tell you something about that time and then I'll never mention it again. You see, I didn't believe your Daddy loved me, and thought he only married me because he felt sorry for me. So, I listened to everything he said and I tried to do exactly what he said, but I didn't tell him I had lost that baby. I thought he'd divorce me if he knew and I didn't have any place to go. Then Kyle came early and your Daddy thought he belonged to that devil, but he was still as good to Kyle as he was the rest of the children." Sally smiled softly. "Ain't that a good man who would do something like that?"

"Daddy is a good man, Mommy. He's a little harsh sometimes and don't give away much, but I love him."

"I love him too, Abby, but I raised you children to fear your Daddy when I shouldn't have. By the way I acted, your Daddy thought I didn't care about him and so he got resentful. Neither of us acted like we should have all because we didn't talk about our feelings and our past. If you marry, Abby, be sure it is to somebody you can talk to and someone who will talk to you," Sally advised and then finished putting the biscuits she had made into the pan while they talked.

Garson came through the door and he too stared at Abigail. "You're up early. Your mother said you was staying home and would probably stay in bed until we left."

"She's changed her mind, Garson. Our baby girl is coming with us to meeting."

Garson went over to the window and looked out. "Damon must be going too. He's out there hurrying around like a hunting dog on a trail. Why, pon-my-honor, if he ain't already milked the cow."

Damon came through the door carrying a pail of milk. "Here's the milk, and the pigs and chickens are fed. Oh! I also turned the mare and her colt into the pasture."

Sally took the pail of milk from him and placed it on the table. "Abby, stir the gravy and put some bacon on to fry while I strain the milk. Are you going to meeting too, Damon?" She looked at him hopefully.

"Nope! Maudie and Joseph Cantrell are taking their family down on Panther Creek to have a picnic and they've invited me to go with them."

"How much did you have to pay for that treat, Damon?" asked Garson.

"I donated five dollars to help on the food. I don't want them to think I'm too tight to pay for what I eat," said Damon defensively.

"It's more like you want to impress that little black-haired Cantrell girl," said Garson.

"I work it out. I should be able to spend it for whatever I want to," said Damon.

"That's fine if you pay your room and board, gas and use of the truck, and the license and insurance on it first," said Garson seriously.

"Room and board! Are you going to start making me pay to stay here?" Damon was shocked and outraged. "What kind of father are you? I'm not even out of high school. I'm working every minute I'm not in school and now you tell me that I have to pay to stay in my own home."

Damon was on the verge of tears and Sally said, "Garson, you quit that tormenting that boy. Damon, your daddy is just fooling with you. He won't charge you room and board."

Garson started laughing loudly and Damon looked daggers at him before stalking out of the room.

An hour later, Garson, Sally and Abigail were crunched together in the cab of the truck and Damon was seated on the back. He had a gym bag containing a towel and his swimming trunks beside him as he sat swinging his legs off the back end of the truck bed.

"Damon is happy as a lark. He's getting to spend the day with his first love. What's that girl's name? I've seen her a time or two, but I don't reckon I've ever heard her name mentioned," said Garson, looking toward Abigail.

"It's Christine, Daddy. She's a pretty girl, but I didn't think she was old enough to have a boyfriend," said Abigail.

Sally grinned and moved her leg so Garson could shift gears. Abigail noticed that he left his hand on Sally's leg a minute before putting it back on the steering wheel. Sally either didn't notice or didn't mind and Abigail asked herself, *Could I ever allow Lucas to do that to me?*

Then she thought that Lucas wouldn't be back so she'd never be put to the test. That made her sad and she tried to get her mind on something else.

"Do you think there'll be a big crowd at meeting today, Mommy?" she asked.

"It's just our regular meeting so we don't have as many people as we do when we have our Union and Communion meeting."

"Probably they all come then, since they know there'll be dinner on the grounds," said Garson, chuckling.

Sally laughed as well. "They certainly do like Aunt Pearl Cooper's pies and I don't blame them. When she's gone we'll never get that kind of pie again."

By this time they were out to the hardtop and Damon jumped off the back of the truck. "I'll be home sometime before dark, but I don't know the exact time," he said, looking at Sally through the side where the glass was rolled down.

"You be careful when you're swimming, Damon," said Sally, and Garson jumped in with, "There's jagged rocks stickin' up sometimes and you could get hurt bad so don't be diving off no high rocks."

Damon laughed and assured them that he would be careful, and then turned to walk out Route 83 toward the Panther Fork Road where the Cantrell's lived.

Garson pulled out onto the highway and soon they were pulling to a stop on the side of the highway above the church. "I'm leaving the windows down, but if it starts to rain, Abby, you high-tail it up here and roll them up," said Garson, getting out and slamming the door.

They started walking toward the meeting house and Garson got behind Sally. She and Abigail turned to look at him. "Why are you walking behind us? Are you ashamed to be seen with us?" asked Sally.

"No, but I don't want to cause no sudden shocks since there's a lot of old people that comes here. Some of them ain't never seen me inside a church house. That's enough to shock about anybody, I reckon," said Garson, laughing merrily.

His appearance did cause quite a stir. Many of his long-time friends slapped him on the back in welcome and one man said, "Well, Sally must have caught you. Your sworping days are over, Garson, cause all these people will recognize you and run back to tell Sally."

Sally tapped him on the shoulder. "Abby and I are going on in."

Garson smiled and patted her on the arm. "I'll be on in when the singing starts."

Once inside, Abigail found several of her friends and went to sit with them. When the singing started they picked up their books and sang as loud as the members. Abigail didn't know about the other girls, but she loved the singing. It always made her feel so peaceful and joyous. On the next song, Angeline Hagerman's beautiful voice rang out like the pure tones of a bell. Abigail found tears in her eyes and didn't understand why, except the singing was so beautiful that no words could describe it.

When Elder Stewart Owens came to the stand, the house became rapt in attention. Elder Owens looked like such a sad, humble, but peaceful person that he inspired respect and awe from the congregation. He began his sermon about love and Abigail recalled reading in John about love casting out fear. *Lord let your love enter my heart so I won't fear anymore*, begged Abigail as Elder Owens continued. He talked about the Lord not loving the wrongs of his people, but still loving the people. "We are his. Jesus bought and paid for us and the price was his blood. Jesus, the only begotten of the Father, full of grace and truth, allowed himself to be hung on the Roman cross so that you and I would have a way back to the Tree of Life, or back to the Eden we left when Adam transgressed the law of God and was driven out. We all long for that fellowship we had with God before the fall of Adam, but what we lost in Adam we gained back in Christ. God is love and he that loveth not, knoweth not God, but if God has moved in your heart and filled you with love, then it's time you take up your cross and follow him."

People were shouting and the congregation was singing and Abigail, without knowing how she got there, suddenly found herself in front of Elder Owens. She started to say she wanted a home with the church, but something seemed to stay her hand, then a young woman with a baby came up and suddenly thrust her baby into Abigail's arms. Then the woman grasped Elder Owens by the hand and said something. Elder Owens put up his hand and everybody became still. "This little sister has asked for a home with the church. Sister, do you have anything to tell the church of your experience?"

"I've lived with hate in my heart and I need to get rid of it. I've been praying and today the Lord gave me peace. It's the only true peace I've ever known. Please may I have a home with you?" The woman, who gave her name as Beatrice Compton, was crying and it was hard for her to talk. She heard someone say, "I move that we accept this sister as a candidate for baptism." Someone shouted a second and then Elder Owens asked who she wanted to baptize her and when did she want to be baptized.

"I want you to baptize me and I'd like to be baptized today," said Mrs. Compton in a firm, clear voice.

The congregation started singing and again Abigail was enraptured with joy unspeakable. Again she began making her way toward Elder Owens, but the Compton baby at that moment decided that he wanted his mother. He let out a mighty squall that not only brought Abigail back to reality, but the rest of the congregation as well.

Beatrice Compton took her son out of Abigail's arms and Abigail walked back to her seat and stood in muted wonder at her experience until dismissal was called. The usual announcements of special services being planned, as well as requests for prayers for the many sick people in the community, were given.

The Elders talked together for a minute and then Elder Owens said, "We will go down to the river below Bradshaw for the baptism." Then singing started up again and Beatrice Compton was welcomed as a candidate for baptism. Then some Elder called dismissal and the congregation starting filtering to the outside.

Abigail stood where she was as the people moved past her. When the crowd was thinner she began to make her way to the door. She saw Garson and Sally going out the door ahead of her, but knew they would be waiting for her outside. She didn't think Garson would want to go to the baptism and was surprised when she reached them to learn that he was going.

Sally smiled. "We're taking a truckload to the baptism. They asked Garson if they could ride on the back of his truck and he told them to climb on. I guess they just took it for granted that he was going and now it looks like he is."

Abigail still felt full of love and as if she was glowing from the inside out. *I don't know what this is. I've never felt like this before. I feel like singing and dancing and thanking God*, she thought as she climbed into the cab of the truck beside her mother.

Garson drove slowly down the mountain, just one vehicle in a long line that reached a mile or so down the mountain. The people on the back of Garson's truck began singing hymns. Every house they passed had people standing on their porches or looking out their doors to see where the singing was coming from. One man ran to his car and soon had joined their line of vehicles.

When they finally pulled in on the road that led down to the river, the younger people jumped off the truck and hurried toward the water. Garson and some other man helped the older women and men from the bed of the truck and soon they all were walking toward the river.

Abigail got out of the truck so Sally could get out, and then stood by the truck until everybody had gone past her. She was reluctant to follow the others for some reason, but couldn't understand why. Mostly she just wanted to be alone and savor this wonderful sense of peace and love she was filled with. She put her handkerchief down on the running board of the truck and sat down. She sat wondering because she realized she had intended to unite with the church when Mrs. Compton put her baby into her arms. She didn't understand why she had hesitated. She heaved a long sigh and stood up. For some reason, she looked back up the road that led to the highway and caught her breath in surprise.

Lucas was walking slowly down the road toward her. "Lucas, oh Lucas," she cried and starting running toward him. Lucas stopped in surprise. "Lucas, you came," cried Abigail again as she reached him and threw her arms around his neck. Lucas's arms went around her and not only was Abigail's body trembling, Lucas was shaking as well.

Abigail released her hold around his neck and stood back. Then she put her hands on both sides of his face and placed her lips on his. Lucas jerked in shock for a moment and then Abigail was kissed by a man for the first time in her life. When Lucas lifted his head, he saw that Abigail's eyes were filled with tears and he felt dampness on his own face.

"Abigail, I couldn't stay away. I love you. I can't live without you. I had made up my mind that I wasn't coming back anymore, but I had to try one more time. Thank God I did." He found her lips again and held her as if he'd never let her go.

Abigail moved back. "I love you too, Lucas. I've lived in such a state of fear for so long that I doubted that I could ever be normal and live a normal life. Oh, Lucas, I'm so glad you came back. I believe the Lord sent you to redeem me from my world of darkness and fear that held me prisoner for so long."

"Honey, this has been the most miserable week of my life.

I've been begging and praying all week that the Lord would send a miracle through somebody to change you. God heard me, but I didn't think he had."

Abigail stood encircled in Lucas's arms and felt no fear. She felt the greatest joy and peace she had ever known. She nestled her head against his chest. "Lucas, the chances of you and me meeting were one in a thousand or ten thousand, but we did. Then how did you know that we would be going down here to the river today? This isn't just a coincidence. The Lord sent you to me and I'm so thankful."

Meanwhile the congregation had gathered at the riverside. During the singing, Sally looked around and didn't see Abigail, and the old fear that some man might scare her came over her. She looked around and when she located Garson, she edged through the crowd to his side. "Garson, have you seen Abigail? I've looked and looked and she's not in the crowd."

Garson, seeing the near panic in Sally's eyes, said, "I'll go find her. Don't get upset." He hurriedly left the congregation while they were singing the song just before the baptism. He went back up the road and just as he reached his truck, he looked up the road and saw Abigail in Lucas's arms. He stood looking in amazement and, almost in tears, he said, "Well, bless my soul. Lord, I thank you."

Abigail saw her father and thought something was wrong. "What's wrong, Daddy?"

"Nothing is wrong. I just come looking for you, but I've found you in good hands," he said, smiling. "Come on down to the baptizing. It'll please your mother to see Lucas."

Hand in hand Lucas and Abigail went walking down the road toward the river. Abigail looked up at Lucas and squeezed his hand. "This is just like the dream I told you about."

By this time they had reached the water's edge. Elder Owens had come out of the water after baptizing Beatrice Compton and was standing on the bank still in his wet clothes. He saw Garson wading through the crowd with Abigail and Lucas behind him. They came to a stop beside Sally, who was about two feet away from Elder Owens. Elder Owens smiled at Garson's happy face. "You look awfully happy. Who's this you've got with you?"

Garson stepped close to Abigail, reached out and took Sally's hand and then smiling, he pointed to Lucas and said, "This is Lucas Sutherland. The Lord sent him to be 'Abigail's Redemption.'"

CPSIA information can be obtained at www.ICGtesting.com
Printed in the USA
BVOW032142231012

303778BV00001B/25/P